WHISKEY & WITCHES

UNLUCKY CHARMS BOOK 2

T.M. CROMER

ISBN: 978-1-7352032-9-4 (EPUB)
ISBN: 978-1-956941-09-8 (PAPERBACK)
ISBN: 978-1-956941-08-1 (HARDBACK)
ISBN: 978-1-956941-10-4 (LARGE PRINT)

Cover Design: Deranged Doctor Design
Edits: Precise Editing Group

This is a work of fiction. Names, characters, businesses, places, events, and incidents are either the products of the author's imagination or used in a fictitious manner. Any resemblance to actual persons, living or dead, or actual events is purely coincidental.

To Kate Bateman:
Thanks for the hours you spent with me at Panera Bread trying to make sense of a non-existent plot.
"Bloody hell, Tara!"

A special shoutout goes to my hubs, Cynthia St. Aubin, Sarah Hegger, and Kate Bateman for taking my sucky blurb and turning it into something readers might find intriguing.

To Brendan, Dani, Tracey, and Alison:
You've helped me create a story I'm proud of. Thank you for knowledge on all things Irish!

PREFACE

Aeden.

The pain was unexpected.

Unbelievable.

Unbearable.

The movement of Roisin's chest was compressed by the immovable part of the vehicle's framework that caged her. Taking anything other than a partial, panting breath was impossible.

Aeden.

She wanted to call out to her son, but she couldn't. Speaking required more air than she could muster with a single inhale. Even had she been able, the ability to draw in any oxygen was hindered by the sudden smoke filling the cab of their Rover. She knew real fear then. Smoke meant fire. It wasn't just the compression of the metal or the thickening tendrils of smoke making breathing difficult; it was the blind panic beginning to set in.

Aeden.

Her beautiful golden boy. She could hear him crying in the

back, and every fiber of her being needed to get to him, but she couldn't. Her magic was gone, and without it, there was no prying herself out of the tangled metal.

His terrified screams rose to a crescendo, becoming more frantic with each passing second. Then, they were no more. She cried out to him, but the sound was an aborted gurgle, and blood bubbled up from her lungs and into her mouth.

Aeden!

Her heart stopped beating.

The physical agony eased with her death, but the anxiety for her son clung to her and wouldn't let her cross to the Otherworld.

Aeden.

She couldn't leave him, not her precious son. He needed his mam.

Her heart thudded once. Stopped. Then started again, the beat thready and irregular. Barely there, like her spirit, but tenacious all the same. She was alive, and she'd stay that way for as long as it took to make sure her son was safe.

Brilliant white-gold light filled the vehicle and felt like it seared her retinas behind her closed lids. The entire right side of her face was aflame, and the initial stinging turned into a raging fire. She gasped and immediately regretted the movement as another bubble of blood filled her mouth.

"Don't move, love. I've got you."

Whoever he was, his was the voice of an angel. Or perhaps a god because she wasn't sure angels existed in the truest sense of the word. Gods did, though. And Fae. She definitely believed in the Fae, those mischievous feckers.

The metal was sheered away, and Roisin had a vague sense of a giant looming above her.

"Jaysus!"

The light was still too great for her to open her eyes, but she turned her face toward the sound of his sucked-in breath. She wanted to speak. Wanted to ask him what was bad enough to cause that type of reaction. But she suspected the wreckage of her body was a gruesome sight.

"Aeden?" she croaked.

"He's safe, never you fear. I'll not let anything happen to him, love."

She managed a hint of a nod.

"Meg," she whispered past suddenly dry lips. She hadn't heard her sister speak or move, and Roisin feared the worst.

"It's okay, Meg. I've got you."

"Sister…" The metallic taste of her blood mixed with the burn of bile, and she swallowed hard as another wave of fierce pain washed over her.

Gentle fingers stroked the hair back from her face. "I'm sorry," he said gruffly.

The salty sting of tears burned the open, raw wounds of her face.

Meg.

Gone.

Somehow, she'd already known that her larger-than-life, sassy sister who held the world in the palm of her hand was dead. Her rebellious sister who only truly wanted the one thing she could never have: *Carrick.* Roisin's beloved husband.

"I'm not a healer, but I can pause the internal bleeding until I get you to hospital for the help you need."

She opened her eyes and stared into the silvery depths of her savior. No longer able to manage speech or movement, feeling her life force fading, she blinked.

"I'm going to need you to hang in there and not die on my watch, Meg."

His hand burned where it rested over her heart, but she felt the suffocating fluid filling her chest cavity recede, and her breathing was marginally easier. Turning her head away from his too-intense stare, her gaze touched on her son lying by the side of the road.

Aeden!

Her panic returned, and she feebly shoved at the thick, muscled chest holding her. She'd been unaware of speaking, but the gentle giant holding her was quick to ease her fear.

"I've put him to sleep. He's not hurt but for a little smoke inhalation. The fire's out now, and he's safe." He touched her hand. "If you know what I am, you know what I can do, Meg. I'm going to use my magic to probe your spine for injuries, and I need you to stay perfectly still for me. You can do that, yeah?"

She didn't have the strength to move or speak, so she simply blinked her acknowledgment, feeling suddenly detached from it all.

A pulse of power, just shy of an electrical zap, slowly traveled from the base of her skull to her tailbone, hesitating around the area of her low back as if it were exploring that area.

"Nothing severe, but I think you have a few fractures, love. I need to get you out of this bloody mess, which means you're going to experience a bit more pain."

She opened her mouth to protest but closed it again as blood trickled out in place of her words.

"I've no choice, Meg. The whole thing could blow."

With great care, he used his magic and large, gentle hands to ease her out of the wreckage, then strode with her to where Aeden was curled up. Bending, he used the hand supporting her legs to touch the crown of her son's head. Roisin's cells warmed, starting with the nucleus and burning outward, heating her entire body as he teleported them away from the crash site.

The sounds of an ambulance in the distance and of nearby shouting indicated they'd arrived at hospital.

As the blackness crowded the edges of her consciousness, she heard her rescuer's smooth, confident tone as he explained the situation to another and handed her off to the medical personnel.

She had enough presence of mind to grasp his hand and squeeze —the only thanks she could manage.

"Aeden is safe," he murmured. "We'll contact his da. Rest now, love."

And so she did.

CHAPTER 1

10 MONTHS LATER

*A*eden O'Malley was playing in the yard when the blonde witch arrived. Even at the ripe old age of seven, he knew what she was. Her light was brighter than most, meaning she was magically stronger than others like them. But even as he watched, it flickered as if it could go dark at any second. As if maybe she didn't have full control over it.

"How are you getting on, Aeden?" she asked, her pleasant smile reminding him of his mother. Everything reminded him of her. But she was gone now. Hurt so badly in a car accident that she was still in life-threatening stasis, unable to have visitors, according to his da.

Hurt by evil.

He'd tried to sneak off and see her once, only to get lost on the way and later be found by his worried da. His father had punished him for "takin' years off his fecking life" and made Aeden promise never to attempt it again. The panic and mist of tears in Da's eyes had made the promise an easy one.

As the witch moved closer, Aeden jumped to his feet and barred the walkway.

Her gentle smile shifted into a frown, and she looked beyond him to the door of the cottage, then back down at him. "Are you all right, Aeden?"

He wanted to ask why she was here. Demand to know why she kept returning to see him, but his vocal cords refused to work most days. His throat had been damaged after he inhaled too much of the smoke from the flames surrounding the vehicle his mother had driven. Six months later, he'd stopped speaking to anyone but his da due to the pain, and he'd learned to sign, communicating with his hands and a few grunts. Once or twice during a nightmare, he managed a terrified scream, and he could still speak, but not without difficulty.

Tears stung his eyes, and he pressed his lips together. Why did *she* get to visit him when his mother couldn't? The witch who was his mother's sister. Aunt Meg had never been nice to him in the past unless she wanted something, and he had no reason to trust her now.

A soft light entered her sorrowful eyes, and she reached out a hand as if to stroke his cheek.

Jerking back, he scowled and slapped her hand away. He wouldn't be fooled by her, and he didn't want her fake kindness. Didn't need it when he had *real* family to look out for him. Turning away, he scooped up his toys and raced for the front door.

"Aeden?" she called, and there was unhappiness in the sound.

He paused just as he reached the entrance to his home, something in her voice compelling him to turn around.

"I can help you." Her smile was hesitant. "If you'd like."

He didn't want her help.

Didn't deserve it.

He was the reason his mother wouldn't wake up. But he couldn't tell her that. Couldn't tell *anyone*.

Aeden ran.

. . .

Roisin Byrne-O'Malley sighed deeply. For the sixth time in a month, she'd come to insist Carrick use her magical services to help Aeden. She'd have done it after waking from her coma, but her husband hadn't wanted to tax her strength. Maybe he'd be more receptive to her cures after so much time had passed. Sure, and she wasn't back to one-hundred percent, but her magic was stronger than it had been, and she was desperate to get their lives back to normal.

Without a doubt, they needed to discuss revealing the truth to Aeden. Their son grew more surly by the day, and he still rejected her overtures as Meg. Granted, her sister had been a raging bitch to him, and posing as her wasn't a comfort to him. Aeden had seen through her sister when she'd been alive, and it appeared he didn't believe she'd had a change of heart now.

Movement in an upstairs window caught her attention. As if she'd conjured him with her thoughts, Carrick appeared. He stared down at her, his corded arms crossed over his impressive chest and a dark scowl on his devastatingly handsome face. Today, he only wore a simple navy-blue t-shirt. Even from this distance, Roisin could see how the material loved his body, conforming to all the well-defined muscles.

Oh, how she remembered the beautiful contour of his chest and abdomen!

Damn, but the man was grand. Always had been, always would be.

Too bad he had no place in his life for her anymore. She felt a literal pang in the region of her heart, and she imagined she could hear another crack as it fractured further. They'd grown distant since she'd woken from her stasis, and separate households didn't help their relationship. It only served as a constant divide as the weeks, then months flew by.

She gave a tentative little wave, causing his frown to deepen to a scowl. Without meaning to, she grinned, mostly to annoy him and cover her heartache. But her cheeky smile disappeared when he ran a hand through his thick black hair and turned away in dismissal. Tears welled up, and she violently wiped them away. Hers was a family she couldn't have anymore, and she was an eejit for thinking she could change things. For wanting everything back the way it had been before that fateful day.

A tingling in her face was the only indication her glamour spell was wearing thin. She released the clip holding her hair and arranged the thick layers to shield most of her scarred visage. Careful to keep the ravaged side away from oncoming foot traffic, she traveled the short distance until she came to the dirt path leading to her cottage. The remainder of the glamour dissolved, and her hair morphed from a smooth strawberry blonde to a wild mass of golden curls. Thank the Goddess, her place was as close as it was; anyone witnessing her transformation would be in for the shock of their lives.

She'd only been home five minutes or so when the banging on her front door commanded her attention.

Carrick.

It had to be. No one else would dare be that demanding of the Witch of the Woods. Not in her own home anyway.

"Open the door, Roisin!"

The challenging tone grated on her nerves. Who the hell did he think he was? *He* had rejected *her*. Now he thought to come here and what? Take her to task for talking to Aeden on an unscheduled day? For trying to reach beyond their poor child's pain and help him heal? For giving in to her need to see her son?

"Go away, Carrick. I'm not accepting callers today," she hollered from the other side of the wooden panel.

"Jaysus, woman, you'd try the patience of a saint! *Open the fecking door!*"

A little devil danced on her shoulder. "Only if you ask me nicely. I'll be expecting a please from you, I will."

She imagined she could hear his teeth gnash together. To be sure, she heard his frustrated exhale.

"Please," he gritted out.

Suppressing the bubble of laughter was difficult, but she managed. She didn't know why she found his irritation amusing these days, but she'd take her jollies where she could get them. When she could speak without inflection, she said, "Please, what?"

"I swear to the Goddess," he muttered. Raising his voice a hair louder, he called, "Please, open the bleedin' door!"

She turned the knob and stepped away, presenting her back. "It wasn't locked."

"You'd try the patience of a saint."

"You're getting repetitive, Carrick, my love. I'd make a concerted effort to find another way to insult me if I were you. It shouldn't be too hard." Without bothering to spare him a glance, she limped to the stove and spooned stew into two bowls. She slapped them on the table and followed it with a crusty loaf of freshly baked bread. "Eat. You look like you haven't had a decent meal in ages."

She sat to his right to hide the direct line of sight to her scarred side. After a long, tense moment, he joined her at the table. They ate in silence, shoulders bumping lightly, and she got lost to another time when the two of them had broken bread together. A time when love and laughter were the themes of the day. A time when they had lovingly fed each other and followed each bite with a delicious kiss.

"I think you have to stop coming by, Ro. You're frightening Aeden."

"I'm not giving up." She struggled to keep her voice steady even though her heart was thumping wildly in her chest, on the verge of breaking completely. "I've never let him see the marks, and anyway, I think he's ready for the truth."

"I don't." Carrick's voice was as grim as his look. "His behavior is worse. And when you appear like you do, lookin' like Meg, you remind him of his mother."

Her stomach clenched in knots, and she wanted to shout that she *was* his mother. "Is that such a bad thing? To let him think of me?"

Carrick set his spoon down with a loud clatter. "Yes, it is. Thoughts of you are bad for all of us."

Blinking furiously, she set down her spoon and placed her shaking hands flat on the table. "You're a complete arse! We were great, Carrick. Those memories are good for him, and if we take the time to explain, he'll understand. He's a clever boy."

"It triggers the night terrors." Carrick shoved his bowl away. "I'm sorry, Ro. I have to do what's best for him, all the same."

"You mean what you *think* is best for him."

"He'll never accept you. Not like this."

She glanced up in time to see the pity in his eyes. Rage clouded her vision, and the plates on a nearby shelf rattled as an expression of her most profound emotions. "Get out of my house and never come back."

"Ro—"

"*Get out!*"

The ground rumbled, and his face grew pale.

"Is this what happened that day? Did your anger take over?" he demanded.

Her fury faded into a black void of grief. "I don't know. I don't remember much."

But she did. She remembered *almost* everything, although she wouldn't say it, not to him anyway. He didn't need to seek out the truth and get himself hurt or possibly killed going after a phantom. But she'd find their attacker, and whoever it was would pay for what he did to her family. For now, she would try to be patient a little longer, but that patience was thinning. Answers needed to be discovered, and soon.

Roisin climbed to her feet with great care. If she moved at a pace faster than a snail, her back would pinch, and it would take the devil's own magic to make the muscles respond to her commands.

Carrick jumped up to assist her.

"Don't touch me," she snapped, her voice raspy and raw. "*Never* touch me."

"I was only trying to help."

"I don't want your help." What she wanted was her family back, and *that* he wouldn't give her. Never mind that she'd initially thought the plan a sound one. She'd quickly discovered they'd erred in their scheming. Aeden was getting worse, not better, and she was never going to heal the scars on her face. Her magic was too erratic and never lasted long.

Roisin shuffled to the other end of the kitchen and reached for the elixir she'd concocted for Aeden. Her back spasmed, and she couldn't prevent a cry of pain. Silently cursing herself for overdoing her exercise today, she gritted her teeth and tried to push through the worst of it.

Warm, strong arms encircled her from behind, and for a brief, heavenly second, Carrick held her to his chest. She didn't have more than a heartbeat or two to savor the feel of his touch before he scooped her up and set her on the kitchen bench.

"Bleeding stubborn to the last." There was a hint of affection in his statement. When he squatted to look at her face, she lifted her hands to shield the damage. "Your scars don't matter to me, Ro. They never have."

"Sure they do. They matter enough that I can't be part of your life. Part of Aeden's."

His expression turned to stone, and he stood. "He has horrific nightmares of that day. It's caused him to shut down. I'll not subject him to anything that could trigger more trauma for him." He softened marginally. "We *both* agreed it was the right thing to do, Ro."

"Yeah." She tried to tell herself he was being a good da and that she was a good mother, but it got more challenging every day. "Take the potion and go, Carrick." She pointed to the bottle she'd tried to reach, then to the envelope at the far end of the table. "There's the spell to go with it." She closed her eyes and sighed. "I'm tired, and I need rest."

What she really meant was that she was exhausted from the age-old argument. He'd made the decision to protect their son from the horror of her face while she'd been in stasis. And when Roisin had woken, he'd presented the plan to her. In her broken state with endless hours of recovery ahead of her, she'd agreed. Not only to protect Aeden's mental health, but because someone had targeted her that day, and she saw no other recourse to keep Aeden safe until she discovered who.

But in the interval, her spirit had been crushed, and her seemingly unbreakable bond with Carrick had frayed, becoming dangerously close to severing. These days, all she ever received from him—when he wasn't shoving her away and reminding her this horrid way of life was better for everyone involved—were rare scraps of affection. She was tired of that, too.

No more.

She refused to meet his probing gaze and kept her eyes trained on the stone floor.

It seemed as if an hour passed before he moved out of her good eye's peripheral.

"What's this?" he asked.

"It's for his throat. I've been working on the proper recipe for months. That should help."

His large hand came down on her shoulder and caused her to jump.

Damned blind eye!

And damned stealthy male!

"What's the dosage?" Carrick held the bottle to the light and squinted at the contents.

"A spoonful morning, noon, and night until it's gone. And

should he regain his voice, he's to continue until there's none left."

"What if he hates the flavor?" he asked dryly. "You don't know what it's like to make that child take—"

He clammed up when she glared. Their gazes remained locked until redness dusted his cheeks. "Right. Sorry, love."

"I flavored it to taste like his favorite sweets. He'll take it without complaint," she told him as he retrieved the envelope with a handwritten spell from the end of the table. "He might not be able to speak that aloud, but have him mouth it, at least." She gave Carrick a pointed look. "Aeden needs to concentrate on the words and the intent behind them. It will give the potion a boost."

"He's an O'Malley. He has no power."

"Oh, you O'Malleys hold more magic than you realize. But the spell is from my family's grimoire and the potion from me. It'll work."

"Will it tax your strength?" he asked.

"Cautious to the last," she muttered. "What does it matter if it does? It's for our son."

Carrick's dark green eyes focused on her, and in their depths, she saw his thanks. Roisin was positive she heard her heart crack for the third time that day. His gratitude made all of this worse; he truly believed parting Aeden and her had been for the best.

Fool.

Once, those stunning eyes of his had been a brilliant emerald color. But since their personal tragedy, they had turned the shade of a shadowed forest. Eyes were a witch's tell. The lighter and brighter the color, the happier or more content the person was. Carrick's told the tale of his pain.

"I don't know how to express my thanks, Ro."

"*Meg.* I'm Meghan now. Roisin is never waking from her stasis, remember?" she said snidely. "And I'm not doing any of this for *you*. I'm doing it for Aeden. And only because I don't want him to know his da is a fecking eejit."

She bit her lower lip as she struggled to her feet. Having Carrick hover over her was a strain on her neck. With her standard shuffling walk, she crossed to the door and opened it. "Goodbye, Carrick."

He paused in front of her. His hand lifted to her destroyed cheek, and she flinched at his touch. As he trailed three fingers along the network of scars, she forced herself to give him a stern look from her good eye.

Wordlessly, he dropped his arm and left her alone.

A sob caught in her throat, and she sank to the ground with her back to the closed door, giving in to her grief. Sitting like this would cause a cramp, and she knew it would be hours before she could move again.

CHAPTER 2

*C*arrick heard Roisin's heartbreak through the closed door. Her sobs became louder with each passing minute. He placed the flat of his hand against the weathered wood and hung his head. As if, somehow, that simple touch could alleviate her pain.

It couldn't.

He found himself stuck between a rock and a hard place. Roisin couldn't maintain a glamour for any extended amount of time, and the sight of her disfigurement would certainly send Aeden spiraling into the dark abyss associated with the accident. As it was, their son was convinced monsters were out to destroy their entire family.

No, despite the fact he loved Roisin, Carrick needed to keep her and Aeden separated until she could keep a disguise in place for longer than an hour or until their son's mental state improved. Their beloved boy was Carrick's number one priority.

As he meandered home, he wondered—not for the first time —if he should have an honest conversation with Roisin. If he should remind her his love for her would never die and beg her to grab what small happiness they could when stolen moments allowed. Even as he had the thought, he discarded it. They'd already been down that path, and she was too proud to settle. Without a doubt, she'd insist he was only with her out of duty.

His heart ached at the remembered sight of her pitiful attempt to cover her scars. The network of raised, angry keloids criss-crossing her face and causing her sightless eye to droop might be grotesque to some, but he saw none of that. Her inner beauty and magic shone too brightly. *He* was the one blinded in *her* presence. If only Aeden could see it the same, perhaps then, they might begin to rebuild their lives.

Carrick's hand tightened around the neck of the bottle Roisin had given him. A tear trailed down his cheek, and he swiped it away with the back of his hand. She'd faced it all—rejection, ridicule, constant physical pain—with a brave heart and a defiant tilt of her chin. The residents of their tiny village had never cared for or treated Meg well, and yet, Ro courageously posed as her much-hated sister as they looked for a way to help fully recover her magic.

To anyone else, her sacrifice might not make sense; however, Carrick and Roisin felt this way allowed her to visit Aeden on occasion and prevented their son from encountering gossiping gobshites without a care for his feelings. Neither Roisin nor Carrick had considered what it might look like when he went to the cottage to check on his wife. The more critical members of their village liked to speculate on his "affair" with Meg.

If Carrick hadn't already loved Roisin before today, he certainly would have after. The elixir in his hand spoke of a genuinely good soul who cared more for a seven-year-old child than she did her own wants or needs.

"Ah, Ro," he whispered to the wind. For the millisecond he was able to hold her, he thanked the Goddess Anu. The bitter-sweet feel of Roisin in his arms, along with the smell of her lilac-scented skin, nearly drove him mad from his need to hold her forever. And for the moment, he believed she enjoyed being held by him, too. The light caress of her fingers through the fine hairs on his forearm, the deep sigh she expelled when her back connected with his chest, and the slight softening of her stance before she remembered to put up her guard, all spoke of a deeper desire to be close.

Carrick opened the gate and smiled at Aeden, who waited so patiently on the stoop for him to come home. "Hello, my boyo."

"Hi, Da," Aeden signed. He had no smile for Carrick. Indeed, his son had forgotten what it was to laugh. Their only hope lay in the liquid contained in the amber bottle and the spell in his pocket.

And perhaps a new therapist.

The old one had done nothing to help him get past the trauma.

Piper Thorne, his brother Cian's American fiancée, stepped out of the open door and graced Carrick with a wide smile. "You're back! That was fast." She placed one hand on her slightly protruding belly and ruffled Aeden's shaggy blond curls with the other. Soon, she'd have another O'Malley child to spoil. "Aeden and I had a wonderful time while you were gone." She cast a quick glance around and said, "I conjured my cousin Winnie's infamous cinnamon rolls. They're as big as a plate and dripping with the tastiest icing you've ever eaten."

Aeden's eyes lit with hero worship as he looked up at her. She smiled down at him with the same expression. Carrick told himself that Piper and his sister Bridget might be all the female influence his son would need. But inside, he knew himself for a liar, all the same. *No one* could replace Roisin.

"Did you accomplish what you needed?" Piper asked.

"Mostly, but I'm not sure it made a blind bit of difference." He gave her a tight smile. No one knew the truth of his relationship with his not-really-deceased wife, and he intended to keep it that way as long as possible. Aeden believed Ro was in stasis. The rest of the world thought her dead. It was for the best until their son healed in mind and spirit.

Carrick held up the bottle in his hand. "I brought Aeden a new medicine to try."

A sullen look settled on his son's hauntingly thin face.

"Look, I'm told it will help," Carrick told him. His resolve was firm. Whatever it took to make Aeden a normal child again, he'd do.

"Wow," Piper said softly, her enchanting honey-colored gaze intent on the bottle. "It has to be a powerful witch to brew what you've got. I can see the pulse of magic from here."

Both he and Aeden frowned at the cobalt blue glass.

"Are you codding me?" Although Carrick could tell a witch from a normal mortal from their glowing aura, he'd never been able to tell if an object was infused with magic or enchanted due to his family's curse. For two-hundred-and-fifty years, they'd been without real power because some thieving O'Connor stole a sword the O'Malleys had promised to protect. The god Goibhniu, who'd entrusted the weapon to Carrick's family, didn't take the loss well.

Piper laughed lightly at his question and shook her head. "If that means kidding you, then not at all. I suppose if you had your abilities, you'd see it. Did a spell accompany the potion?"

"Yeah, it did." He wasn't sure why he was hesitant to pull the paper from his pocket, but he was.

Her narrowed eyes assessed him, then the bottle.

Wordlessly, he handed her the written note from Roisin. She studied what he'd given her in silence.

"Well?"

"I can't see where it wouldn't work." Piper handed the paper back. "It's worded correctly."

Carrick expelled a long breath in his relief. He wasn't sure why he feared failure—maybe because their family's luck had been shite for what felt like forever—but he had. Perhaps there was a subconscious worry what Roisin gave him wouldn't work, and once again, he'd let down his son.

"I'm happy to lend my magic to the cause," Piper offered. "I know Cousin GiGi would help as well. She's the most skilled healer I've ever encountered and would willingly confer with the witch who gave this to you."

Embarrassment caused Carrick's neck to heat, and he scratched behind his left ear. His wife would've teased him had she been around to see. Roisin never missed those small gestures that gave him away and used to delight in every one. A fresh wave of sadness washed over him, and the air seized in his lungs. The first indication of a panic attack began with the crawling sensation under his skin and his need to be anywhere but where he was. He'd started having these episodes when Roisin failed to wake after the wreck. They were rare but tended to creep up on him at the oddest moments, like now.

For seven full years, he'd believed the ill-luck haunting the O'Malleys had passed him by. But the accident changed his thinking and had left him wondering why he'd been arrogant enough to dream he, of all people, was special.

He took a few deep, calming breaths and counted back from ten.

"Carrick? Are you okay?"

He shook his head in an attempt to let go of the past and dispel the remaining anxiety.

"Sorry." A glance showed Aeden watched him, his blond brows drawn together. Carrick forced a smile for his son's benefit and held up the potion. "Ready to craic on?"

ROISIN WAS ALERTED AT THE EXACT MOMENT HER SPELL HAD BEEN used. She'd charmed the elixir so she'd know if Aeden was taking it as prescribed. If he wasn't, she'd intended to blister Carrick's ears.

Swiping a hand over the silver-framed scrying mirror in front of her, she watched her small family as they performed the ritual. She saw the dark-haired witch interact with Aeden, and for the first time since she'd been spying on her husband and son, she witnessed Aeden's pink lips twist in a semblance of a smile for Piper Thorne.

Roisin's heart spasmed to know he'd never again look at her with such unguarded love. No, she'd frightened him the day of the accident and in the days that followed. Some inner part of him recognized she was responsible for all his woes. It didn't stop her from scrying or from seeing Carrick's eyes fill with something other than pain for the first time since she woke.

On rare occasions, she'd seen a fleeting glimpse of more in his green eyes. Eyes that, when happy, rivaled the rolling emerald fields of *Éire*. Eyes that saw through her most times.

She shivered.

Should he ever guess the truth, those magnificent eyes would be forever dark; she failed to protect their son when it counted. As it was, he couldn't understand why she'd been traveling with Meg to begin with. He'd known all about their continual strife. But he didn't know about the rest, and until she unraveled the threads of the mystery herself, she would keep silent.

With a swipe of her hand, Roisin hid the sweet scene at Carrick's from view. She didn't want to see another woman in the role she coveted for herself, whether it was an innocent relationship or no. Roisin chided herself on her foolishness. Jealousy had no place in her current, miserable existence, and she needed to keep her stronger emotions in check.

Heaving a heavy sigh, she returned the mirror to the sideboard between her tiny kitchen and living area. She added the trio of candles on top. Should she ever have a visitor, they wouldn't see it as anything other than decor, certainly not the instrument she used to torture herself daily. They'd simply see Meghan Byrne, the surly Witch of the Woods who made potions for people for money and who despised their village as a whole.

A glance out the window showed the afternoon weather was mild and the sun shining. A perfect time to work in the yard and get her mind off what might never be. She gathered a basket, gardening gloves, and a straw hat. Within twenty minutes, she'd pruned all the bushes and discarded her gloves to get lost in the sensation of dirt sifting through her fingers.

Goddess, she loved gardening, as did all earth elementals. The soil fed her soul and strengthened her magic. Working this patch was the only time she felt truly centered and as if she were part of something greater. Although, what that larger thing could be, she was clueless to know. Her life had taken a tragic turn, and she was as isolated as any living being could be. Alone. No friends. No lover to whisper sweet nothings or to caress late at night when she missed human contact the most.

"Evil witch!"

Taken by surprise, she didn't move fast enough, and a large, jagged rock hit her on the shoulder. She twisted in time to avoid the second stone, narrowly avoiding having her unmarred cheek struck.

"Husband stealer!"

Whack! Another rock.

"Skanky hag!"

Those little feckers must've searched for the sharpest damned stones they could find. Two more hit her in rapid succession before she had the presence of mind to react. Placing her hands on the ground, she directed a blast of energy toward the three teenage boys. The trees' branches swept dangerously close to their heads, and the ground buckled, knocking her attackers flat on their backsides.

Their cries of fear gave her a fierce sense of satisfaction. As Roisin, she'd never have thought to retaliate, but posing as her sister, it seemed like every day she turned meaner, more Meg-like. She experienced a small pang of regret that she'd never tried to understand her sister better. Meg had her reasons for her bitterness and anger, but Ro had stopped trying to get through to her years before. Or she had until the day of the accident, when Meg insisted they talk, that she had something important to relay. But she died before she could, and the fact tormented Roisin daily. Whatever Meg had intended to say had died with her that day.

She couldn't climb to her feet because her back had gone into spasm when she'd twisted, but she continued to send milder shock waves toward the boys until they scrambled up and ran down the dirt lane. When she knew she was safe, she sent her thanks and the last remnants of her magic to the trees to repair what her anger had wrought. Easing onto her back, she watched the clouds gather in the late afternoon sky.

A lone tear rolled down from the outer corner of her eye into her hairline. She was so lonely. Why did she stay in this goddess-forsaken place? She had the power to go anywhere in the world. Why did she torture herself and allow the ridicule from those ignorant of who she was?

"Ro!" Carrick's concerned cry reached her seconds before he did.

He was why she stayed.

And Aeden.

Goddess, she was an eejit.

Kneeling beside her, Carrick cradled her face within his palms. "Tell me where you're hurt. Where's the blood coming from?"

Blood? She tilted her head as much as his hands allowed. The rock to her shoulder had cut her sleeve and nicked her skin along with it.

"I'm grand, Carrick." With impatience and a strength she

thought had deserted her, she brushed his hands away. "Just some little feckers out to teach the evil witch a lesson."

"Jaysus, Ro! Who were the boys? I'll see they're punished."

The temptation was strong to let him, but she shook her head. "I'll deal with it in my own time." And although she hated to ask, she needed his help to stand. "Could you… give me a hand?"

He surprised her when he laid down beside her and folded his arms over his chest instead.

"Are ya mad? What are you doing?" she demanded, turning her head to look him in the eye.

"It's occurred to me, we haven't done this in a long while."

"This? Get stoned by a couple of juvenile delinquents?"

Anger pulsed from him, and Roisin gasped her shock when it lightly smacked into her body. "Carrick! When did you learn to do that, now?"

"Do what?"

"The magic."

"What are you talkin' about, Ro? I didn't perform magic."

"Ya did! I felt it, I did."

He rolled to his side, propped up by his elbow, and gazed down into her face. "What are you going on about?"

"Your anger… just now. I felt it," she repeated. "It burst out of you."

Carrick stared, nonplussed. "Yeah, I experienced a tingle, but here, I thought it was you."

She grinned. "It was all you."

It was easy to tell he didn't believe her by his doubtful expression.

Then his moody green eyes dropped to her smiling lips.

Uh oh! She recognized the look. *Carrick O'Malley was feeling amorous.*

Maybe the magic coursing through his system was affecting him in other ways.

Roisin's pulse sped up considerably.

In a lightning-fast move, he was kneeling over her, a hand braced on either side of her head. Trapped, she couldn't move even had she wanted. And if she were being honest, she had absolutely no desire to escape the cage created by his beautiful, sculpted forearms. After a lifetime together, she recognized the sign; Carrick intended to steal a kiss.

A kiss was a bad idea.

The worst.

Top-of-the-charts terrible, in fact.

But she didn't say no when his eyes begged permission. *Hell, no!* She wanted this. Wanted him.

Tangling her fingers in that rich, raven-colored hair, she pulled him to her. Chest to chest. Lips a tease away. She closed her eyes and inhaled when his mouth met hers. His delicious scent reminded her of a delectable banana loaf, with hints of cinnamon and allspice—*and he tasted even better.*

How long their tongues danced in their lazy waltz, she had no idea. She got lost in the sweeping back and forth. The seductive give and take. Moaning into his mouth, she strained for more. Back pain be damned!

Carrick broke the kiss and nibbled little love bites along the left side of her jaw. She arched her neck to allow him access to her throat, celebrating the feel of his velvety-soft lips—so at odds with the man himself. He devoted his attention to the deep valley between her breasts, and Roisin gasped when he licked the skin there. She hadn't been aware of him unbuttoning the top of her blouse, but she was all for it.

He leaned his body into hers and ran a hand underneath her shirt, lifting her bra enough to access her breast. As he cupped her and gently squeezed, as if familiarizing himself with the weight in his large hand, he met her gaze again.

Desire darkened those heart-stealing eyes of his, and Roisin thrilled to see it. Lowering his head, Carrick sucked her nipple through the aged material of her button-down top. Passion bested her, and the ache between her thighs became unbearable, mercilessly prodding her to do something about her long dry spell.

As one of those talented hands of his found its way past the waistband of her knickers, reason returned.

What the hell did she think she was doing?

Hadn't she firmed her resolve and told herself she wouldn't settle for scraps anymore only thirty or forty minutes ago? Not from him. Not from anybody. With a burning regret, she forced the words from between kiss-swollen lips. "Carrick, no."

CHAPTER 3

*I*t took a pulse-pounding second or two, but Roisin's rejection penetrated Carrick's fevered brain. With great care, he withdrew and straightened her clothing. There was nothing he could do about the damp spot on her blouse. Neither would he feel guilty for giving in to temptation and kissing her. He'd wanted her for too long and Jaysus, did he miss her!

Rolling onto his back, he adjusted himself to allow more room for his erection and slowly blew out a breath. No was no, and he'd respect her wishes, but damned if he wouldn't be a bit sulky about it.

"What's with the blast of cold, pet? The signals you were giving were clear."

"It's hard to say no to you, Carrick, but this isn't going to do either of us any good."

"I beg to differ. It will do us both a great deal of good." He turned his head to meet her searching gaze. "We'd both enjoy a hearty shag and be more relaxed for it."

"Sure, if it were only about the physical. We both know what we shared was more. Once."

He sat up and hooked his arms around his bent knees, clasping his hands together. Roisin was right, of course she was, but her response wasn't any less galling. All these months without sex had made him a bit irritable.

"I'm sorry, Carrick."

"Don't apologize," he snapped. With a deep inhale, he purposefully softened his expression. "A woman never has to feel bad for saying no. You know that."

She nodded but didn't look convinced, and Carrick hated the insecurity flowing from her.

"Ro? Has someone..." His mouth went dry. "Did someone... since...?"

"What? No!" She shook her head and swatted his bicep. "You know I'd cut off a man's bollocks if he didn't respect my wishes."

Relief, swift and fierce, swept through him. She'd been hurt enough, both by him and the incident that scarred her. Because most of the town knew he sought her out without knowing the why of it, they treated her poorly, and he was constantly worried on her behalf. It was why he stopped back by today. The nagging feeling something was wrong wouldn't leave him.

"Who were the boys, Roisin?"

"And didn't I say I'd deal with it in my own time, Carrick? Let it go."

"I'll not stand around while others harm you. Don't ask me to." He frowned because she still hadn't moved. "Your back's seized again, hasn't it?"

"A little."

Cursing under his breath, he lifted her into his arms. It cost her plenty to admit she was in pain, he had no doubt. The least he could do was see to her comfort.

"It's not your job to take care of me, Carrick. Not anymore."

"Look, I'll not be havin' this argument again. If I can make life easier for you without cost to Aeden, that's what I'll be doing."

She went still, and he could feel the stiff tension in her body. With an internal sigh, he strode into the ramshackle cottage. The place was tiny and could use updating, but she'd made it quaint with her little touches here and there. Roisin knew how to transition brick and mortar to a home, using only bright curtains, a pot of flowers, and a heart full of love. He made a mental note to bring his toolbox back with him the next free time he had.

"Couch or bed?"

"Bed, please."

After he'd laid her on the mattress, he rifled through the top drawer of her dresser for the liniment she usually created by the liter. Finding it, he opened the lid, took a whiff, and grimaced. "It still smells like shite. You'd think you'd have found a better fragrance for the bleedin' stuff."

She grinned as she held out her hand. "Lucky for you, you're not the one who'll be wearing it."

"And I'll be thanking the Goddess for that." He rolled his eyes skyward to emphasize his comment. "Can you remove your clothes and turn over, or do you need help?"

"Carrick, you don't—"

"Jaysus! Can you not stop arguing with me for five minutes, woman?" Carrick set the pot of ointment on the bedside table and gently sat her up. When he began unbuttoning her top, she smacked his hands and growled. He fought a smile and averted his eyes until he heard her clothing drop to the floor.

She attempted to shift, but her sharp hiss gave her away along with her difficulty.

Careful not to move her too fast, he eased her legs straight and her back flat. Then, he rolled her onto her stomach with another glance skyward. This time he added a few silent curses that he couldn't take advantage of his wife's naked state.

He scooped up a euro-sized amount of the goop and warmed it between his hands. Her flesh quivered in direct relation to the cold air, or perhaps his nearness, and goosebumps formed from the base of her neck to her ankles. Scars marred the previously unblemished body all down her right side. It was the first time he'd seen some of the accident's reminders carved into her delicate skin, and it made him ill to think of the pain she'd gone through—was continuing to go through.

"Cold?"

"A little," she admitted.

He pinched the sheet between his index finger and thumb and drew it up to cover her legs, in addition to the bottom half of her bum. Regret struck at being forced to cover her loveliness.

Carrick skimmed his palms over her back. After a liberal application of the greasy mixture, he used his thumbs to work the kinks from her muscles, and her soft moan of pleasure caused him to smile.

"You can thank me for insisting," he teased.

"Your head will swell."

"My head is already swelling, but probably not the one you're thinkin'."

She snorted a laugh. "Then it's a good thing for me you'll not take advantage."

"Good for you, bad for me."

Roisin tried to hide her smile in her forearms, but he caught the fleeting grin.

"Thank you for insisting, Carrick," she murmured a few minutes later. Her voice was sleepy and, for once, without an edge of bitterness.

He missed this side of her. "My pleasure, love."

"Am I?"

Her whispered question held a ton of angst, and it cut him to the quick that she had any doubt.

"Always, Ro." He kissed the crown of her head. *"Always."*

LATER THAT EVENING, AS ROISIN WAS HEATING UP LEFTOVERS FROM lunch, a wave of loneliness struck. Carrick had been lovely earlier, and his massage had worked wonders for the tight, painful muscles of her back. She'd forgotten to ask why he'd come by, but if it was important, she'd find out in due time.

At some point after she'd fallen asleep, he'd left her, but not without writing her a note and propping it up beside a single rose in a drinking glass. She hadn't been able to bring herself to read it yet, knowing the sharp, bittersweet blade would impale her heart and make her cry. His sweet gestures always triggered strong reactions in her.

A short while later, as she stared at her meager dinner, trying to work up an appetite, her eyes drifted back to the folded paper. Giving in, she opened it, already knowing what it contained.

Carrick & Roisin 4-Ever

The tears came, but she smiled anyway. From their first day of primary school, he'd been writing her these little notes, and she'd kept every single one.

Goddess, she loved him.

With his dark hair and laughing eyes, he could've had anyone, but for some reason, he wanted dull Roisin with her stubby braids and hand-me-down clothing. Too shy to speak to him, she'd smile her greeting and allow him to do all the talking. Oh, the stories he'd tell. His mind had been ripe with imagination, and he'd thrilled her with his tales of the fae. When they were grown, she encouraged him to write children's stories. And when he signed a contract for a three-book deal, he'd swept her off her feet and said he couldn't have done it without her. It was the same day he'd proposed marriage.

Roisin wiped away the moisture from her cheeks and gently folded the paper in two. No good could come of recalling the past with such frequency and longing. Dwelling would get her nowhere fast. With a wave of her hand, she sent the paper fluttering upward to the cardboard box, decorated to hold her memories. A flick of her finger lifted the lid for the air current to deposit the note inside. She snapped to put the box back to its original state then dusted her hands together.

That was that.

A sharp rap on her door caught her attention, and she frowned at the urgency behind the sound. With a grimace and curse for the visitor on the other side, she ambled her way over to answer.

"Who's there?"

"I'll give you one feckin' guess, Roisin Byrne-O'Malley!"

She'd recognize that strident tone anywhere. Bridget O'Malley. *Her sister-in-law.*

"You'll open the bleeding door, or I'll kick it down, Roisin!"

After admitting her, Roisin winced when Bridget connected with her injured shoulder as she passed by.

"How did you know it was me, Bridg?"

"So it's true then? You've been lying to everyone—*me included*—while pretending to be *her?*"

Meg and Roisin had always looked similar enough for her to pull off the ruse. The only difference was their hairstyle and the scowl Meg had preferred to grace everyone with. Their height, build, eye color, and facial features were nearly identical. The scarring helped. No one was comfortable looking at her face for long.

Refusing to answer Bridget's fury-packed question, Roisin lifted her chin. They stared at each other, both unable or unwilling to cross the divide of their differences and Bridget's anger.

"What are you doing here?" Roisin demanded.

"Carrick wanted me to stop by and bring you dinner. He said you had nothing worth eating in that temperamental refrigerator of yours." She tossed back her gleaming auburn locks and nodded toward the antiquated appliance with a grimace.

Her husband's sister was as prickly as she was beautiful, and Roisin deeply regretted the loss of their friendship. But she'd had a part to play and couldn't risk anyone finding out she was alive. Bridget knew her almost as well as Carrick had, so the lie was necessary to keep her away. Everyone in their town knew Bridget had hated Meg with every cell in her petite body and wouldn't seek her out if her life depended on it. Roisin had been banking on it when she convinced Carrick to tell everyone besides Aeden she was dead.

"You didn't need to do this," Roisin said, accepting the dish. Saliva pooled in her mouth as the drool-worthy smell hit her olfactory glands. People could say what they wanted about Bridget being a salty bitch, but the woman could cook.

"I know I didn't, but I promised my no-good brother. When I refused to lift a finger to help 'Meg', he broke down and confessed to me, not an hour past, that you're still alive and living in this hovel. Apparently, he's worried about you, although why he gives a shite after what you pulled is beyond me."

"What *I* pulled?" Roisin ground out. As quickly as her ire rose, it receded. Weariness settled in her heart, and she sighed her emotional exhaustion. "You want to do this now, Bridg?"

The other woman's gaze, so like Carrick's, shrewdly scanned her face before taking on a look of sympathy. "No. Not really. You'll tell me soon enough. That's your way." Bridget wrapped her in a tight hug. "Fecking hell, I missed you. *Ten months*, Ro. Bollocks!" Winding down from her second rant, she asked, "Want company for your meal?"

Roisin bit her lip against the emotional tide rising up.

Once, they'd been besties. Now? Who knew? It seemed like Bridget was offering an olive branch, and Roisin wasn't inclined to reject it. "Yeah," she said gruffly. "I'd like that—if we can shelve the animosity for a few hours."

"We can *if* you have some of that blackberry mead I'm so fond of."

"So it wasn't me you were missing but my mead."

"Well, sure, you were the only one who made it proper like."

Roisin's lips twitched. "I'll get the wine; you get the glasses. Right over the sink there."

They drank in companionable silence for a few minutes, but she knew it wouldn't last. She was used to the quiet, however Bridget was not.

"Does it still hurt?" her sister-in-law asked.

"My face, my body, or my spirit?" She snorted as her friend winced. "Yes. They all three still pain me."

"What happened that day, Roisin?"

"You mean you don't know?" There was a nasty edge to her voice, but Bridget—along with the rest of the town—had treated her like a leper, and Roisin was sick of it all. Sure, and it had been part of her plan to ferret out the orchestrator of her accident, but naught had come of it in all this time, and she was lonely as feck. She needed someone to confide in, and Bridget was the best listener. Roisin had to fight the urge to tell the entire truth.

She drained her glass with a grimace. Perhaps she *should* leave. Go far away where no one knew her and start over. Try to forget what she was leaving behind. As soon as the thought occurred, she dismissed it. If all she could ever see of her son was a handful of stolen moments, then she'd take them and be grateful. Leaving him permanently would never be a true option. At least not until she was certain he was safe and certain she wouldn't be able to have these scars removed.

"I will if you tell me," Bridget said softly. "You must have a powerful good reason to hide."

"*Now* you believe there must be a reason?" Roisin snorted. Shoving aside her leftover animosity for how the O'Malleys had so recently treated her, she said, "The truth is I'm not entirely sure what happened. Meg and I were in the car, with Aeden in the back. There was some sort of argument. Over Carrick, I think." She frowned. "But it was like she was purposely taunting me to distract me, now I think back on it. It was her way to dance around the real issue before she would get to it." Roisin shook her head. "The brakes went out, and the next thing I knew, I was in hospital, waking from surgery."

She omitted the ominous sight of a man in the road, one she couldn't see clearly, and she wouldn't mention the hazy memory of the stranger who saved her and Aeden until she was positive it hadn't been her imagination. If she hadn't imagined him, why hadn't he come forward?

"But you're a powerful witch in your own right. Why didn't you stop the accident? Save Meg and prevent all of this?"

Roisin chugged her wine, swallowing self-hatred and regrets. Her sister had died, despising her. Her son was tortured with the memories of the crash and his monstrously disfigured mother.

"Ro?"

"It was gone. My magic, my ability to prevent what happened to us. All gone." Although she didn't have the ability to freeze time, she could've easily teleported them all to safety had she been able.

Bridget paled. "How is that possible?"

"Meg? Maybe she set me up. I don't rightly know. You remember she'd developed the sight? Maybe she foresaw what was to happen. Maybe she put a spell on me and bound me in some way so I couldn't save her." Roisin toyed with her glass, rolling the last of the liquid around in small circles. "She was depressed toward the end, I think. I'm guessing she saw it as a way out, knowing she'd go mad eventually. And I avoided her, never trying to help her through it."

Roisin's guilt was great. Rather than subject herself to her sister's awful moods, it had been easier to stay away. To tell herself that Meg's life choices were to blame for her predicament.

"So you still have no magic?"

"It came back the day Meg was buried. Or partially. It's sporadic."

Both women shivered as if merely saying Roisin's younger sister's name would bring with it evilness.

"We both loved Carrick. She hated that he loved me and not her."

"Why the pretense? Why make yourself look like her when you're in town?"

"In a word—Aeden. He was stuck in the car with us for over a half hour before it ignited. Then, in a blink, help arrived." Meg had already been dead, her eyes sightless and eerie. "I still have nightmares, Bridg, so I can imagine what he's going through." Roisin refilled her glass and drained it half as quickly. "I was a sight, I'm sure, with the metal sticking out of my eye socket, torn flesh and blood covering two-thirds of my face. Carrick told me Aeden wakes screaming."

Bridget nodded. "Aye. He does. And he won't say a word otherwise."

"It's the damage from the smoke. I'm working to fix it."

They both refilled their glasses, content to drink their dinner.

Her sister-in-law sat frowning down at her wine.

"What?"

"I was told about the fire, but I assumed it happened right away and was put out. How did it ignite so long after?"

"I don't know the timing of it all. I faded in and out, unable to move."

"So Aeden is why you pretend to be Meg, but why, Ro?"

"Were you not listenin'? My face terrifies him, Bridg. I can't force that on him."

"And what about a glamour?"

"I can't seem to sustain it long enough. It could be the pain ruins my concentration."

Bridget snorted and rose to pace. "So let me get this straight. You pretend to be Meg, the woman this entire town despises, all in an effort *not* to terrorize Aeden because Carrick is a dumbass and thinks it's best?"

"I didn't mention Carrick," Roisin denied hotly.

"You didn't need to, Ro. This harebrained idea has that eejit's name written all over it."

CHAPTER 4

*a*fter Bridget left, Roisin thought about what she'd said. Maybe continuing on this unproductive course to protect Aeden was foolish. Perhaps part of why their son hadn't recovered was because he believed his mother to be the one who'd not woken up. Maybe if he saw her, saw she wasn't a monster, he could learn to come to grips with the reality of her scars and still understand she loved him with her entire heart.

She rested her unmarked cheek on her folded arms and sighed. Bridget's parting words were on repeat in her mind and refused to stop.

"You're doing everyone involved a mighty disservice, Ro. Aeden needs his mam, and Carrick is a sad sack, unsure how to help your boy."

Tomorrow she would confront her husband and work this out for the benefit of everyone involved. If her face truly gave Aeden nightmares after they revealed the truth to him, then she'd go away once she discovered the engineer of her accident. No point in torturing her sweet son any more than he already had been. Maybe she'd be able to find someone with enough magic to heal her. The Thornes were rumored to have extraordinary abilities. Perhaps she could talk to Piper and see if she had a solution to the problem.

She'd just locked the door and turned out the lights for the night when the smell of smoke drifted to her. As an earth elemental, she was great at growing herbs and creating potions, not so much at controlling flames or the water to extinguish them. And with her unreliable magic, her abilities were questionable at best.

As swiftly as she could, Roisin checked the oven and, not finding the problem, looked out the side window to see if the smoke was from an external source. A crackle overhead urged her head up, and she saw the first lick of fire dance across the ceiling.

Shoving away the instinctive panic, she closed her eyes and concentrated all her energy on the roof. The wooden rafters still contained trace elements of the earth, and she should be able to manipulate them with a major push of magic. It would deplete her, but she had to try.

Lifting her hands, she went to work.

"Anu, hear my plea and assist me in this time of need..."

The beams curled up on themselves and created a large wooden ball, similar to the Hol-ee Roller dog toy. Galvanized nails scraped her skin and pinged where they hit the tiled floor, but Roisin didn't let the raining metal break her concentration. It required all she had to levitate the ceiling and alter the shape of the shingles to provide a protective outer shell that would contain the fire inside for the few precious minutes she needed. With one last push of her power, she shoved the entire ball away from the house and into the open field beyond.

Through the window, she witnessed it bounce and burst open to reveal the raging inferno within, and Roisin worried it could burn its way back to her home. She didn't have time to stress it, and she turned her attention to maintaining the integrity of the walls. A quick magical probe revealed the threat of fire to the remaining structure had passed.

Now, on to the tea rag responsible!

Shoving her fear deep down, she unlocked the door and stepped outside, her hands raised and ready for battle. The glow from the blazing pasture revealed a shadowy figure running away, down the lane. Her fury gave her the boost her fear hadn't for her next blast of power. Palms face down, she called to the tree roots cradled lovingly within the earth's rich layers of dirt, then flipped her hands upward, urging the strongest to the surface and into the path of her vandal.

She smiled her satisfaction when he toppled with a strangled scream. The fecker would feel *that* in the morning! And perhaps they'd still be sporting the bruises for the length of time it took her to discover who it was.

"And don't come back or I'll bury you, you scaldy bastard!" She released a high-pitched, wicked cackle, hoping to make whoever it was soil their pants. If it took instilling terror in others to protect herself, that's what she'd do. Served the gobshites right.

She watched until the shadows swallowed her arsonist, then faced her poor abused home.

"Dear Goddess, for once, don't let it rain tonight." Roisin would do well to cover her valuables with an oilcloth tarp if she could dig one up. This was once her grandda's cottage, and the man had never parted ways with a single thing he'd acquired. He was known as a hoarder, so those old protective coverings had to be here somewhere; he sure as shite never repaired anything if he could take the lazy way out and cover it. Thank the Goddess, Carrick was handy with a hammer and nails or she'd be living in a true hovel.

Grandda had been a lot of things, with a drunken lout being the top of the list. Meg had voiced her complaints too many times to count both before *and* after he'd passed. She'd once created a bonfire in the pasture to get rid of what she didn't want, and Roisin had to stop her from torching the cottage with it. Right now, Roisin prayed rain gear and tarps weren't one of the casualties of Meg's previous mood swings. Sure, Roisin could try and conjure what she needed, but she was dangerously close to the last of her energy.

A small squeak sounded behind her, and she spun around, ready to strike. Pain, like a hot poker, burned through her muscles and left her gasping. What air remained in her lungs whooshed out in a single breath when the moonlight and fire's glow showed Aeden huddled by a nearby bush.

She had no more power to glamour and hide her scars, but she flung up a hand to hide the worst of them. "Aeden? *Mo stór*, what are you doing here, so far from home?"

He stared at her, transfixed, and Roisin feared her face had terrorized him. Slowly, with great care, he inched forward, only stopping when he was a foot away. His mouth worked to form soundless words.

She knelt in the dirt with her arms to her sides. Her goal was to appear as nonthreatening as possible. It seemed to work, and he shifted closer.

"Why did you come to see the Witch in the Woods, darlin' boy?" she practically whispered the question, fearing she'd lost what was left of her mind, and her son wasn't standing an arm's length away.

He touched the unmarked side of her face in wonder, then her curls. He worked the strands through his fingers like he'd done when he was a *wean*. He'd always been fascinated with the golden shine and would stare up at her in wide-eyed wonder as he consumed her breastmilk.

"Anu," he croaked.

"Anu? The Goddess?" Roisin had heard the story from Carrick, who'd heard it from Bridget, that Aeden had been instrumental in helping save his uncle Cian. Apparently, Piper

Thorne believed Aeden had a gift and the ability to speak directly to Anu, though Roisin had never seen hide nor hair of that talent in the years she'd raised him. But she knew better than anyone that powers could develop or wane over time.

Aeden nodded, still mesmerized by Roisin's hair.

"*Mo stór,* can ya tell me what Anu said to ya?"

He shook his head, and tears filled his eyes.

Roisin wanted to smack herself on the forehead. *Of course, he couldn't say!* Not without great effort and pain. His vocal cords had been damaged. "I'm sorry, darlin'. That was insensitive of me, to be sure."

His wary gaze lifted and met her good eye. He focused there as if afraid to look anywhere else.

"These scars aren't meant to scare you, Aeden," she said as gently as she could. She didn't dare confess they were from the accident he'd been involved in. There was no telling how he'd react. "I can glamour them away for a bit if they bother you," she offered as a resurgence of her magic began to build within her cells. She could probably maintain a disguise for a short time. Long enough to get him back to Carrick.

Although the rate of his breathing increased, he shook his head.

"You're a brave, boy," she said, her voice full of pride.

AEDEN STARED, UNBLINKING, AT THE WITCH AND WORRIED ANU had lied to him. This woman couldn't be his mother, could she? Mam would never leave him alone in the dark for all time. She'd always been there to sing him to sleep and chase away his deepest fears.

Tears blurred his vision, and all he could make out were the blond curls, so like Mam's. When she'd appeared earlier today, her hair had been straight and more ginger in color, like Meg's. He clutched the lock he held tighter, tangling his fingers between the strands, and gave a sharp tug.

She didn't scream or lash out the way his aunt might've, but instead, she tenderly gripped his hand and eased open his fingers —*the same as his mother had done when he was a small child.*

"It's a mighty fine grip you have there, mo stór," she'd always say before kissing the tips of his fingers.

His racing heart about stopped when the witch said the same thing. She didn't kiss him like Mam, but she smiled as if she were sad. The kind of smile Aunt Bridget gave when she thought no one was looking as she watched Ruairí O'Connor. *The smile of someone who was afraid to show their love.*

But why would his mother be afraid of *him*? The accident he'd caused?

Aeden desperately wanted to ask, but his voice failed him every time he tried to speak. He did the only thing he knew how to do; he flung himself into her arms. If she hugged him like Mam, if she smelled the same, he'd know if it was her or not.

A harsh sob escaped him and was echoed by the witch as her arms clasped him tight, and even with the lingering smell of smoke in her hair, she shared Mam's flowery scent.

Mam.

Aeden would know her smell from anyone's. It was the one thing that always calmed him most when he was afraid. Anu had told him the truth. She'd said he'd find what he was looking for at the end of this lane and that tonight, the Witch of the Woods would have what he sought.

He squeezed his eyes tight and scrunched up his face, trying his best not to be a baby and cry. But the tears burned his lids, and his nose grew stuffy then runny. He pulled back to swipe a sleeve across his face.

The love shining from the witch's non-blind eye made Aeden's heart ache and eventually, his stomach hurt. The pressure built in his chest. It made him angry that she'd lied and stayed hidden all this time. Rage flared to life inside him, and he struck out, shoving her backward.

"Hate... ya!" he croaked in his fury.

He didn't understand this weird desire to wipe the tender expression from her face or to hurt her as she'd done to him by staying away when he needed her most. He only knew he was upset that she'd abandoned him to his night terrors. That she'd found fault in him and didn't want him anymore. What was wrong with him that she wouldn't come home?

He swung his fist at her, but his arm was caught in a hard grip, and he never made contact. Terrified, he looked up... and up.... until he caught sight of his da's enraged face. His fear doubled. Never had he seen his father look so scary.

"What the bleedin' hell do ya think you're doin', Aeden?" Da's voice trembled with anger. "We don't strike women and especially not your—"

"It's all right, Carrick," Mam said swiftly. "No harm done. But it's late now, and I'm certain Aeden should be snug in bed, yeah?" Her smile looked forced, and her one eye held enough sorrow for two.

Aeden had never felt so ashamed, and he ducked his head to focus on the tips of his trainers.

"Aeden?" Mam's sweet voice caused his chest to ache. "I'm sorry if I frightened you, *mo stór*. It won't happen again."

He looked up sharply. *What had she meant by that?*

CARRICK WATCHED THE PLAY OF EMOTIONS CROSS THE FACES OF HIS wife and son. They were each trapped by circumstances beyond their control, and he had a moment's doubt as to the plan to keep them parted.

Had it done them both more harm than good?

When he went to tuck Aeden in, he'd found him gone. A look outside had shown his son creeping down the road toward

Roisin's cottage. Carrick had followed at a slower pace, careful to keep him within his sight, to see what the boy had planned. And when he'd come around the bend and saw him approach Roisin, he waited to see how the boy would react. He didn't understand why Aeden had snuck off tonight, but he intended to find out. He opened his mouth to ask, but the fire behind Roisin caught his attention. With a quick scan of the area, Carrick looked for any lingering threat but immediately noticed her missing roof.

"What the feck happened here, Ro—uh, Meg?"

He felt Aeden's hand jerk within his, and he looked down. The confusion on his son's face was disconcerting. His troubled gaze darted between Carrick and Roisin as if he were trying to figure out a puzzle, and Aeden reached for his mother's hair, reverently running a finger through one of her corkscrew curls.

A breath caught in Carrick's chest, and his gaze locked with Roisin's. Her confusion appeared equal to his.

"This is the second time tonight, Aeden has become enthralled by this unruly mop of mine," she said softly with a sweet half-smile.

She tried to stand and ended up staggering forward. Carrick released Aeden to catch her, and he held her steady within the circle of his arms. He unwittingly buried his nose in her hair, and the sweet lilac scent caused him to close his eyes and savor the fragrance. Only Roisin had that unique scent, one she concocted from the flowers in her garden. It brought him back to better times, and he never wanted to let her go.

Her fingertips brushed his jaw, butterfly soft, then she whispered, "Don't show any reaction for Aeden's sake, but to answer your question, my house was torched tonight, Carrick. That's the fire you see in the field."

He exhaled in a harsh breath and struggled to suppress his blinding fear and resulting rage that she'd been attacked twice in one day. Seemed some scumbag was upping their game.

With a nod and a light kiss to her temple, he set her away

from him, keeping hold only long enough to make sure she was steady on her feet. Other than gingerly steps, she appeared able to move without assistance. But he couldn't resist holding her again, so he scooped her into his arms and ignored her outraged squawk. "Let's get you out of the cold."

She'd blister his ears later, and he'd take his punishment, but there was no way he intended to let her suffer in pain a moment longer than necessary.

"It's just as cold in the cottage," she replied dryly. "I'm afraid the new opening has let the evening mist settle inside."

Carrick stopped short as he registered the truth of her words. He looked from her to Aeden to the fire to the cottage and back at her. "Sure, you'll come home with us then."

CHAPTER 5

*R*oisin stared at Carrick as if he'd lost his fecking mind —and likely he had. She hadn't realized she'd said it aloud until he laughed. Jaysus, she missed that deep, all-encompassing laugh. It was like a warm hug, wrapping around her and stirring up all the old feelings: love, happiness, togetherness.

A glance back at Aeden showed he was bemused, but his lips were no longer turned down, and he seemed okay with the fact his father was carrying her. Of course, she wasn't disguised as Meg with her flawless complexion and straight reddish-blonde hair, but Aeden appeared to like Roisin's wonky hairstyle better anyway. His fascination was reminiscent of when he was a baby, and for a moment, she almost believed he'd recognized her.

But then his temper had emerged, and he'd shoved her backward in the dirt. Her heart silently wept when he raised his fist to her and she once more became the hated Witch of the Woods. Shock had held her in place, or she'd have stopped the tantrum immediately. Thank the Goddess, Carrick had arrived when he had, or the incident would've been that much worse.

She briefly wondered where Aeden's temper had stemmed from. Her son had never shown that type of strong emotion in his entire life. He'd always been a good-natured happy child. However, things weren't normal anymore, and she had to remember to tread carefully.

"What has you thinking so hard, Ro?" Carrick's voice was pitched low for her ears alone.

"Aeden. He had a right powerful rage when he struck out. I haven't been able to reason why."

"We'll ask him in due time. I'll not have him hitting women or those who won't defend themselves, all the same." He gave her a pointed look. "You'll not take abuse from anyone, love. I'll not have it."

Her lips twitched. "You'll not, huh? Well, Carrick O'Malley, I thank you for your timely intervention, but I'd have handled it in my way, *all the same.*"

"Jaysus, I want to kiss your smart mouth right now. I would, too, if our shadow wasn't watching us as closely as he is."

"You'll keep your kisses to yourself. Nothing's been resolved between us."

"Ro—"

"Just take me inside and summon the Thorne witch. Perhaps she can loan me some of her magic to secure a new roof."

"You're not staying here," he said sternly.

"It's my home, Carrick."

He jerked as if struck and stopped walking. His mouth opened and closed as if he wanted to argue, but he had to know it wasn't the time with their son inches away and his ears tuned in to every word they spoke. Jaw like granite, Carrick strode into her humble abode and eased her onto the table.

He called out to Aeden and stopped him before he could come inside. "There are nails scattered on the floor. Wait where ya are."

Aeden's expression remained closed as he studied the inside of her tiny cottage from the doorway. He narrowed his eyes on a small blue blanket by the bed.

A replica of his.

The baby blanket didn't hold his scent, of course, but it comforted Roisin all the same on the nights when she couldn't hold her son and sing him to sleep.

Seeming to forget or outright ignore his father's dictate that he remain by the door, Aeden moved toward the bed.

Carrick caught him up in his arms before he reached his goal. "What did I tell ya?" he growled.

Fixing his face in stubborn lines, Aeden gestured to the bed. "Mine," he croaked.

"Similar," Roisin acknowledged. "But not exactly the same."

Following the direction of Aeden's pointing index finger, Carrick crossed and picked up the blanket. He handed it off to their son without comment, but his concerned gaze locked on her across the short distance. The baby blanket on her pillow was telling. Raw emotions closed her throat, and she wanted to sob for all she'd lost. Unable to bear the weight of his worry, she looked away.

"I think you should come back to the house tonight, Roisin," he said. "You can't sleep under an open roof and subject yourself to the elements."

Panicked that Carrick had slipped and used her real name, she looked at Aeden. Her son watched her with an old soul's eyes. He either hadn't noticed the mistake, or he knew exactly who she was. Their stare-off ended with Aeden clasping the blanket to his chest and resting his head on his father's shoulder.

Roisin weighed the pros and cons of returning home and found she just couldn't do it. If she went back, she'd never want to leave when the time came. She wasn't strong enough to abandon Aeden a second time, regardless of the reason.

"I'm afraid this scarred face of mine might cause poor Aeden nightmares should he encounter me in the dark," she said in a false teasing tone. "It's probably best I stay here."

Aeden immediately averted his face and curled into Carrick, wrapping his arms around his da's neck.

To hide her reaction to her son's rejection, she turned her attention to the floor and counted the bent nails. Cleaning didn't take much magic, but healing the sole of a foot after it was punctured would. Closing her eyes, she held out her hands, palms down, and brought them together with a loud clap. Flickering gold light solidified into the shape of a broom and swept all the debris into a neat mound. Waving a hand, she manipulated the broom to push the entire pile outside and to the left of the entry to prevent anyone from mistakenly stepping on it.

"'Twas a grand trick, Ro," Carrick said with a light laugh. "What I wouldn't give to have a bit of that power. Perhaps I might have my stories write themselves as I lazed about all day."

She gave him a small smile but didn't respond. His lack of magical ability was an old joke between them. He always conjured creative scenarios of what he'd do if he could.

"It's probably best if you get Aeden home to bed now, Carrick. It's been an eventful night."

Her husband stared at her for a long moment, and all the things they couldn't resolve were in his eyes. She wanted to tell him not to come back. Contrarily, she wanted to beg him to take her with him. But mostly, she wanted to turn back the clock ten months to a time when they were exceedingly happy. A time when her boy was always laughing and joyful.

CARRICK KNEW HE WAS BEING OBSTINATE IN TRYING TO GET ROISIN to come home after all this time. He'd been the one to insist she stay away so she didn't terrify Aeden worse. Yet, their son didn't seem scared of her now, and the damage to the cottage was substantial.

And Carrick missed her dreadfully.

He missed many things. The sunshine her laughter brought. The warmth of her smile. Her passion for life—both in and out of bed. But the thing he missed the most was the constant companionship. Until this year, they'd always been in sync. From the day they'd met, they'd been simpatico on every level. It was not to say they hadn't butted heads on occasion, but they usually patched things quickly and enjoyed the make-up sex afterward.

However, that wasn't the case these days.

"Da." Aeden's choked voice drew Carrick's focus away from Roisin. "Not... afraid."

He sought his wife's gaze. Her pain and longing were difficult to witness, and he extended his hand for hers. She quickly and carefully blanked her face then crossed her arms. Once again, she'd effectively shut him out. She tended to do that a lot lately, and it broke his fecking heart. His beautiful, open wife was a closed book, a distant stranger. The one woman who understood his soul, who never resented when the creative muse ensnared him and who loved him with every fiber of her being, had shut the cover and shelved their love story.

All because Carrick had insisted they put Aeden's needs above hers. Wasn't that what good parents were supposed to do? Take care of their children before themselves? And didn't that make him angry and bitter? They were broken, the two of them, their binding cracked, and he didn't know how to repair the damage. A man whose living was made with words found it next to impossible to find the ones needed to bridge the gap and heal their relationship.

The accident and Aeden's resulting fear had frayed the ties of their marriage. Maybe his bravery would help Carrick rebind those ties and resurrect what once was.

"That's my boy," he said as he rubbed his son's boney back, barely managing to curb a wince at the feel of Aeden's knobby spine. Most days, he had to encourage his son to eat. His cooking wasn't anywhere near as good as Roisin's, and Aeden was picky about his food. "How about we invite your—uh, Meg back to the house for the night until we can repair this roof of hers?"

A tremor shot through Aeden's body, and he stiffened his arms in an effort to be away from Carrick.

"Lies," Aeden whispered angrily.

Carrick's heart stumbled in its steady beating. He placed Aeden on the table next to Roisin then tilted up his tiny, pointed chin so he could meet his angry gaze. "Explain."

But Aeden shut down, crossing his arms and scrunching his eyes tight. Not so different from his mother. With a stern warning infused in his tone, he said his son's name. But it seemed their boy had inherited Roisin's stubbornness, too. Carrick almost said as much, but she gripped his wrist and squeezed it in warning before releasing him.

"Aeden," she said softly, turning her full attention to their son. "Sometimes adults hide the truth for the benefit of their children." She stared at him intently. "They believe they're doing a good thing, but it turns out, it may have done more harm than good."

Aeden's lower lip trembled, and tears cascaded down his pale cheeks.

Carrick had the damnedest time not pulling the boy into his arms to help heal the hurt. "Sure, and Meg's right."

"Not Meg," Aeden signed frantically, his throat and mouth working as if he wanted to yell the words. "She's not Meg."

"You're right," Roisin signed and spoke in return. "I'm not."

Shaken, Carrick plopped heavily onto the bench and rested his head in his hands. He had no idea when Roisin had learned to sign, but not only had she read and responded to Aeden, she basically told him the truth about who she was.

"This is fecking grand," Carrick muttered.

"Why?" Aeden's croaked question caused a literal ache in Carrick's chest.

What could he say? The truth would make Aeden feel worse than he already did.

"Bad people were after me," Roisin replied for him. "Maybe

still are. As you can see by my new skylight…" She tilted her head back and lifted her face to the stars.

A faint moonbeam found and caressed her skin, and Carrick was envious.

With her eyes closed and her lips compressed, she looked like she was trying to stem off her own tears. After a deep inhale, she lowered her head and met Aeden's questioning gaze. "And because when you came to the hospital those first few times, you were terrified of me. It broke your da's heart every time you looked at me and relived the accident. It was better if you believed I was sleeping until I could find a way to heal these." Roisin gestured to her scarred face, although it was mostly turned away from them.

"My fault," Aeden signed as silent sobs shook his slight frame.

She bundled his fists and pressed them to her lips. "No, *mo stór*. Never." Shaking his hands to emphasize her point, she ducked her head to make her face level with Aeden's. "None of this was your fault, not then, not now, not ever, my darlin' boy."

Seeing his son so lost and tormented practically crippled Carrick, the pain was so great. "It was my fault," he said hoarsely. "Not your mam's. I made the choice to keep you separated, so if anyone's to blame, it's me."

Mother and son stared up at him, mouths agape.

Roisin recovered first, and her lips twisted in a sunny smile. Carrick could almost feel her relief that she'd not be viewed as the bad guy in all of this. "Sure, it's not often an O'Malley shoulders the blame. Mark this moment down, Aeden. You'll not see its like again."

"True enough." Carrick cupped her beloved face and held firm when she tried to turn and hide. "But now I want you home where you belong. Where you're safe."

CHAPTER 6

"*B*ridget is cross with me," Carrick told Roisin as they settled their sleepy son on her bed in order to gather her things for the night.

"Yeah, it's the impression she left me with, to be sure." She stared down at Aeden, smiling as he fought to stay awake. For a brief moment, Roisin's heart was full. But the feeling was only temporary. The real test would be if Aeden's night terrors were triggered by seeing her damaged face in all its glory. Any progress gained could easily backslide. "You should take him home, Carrick," she said quietly. "I need to try to patch this roof."

"No. Look, you'll need help to tarp your things before we head back—I'll not see your precious items damaged by rain— but you *are* coming home, all the same."

Roisin rubbed the spot between her brows. Carrick could test a saint with his stubbornness. "I'm not going back with you."

"You are, and that's the final word."

"Carri—"

"Ro, stop!" He stood up from the edge of the mattress and gripped her shoulders. When she tried to pull away, he tightened his hold but not enough to make her uncomfortable. "Someone was out to cause mischief tonight. Why, I don't know, but had you been tucked in your bed, you could've been seriously hurt or even killed. You're too precious to this family, and I'll not leave you out here alone again."

"My magic put out the fire," she reminded him. "And thank the Goddess for it because it wasn't as if I could run away after the day I had." She thumped his chest. "But you're not the boss of me, Carrick O'Malley. You never were, and you never will be, so you can get that right out of that thick head of yours."

His lips twitched.

And like a Pavlovian response, hers responded in kind. "Sure, and now you'll be thinking of thick heads, you plonker," she whispered.

"You're the one who mentioned my thick head, darlin'. Clearly, it's heavy on your mind."

She punched him lightly in the belly. "Go on with you!"

Abruptly, he became serious, and her stomach lurched.

"Ro, please come home with me. It's not safe for you here now."

"You don't seem to understand."

"Then explain it. Because for a long while, you've been wanting to be where you belong, to tell Aeden the truth, and I've been the eejit who thought you should stay out here. I'll gladly admit I was wrong and that our plan might've been a bad one." He touched his nose to hers. "I'm sorry I stole all this time from you. It was for him. You had to know that."

"And you," she couldn't resist adding.

"*What?* No!" He drew back in his astonishment. "*Never* for me. Why would you say such a thing?"

"Many a night, I laid right there—" she gestured feebly to the bed "—and wondered why we couldn't make it work. Why we couldn't sit Aeden down and explain his mam was scarred but not a monster." She swallowed hard. "And whenever I brought it up, you were adamant that I remain here," she ended on a choked cry.

"Oh, Ro. No, darlin'. No." He gathered her close, but she made no attempt to return his embrace. "I've loved you from the first. You, with your hair in ponytails and wearing your wildly mismatched socks. And I'll love ya 'til the day I'm toes up in my grave. Then, I'll love you longer still."

With a gentle smile and tender eyes, he used the sleeve of his jumper to dry the tears she didn't realize were cascading down her cheeks. "The reason I was adamant was because you needed time to heal without the demands of a family to care for. But mainly because when Aeden reacted as he did after seeing your... well, *after*..." He sighed and rested his forehead against hers. "Jaysus, Ro. You don't know what it was like. You were unconscious, and he was screaming his fecking head off. They had to give him medication to calm him, and still he sobbed in his sleep." His voice was an aching whisper as he said, "And his nightmares have spilled into the daylight hours. He's seeing evil in strangers' faces."

She'd heard the first part before. After she woke from her coma and demanded to know about Aeden, Carrick broke the news to her. Twice more he tried to bring their son by, each with a similar result.

"But I woke up, Carrick. I woke up, and we should've explained to him nine months ago. He thought he was looking at a corpse, for St. Peter's sake!"

Her husband's expression tightened, but he didn't speak.

"All these months! All these months, he's believed me to be in stasis, and he's feared the Witch in the Woods. He's missed his mam to kiss his hurts and singing him his favorite lullabies." Her anger grew with every word, and she was startled when he grabbed her balled fists to stop her from striking his chest another time. She hadn't realized she was physically taking her anger out on him. "It was torture for us both, Carrick. But not for you. You had our son at home and, whenever you remembered, me here on the side. *I had nothing.*"

"What we have is not nothin'," he retorted emphatically.

"It is now."

His shock was complete, displayed in his wide, hurt eyes and slack-jawed response. The sight made her a little ill. Her temper had gotten the better of her—again. It seemed to happen a lot more frequently since the accident.

CARRICK'S BODY WENT COLD, HOT, THEN COLD AGAIN. AND IF HER harsh words weren't evidence enough, the fierce anger on Roisin's face left him in little doubt of her feelings.

He dropped her hands and stepped back, but he was unable to stop staring at her. She wasn't the woman he'd known. His Ro was kind and loving, not twisted with hate. If he didn't know better, he'd believe it was her sister Meg standing before him.

"Car—"

He lifted his hand to prevent whatever excuses or accusations she intended to spout. Most likely, it would pour salt on his already raw wounds. "You've said what you've said, and it's all I can take for tonight, Roisin. I understand you don't want to sleep in my bed, and I'll not ask you to. When we return, you'll have a room at the Black Cat until we figure out our next steps."

"I—"

"*Jaysus, Mary, and Joseph!* I'm bleedin' here, Ro. Please, stop fighting me on this. Would you have us all sit here in this fucking house and freeze to death? I'm sure as hell not leavin' ya here alone."

He turned away at her lack of response and noticed Aeden was awake and watching them from the bed, wide-eyed and wary. Carrick felt lower than low. Nothing he did lately was right for anyone he loved. He tried to offer up a reassuring smile, but he suspected his son saw right through him.

"Mam," Aeden signed. "She'll come home?"

Carrick felt a hundred years old and weary down to his soul. "You'll have to ask her," he said aloud and headed for the door.

"Yes."

He stopped short when Roisin's hesitant confirmation registered, but he didn't turn back. "Yes, what?"

"Yes, I'll come home," she replied hoarsely.

"Fine." The word almost stuck in his throat. "I'll look in the shed for the tarps. Here, you gather a few things for tonight, and we'll be back for the rest in the morning."

He stalked outside and straight to the outbuilding, only to find it securely locked. In a temper, he tugged forcefully on the lock and released a guttural yell. Lightning flashed in the distance, and the sensation of... *something* ran the length of his arm to his fingertips. The metal sparked.

Carrick stared in stunned disbelief as the mechanism disengaged and the padlock clicked open. A check over his shoulder showed him Roisin hadn't been there to give him an assist, and it registered he'd accidentally channeled magic. He shouldn't have been able to do it.

A minute later, Roisin limped out of the cottage with a flashlight in hand. When she got to him, the surprise on her face was priceless. "How did you open the lock?"

"Magic," he said softly, still not believing he performed such a feat. "Ro, it was like a bolt of electricity down my arm and then sparks. Sure, and the lock just dropped open."

"That's the second time today that you've channeled it."

She was right. In all the madness, he'd forgotten about when they were lying by the garden earlier. "I've no idea what it all means."

"I might." Her response was cryptic, and she shoved the flashlight into his hands. "Look in the back, on the right side. I think that's where the tarps were always stored."

The desire to question her further was strong, but Carrick

shoved it aside. Nothing needed answering immediately, and he had to protect the interior of her house as best he could until he could get up there to replace the roof or hire someone who could. *Éire's* weather was too unpredictable.

After he'd retrieved what he needed, he snapped the lock closed, shook his head at what he'd been able to do, and returned to the house. Roisin had a small bag of things gathered and placed on the wooden kitchen table, and Aeden sat in the corner of the bed, the blue replica blanket tucked under his chin. Although sleepy, he had a guarded look in his eyes as he watched her shuffle about the room.

"What's wrong, Aeden?" Carrick asked gently.

His son shook his head and averted his eyes. Whatever demons plagued him, he didn't care to share at the moment.

IN THE NEXT TOWN OVER, SEAMUS MCCLEARY NURSED A PINT AND tried not to wince every time he shifted his abused body. Those fecking tree roots had surprised the shite right out of him and sent him scrambling for safety. The fact the Witch of the Woods used earth magic in place of the air magic she was known for told him a lot.

In all his spying today, he'd discovered important news to relay to his cousin, Ronan, though he wasn't sure he should. That wanker had locked him in the tower for a month with only the bare essentials to survive. Moira's inescapable screams of fury had nearly sent Seamus over the edge of sanity. Every moment was a struggle not to give in to the madness as she had.

He drank more of his Guinness and allowed the rich taste to slide down his parched throat. He closed his eyes to savor the sensation. Oddly, he missed the O'Malleys' homemade brew. And perhaps if he was being honest, he missed Cian and Bridget, too. In the years he'd hung around their pub, waiting to see when or if that cursed prophecy would unfold, he'd become fond of the brother and sister duo. Bridget, with her fiery temper and sassy mouth, was always fun. And Cian, with his friendly, welcoming smile and lively tunes, was as entertaining as they came.

But all that easy camaraderie disappeared once Seamus had been found out. He cursed the day he ever threw in his lot with his cousins Moira and Ronan. His life had been nothing but misery ever since.

He snorted to himself.

If he were being honest with himself, his life was truly miserable from the moment of his birth. Parents like theirs were created by the Devil himself. No child should endure the upbringing the three of them had suffered through.

His thoughts turned to Aeden O'Malley, and a shiver of unease danced along his spine. Nightmares of Roisin's destroyed face with the metal sticking out of her eye had haunted Seamus. The discovery today, that she hadn't died and that it was really Meg who'd perished, had shocked the bejaysus out of him.

The truth explained why the woman he'd believed to be Meg wouldn't give him the time of day since the accident. Until a few hours ago, he'd swallowed the tall tale the O'Malleys had put out: Roisin was dead, Meg was the mad, scarred Witch of the Woods, and Aeden refused to speak.

Meg.

Seamus's wild lover.

Sure, he'd never forget the shock on her face when he stepped into the road armed with a spell and enough magic to flip their car. The duplicitous Moira had lied to him—*no surprise there*—and had told him Ronan ordered it done. Normally, Seamus wouldn't dare go against Ronan, but because of one falsehood and despite his better judgment, he attacked the Byrne sisters.

Yeah, Meg hadn't loved him—*and didn't that sting?*—but she'd shared her body freely, and Seamus told himself she cared for him in her own, detached way. He still refused to believe she wanted Carrick, despite the fact she'd never lied about her preference. But gods how he missed her. She'd listened to his hopes and dreams without judgment, and she'd given him a small, secretive smile in return, as if she knew he'd one day accomplish them.

Misery encased Seamus's heart. He'd hurt a small child; something he'd promised himself he'd never do in the process of claiming the O'Malley magic once and for all. In addition, he killed the only woman who'd ever seemed to give two shites for him. But now, he had to clean up his mess. He had to stop Aeden from sacrificing for "The One"—whoever the fecking hell *that* was!—all without harming the boy.

An impossible task.

But like Ronan, Seamus wouldn't stop until the power was theirs and he possessed the level of talent the Thornes bragged of. The O'Malleys' ancient magic could make that happen.

Resignation heavy on his soul, he drained his mug and motioned for another. Sure, and he had to work up the courage this night for the next job he had to do. It wouldn't be easy by any means, but it needed to be done to get him what he wanted, all the same.

CHAPTER 7

$\mathcal{W}$alking through the door to her old home, Roisin experienced a surreal moment. It was as if time had stopped and nothing had changed, yet so much was different. The place was a little messier than when she ran their household, but then Carrick could be absentminded when the writing muse took him. Likely Bridget and Cian helped keep him on schedule most days. And a child Aeden's age couldn't be expected to maintain order.

"Do you want to join me, tucking him in?" Carrick's look was expectant.

Roisin grimaced. She wanted nothing more than to see Aeden snuggled down and to read him a story, but managing the narrow staircase after the day she'd had would be torturous. "It's probably not for the best," she said with a resigned sigh. "I'll never get back down again."

"I'll help you with whatever you need, Ro."

She almost snapped that she didn't want or need his help, but it wouldn't be true. She might not like it, but she absolutely *did* need assistance when it came down to it.

"He's already asleep. I think he won't miss me this time." She managed to keep her voice even and to not show her torment.

"Mam," Aeden stirred and whispered, contrary to her belief.

"What is it, *mo stór*?" Roisin brushed back the mop of hair from his brow.

"'S'alright."

Her eyes burned with the sudden onslaught of tears. The consideration and acceptance, after what he'd been through, was awe-inspiring and humbling. Literally every word he spoke caused him discomfort, yet he was determined to put her at ease.

"Maybe you and I could sit for a while down here?" She'd give anything to cuddle him like she used to.

When he lunged from Carrick's arms to hers, she almost lost her balance. Yeah, she'd be feeling that tweak in her back sooner rather than later, but she didn't utter a word of protest and instead sent up a silent prayer of thanks to Anu as she clutched her son close. She didn't care if his thin but exceedingly strong arms were strangling her. The feel of his little body against hers, the faint scent of the ginger and lime shampoo she'd made and batched last year, clinging to his mussed blond hair, and the fierce love pouring from him brought sobs from the deepest part of her soul.

As she sank to her knees, Carrick caught her, and they all cried as a family. Although she hated to show weakness, it was therapeutic for her to a large degree.

"I'm sorry... I'm sorry... I'm sorry," she mindlessly repeated over and over.

When they were all depleted of emotion, they moved to the sofa—Roisin with the help of both Aeden and Carrick. Once again, she snuggled her son close as she rested her unmarred cheek on his silky head of curls.

"It is all right, isn't it?" she murmured. "You're not afraid, are you, my brave boy?"

The tiniest movement of Aeden's head was his answer, and gratitude filled Roisin's heart.

There was still a place reserved for resentment, but now was not the time to be cross with Carrick *or* herself. Her gaze met his where he sat on the other side of Aeden, and his eyes were red-rimmed and swollen. He looked contrite—and lost.

Roisin told herself she wouldn't feel sympathy for him. All this angst could've been avoided if they'd only spoken to Aeden when she woke up. Yet the largest part of her, the one that had loved Carrick forever, wanted to offer comfort and forgiveness. His actions hadn't been spiteful. For sure, he wasn't wired that way, but they had hurt, all the same. And so the smaller part of her, the one that was aggrieved by the lost year, wasn't ready to be kind.

Mostly, she couldn't forgive *herself*. She'd had a hand in all of this, too. The idea that she could uncover her attacker without help might've been a foolish one. Tomorrow, she'd visit the idea of telling Carrick and the O'Malleys what she suspected, and maybe a fresh perspective from them could help her see what she was missing.

"It's late," she said, her throat scratchy and sore. "And we all need rest. Why don't you take Aeden upstairs, and I'll put on the kettle?"

Her son lifted his head, fatigue showing on his thin, elfin face. For the first time since he'd arrived at her cottage, he looked at her scarred cheek. With the gentlest of touches, he traced the crisscross marks.

"Aether," Aeden said, his voice stilted and raspy with disuse. His gaze was intense and penetrating as if he wanted to make sure she received the message.

She nodded her understanding and kissed his forehead. "Thank you. Now off to bed with you. Tomorrow will be here before we know it."

· · ·

CARRICK CLIMBED TO HIS FEET, PREPARED TO ESCORT AEDEN upstairs, but his son violently shook his head. The glittering anger in Aeden's stormy green eyes hurt, damned if it didn't. But the boy had a right to his resentment. After all, Carrick had denied him a mother's love for almost a year of his young life. It was unforgivable.

"Aeden," Roisin called out when he'd gotten to the base of the stairway. "It's no one's fault. Not yours, not mine, not your da's. What was done was done for love, not in spite. Please try to remember that, yeah?"

Aeden's eyes glinted with unshed tears, and he gave a single nod before darting away.

"He's got a right to his anger, Ro."

"Yeah, I know. But you and I have enough rancor between us to last a lifetime. He doesn't need to carry those feelings around in addition to everything else." She eased her legs straight, then attempted to stand. Her abused body seemed to have other ideas, and she halted mid-movement.

"Will you let me help you, pet?" he asked gently, unable to stand by and do nothing to ease her suffering.

"Will you grab the ointment from the box?" She winced as she shifted to point. "I could use another application."

He left her to retrieve it from the things she'd brought with her. When he returned, she'd managed to stand upright. "Do away with your shirt, and I'll smooth this over the sore spots."

With a snap of her fingers, she exposed her back.

He repeated the same process he had earlier in the day, rubbing the knotted muscles. "You've had the workout, haven't ya?"

"Sure, and I have. I'd sleep for a week if it wouldn't be impossible to get out of bed after."

"How many hours do you get a night, Ro?"

"Five, maybe six total."

"That's not enough to heal." Her answer was a heavy sigh. He figured he wasn't telling her anything she didn't already know. "Aeden mentioned the Aether. I'm assuming he meant we should call on the man, see if he can remove your scars and help heal what won't on its own?"

"I believe so." Roisin moaned when Carrick massaged a particularly tight spot.

"Sorry, love."

"It'll help in the long run."

The pregnant pause was filled with silent speculation, and he sensed she was working through the problem of Damian Dethridge in her mind. Her voice was tentative when she asked, "Do you think Piper would call him for me? They're distantly related, if I've the right of it. Perhaps he could tell me one way or another if my face can be restored."

"I've met the man once, and from the energy radiating off of him, I can promise you that if he can't heal you, no one can."

Roisin's body tensed. "Do you think it's possible, Carrick?"

"Look, I don't want to give you false hope, Ro. But even if he can't, it doesn't matter. Not to me."

She stepped away and waved a hand. In a blink, she was fully clothed. "It matters to me."

"Why?" The question came out rougher than he'd intended, but he wouldn't soften it with an explanation. Not yet. He needed to understand why she was constantly rejecting him when all he'd ever done was try to keep his ragtag family safe during the worst time of their lives. Yeah, they weren't all under one roof— they couldn't be prior to Aeden learning Roisin was alive—but they'd been round and round this topic, and he was growing sick of it.

"I'm not me. Not anymore. Some fundamental part of me has changed, and I can't find my way back."

Her confession pulled the rug out from under him. He simply stared, his heart beating like a bass drum at twice its normal speed.

"I love you, Carrick. That's not going to change. But I need to stop hating myself, yeah? And if I'm being honest, a small part of me despises you, too," she said in a ragged little voice.

"Because of Aeden," he stated grimly.

"Because you didn't trust me to do what was right for my own son. I lost everything with that accident, and I don't know how to believe in this small bit of hope you're offering. I'm not convinced it's not a dream." She angrily swiped at her tears, and it registered on him that he'd seen her cry more in this one day than he'd seen her cry in their entire lifetime together. It gutted him.

"I was wrong, Ro."

The confusion in her eyes was almost amusing. Likely, she thought he'd argue the point or try to make her see his side as he had in the past. But the truth was, he *was* wrong. He'd been a fecking eejit to insist on the separation instead of immediately seeking different therapy options for Aeden and a healer with capabilities like the Thornes or Damian Dethridge. Although there wasn't anyone in the world with powers as strong as the Aether's.

"If you let me, Roisin, I'll spend the rest of my life making it up to you both." He held out his hand, silently begging her to take it. With each second of the clock that ticked by, his hope dimmed. After a full minute, he dropped his arm. "It's too late, then?"

"I don't know."

CHAPTER 8

*C*arrick spent the remainder of the night tossing and turning in the bed he once shared with Roisin. Inasmuch as he'd washed the sheets weekly, he still fancied he could smell her light floral scent on the bedding. He'd been crushed when she rejected him tonight, but he hadn't been surprised. The kind and caring woman he'd always loved was buried under a hardened shell. Somehow, he had to help her rediscover the old Roisin. And maybe, once he did that, she could find it in herself to trust him with her heart again. Perhaps they could rewrite their future with the happily-ever-after they deserved.

He crushed her pillow to his chest and held on tight, as he did most nights. The longing for her never went away, and if she decided they were done, he'd probably continue with this pathetic half-existence, penning lackluster stories until the day he died. His creativity had dried up, and he'd produced nothing but shite in all the time she'd been gone. Ro had always been his muse.

And as for love, she was it for him. She'd been all he'd ever wanted from the moment he'd set eyes on her—as if his soul recognized its counterpart. Together, they made a whole, and without her, there was no satisfactory ending to his story.

A muffled noise by the doorway caught his attention, and he sat up to peer into the darkness. He always left a nightlight on for Aeden, but it wasn't currently glowing. Although it was on a sensor, bulbs burned out on occasion.

After shoving back the covers, he padded to the stairs and listened, worried Roisin had decided to climb them, despite her condition, and that she'd possibly injured herself further. Earlier, she'd elected to stay the night but refused to sleep in their bed, instead choosing the sofa. No amount of arguing changed her mind.

"Stubborn fecking woman," he muttered.

A shiver of awareness hit him a second before the attack. That slight premonition saved him from a bashed skull, and he ducked. A hurling stick slammed into the wall beside him. The instinctive need to protect his family clicked into place, and he went into defense mode, rising up and balancing on the balls of his feet.

His brother Cian had trained him well, and Carrick had a surprise move or two up his sleeve. His first was to bend sideways and kick out toward his assailant's midriff. The whoosh of air from the guy's lungs was satisfying to the extreme, and Carrick followed it up with a front kick to the man's chest, sending him crashing into the wall.

Upstairs, the sound of his son's running feet could be heard, and Carrick hollered a warning. "Hide, Aeden! Don't come out until I call for you!"

Feeling as if he were in a fight for not only his life but for that of his son and Roisin, Carrick channeled his fear into a deadly calm. But what was left of his prickly anger built inside him, and one by one, his cells warmed to just shy of burning. Acting on pure instinct, he held his hands roughly a foot apart and allowed the tingling heat in his body to gather between his palms. A pulsing cobalt ball formed and crackled. Tiny sparks of steel-blue flames flared higher until the room was lit with an eerie glow and revealed the intruder.

Seamus McLeary stared at the energy ball in horror. His wide, terror-filled gaze then locked with Carrick's arctic one.

"You *dare* attack my family, Seamus McLeary? We welcomed you into our pub. *Into our homes!* And this is the repayment you see fit to give?" Rage ruled Carrick now, and he wanted to maim. But the small, still-sensible part of his brain required answers. "Why? What have we done but offer you friendship?"

"It's not personal, Carrick. Ya should know that." A look of chagrin came and went on the man's anxious face. "Ya own what I want, 'tis all."

Blinding fury filled Carrick, needing an outlet, and without a second thought, he flung the magical weapon he'd conjured.

Seamus must've recognized the intent, and he saved himself without a second to spare. He dove for the open side door as Carrick gave chase.

"Da!"

Aeden's hoarse scream stopped Carrick's pursuit, and he swung around to see his son huddled on the top step.

"Here, and I told you to hide," he admonished. He cast one last glance at the door and took the stairs two at a time to reach his son. Scooping him into a tight embrace, Carrick thanked Anu he woke when he had. "Where's your mam? Did you see where she went?" he asked as he scanned the living room from the upstairs landing.

Aeden, in his high state of agitation, couldn't answer. He attempted to move his hands, and Carrick eased his hold to allow his son to sign.

"Outside."

Carrick's blood ran cold.

Seamus had run out back!

If he encountered Roisin, would he try to hurt her?

"Get in your room and lock the door," Carrick ordered and wasted no time tearing down the stairs to find his wife and assure himself she was all right. When he couldn't find her immediately, his heart plummeted to his stomach.

"Roisin!" He didn't care if his bellow woke the entire fucking village at this point. He needed to find her. *"Roisin!"* Frantic and on the verge of a complete meltdown, Carrick raced to the front yard, but his wife was nowhere to be found. *"Roisin!"*

Adjacent to his property, the O'Malley's Black Cat Inn came to life. One by one, lights flipped on and shone from every window.

Bridget rushed out to join him on the lawn. "What is it, Carrick? What's happened that you're screaming loud enough to wake the dead?" She seemed more worried than irritable as she cinched her robe and shoved back her messy mass of hair. "Why are you shouting for Roisin?"

"She's missing."

"Missing?" His sister looked taken aback, and she surveyed the surrounding area then drifted toward the road that led to Roisin's family cottage. "I don't understand."

He gripped fistfuls of his hair and growled. "I've not time to explain, Bridg! I've got to find her!"

Beside him, Aeden—who clearly disregarded his order to stay put—signed an explanation to Bridget. His hands moved at such a rapid pace, even Carrick had a difficult time keeping up with the conversation.

"Seamus McLeary paid us a visit tonight, hurley in hand. He tried to use my head for practice," Carrick told her impatiently to clear up her confusion. "I need to find Ro. Aeden said she was outside, and I fear she may be hurt."

"Then we'll all look, yeah? I'll place a call to Cian and Piper, and they can search the property to the fence line. She can't have gone past that, not this fast." Bridget clasped Aeden's hand in hers. "You go to her cottage, Carrick. I'll mind Aeden until you return."

"Get inside the Black Cat and lock the doors, Bridg," Carrick ordered. "And get Ruairí to come stay until I return."

"I'll not have that dope in my home," she snapped. "And you shouldn't even consider giving him the steam off your piss. That fecker." Giving Aeden's hand a light tug, she said, "Come, Aeden. We'll wet the tea and have scones ready for when your mam gets back."

She muttered all the way back to the door, calling back with a few choice words about Carrick's judgment and sanity and how his mind must be away with the fairies. If he hadn't been half out of his head with worry for Roisin, he'd have laughed at his sister's misplaced indignation. Ruairí O'Connor was a decent sort. Likely the only one from that line.

With a shake of his head, he made one more quick search of the house and grounds, then jumped in his car to race for the cottage.

***

ROISIN WOKE TO THE SOUNDS OF SEAMUS MCLEARY ARGUING WITH a woman, her head practically throbbing from the pain. She remembered his voice well enough from Lucky O'Malley's Pub when she'd picked up the extra shifts to help Bridget since the man never stopped jabbering on.

"You couldn't just kill her and be done with it, you fool? You had to bring her back here?" the woman yelled.

"Shhh, or you'll wake Ronan with your screeching, ya banshee! It's enough to make me ears bleed." Seamus growled. "Besides, we don't know that she's 'the One', now do we?"

The female snorted. "You abduct Carrick's woman—one you failed to kill in that bleeding accident like you should've—and bring her back here to *Ronan's* home? You're missing brain cells, is what you are. Not a lick of sense in your potato head. He'll not let you hurt her once he discovers she's here." The sound of hands slapping on the table echoed in the space around them. "Yeah, that's just fecking grand."

Roisin recognized the voice, but from where, she failed to recall.

She couldn't seem to open her eyes, and a tight, cloth gag across her mouth prevented speech. Try as she might, she couldn't move, and a clawing panic snaked its way through her. Putting herself in Seamus's path to gain information hadn't been the wisest course of action. Yes, she finally learned who had been targeting her, but she had a too-stupid-to-live moment when she failed to hatch an escape plan. She also hadn't counted on him knocking her out when he snatched her, the scaldy bastard. But he'd pay for that along with all the other trespasses against her family soon enough.

Think, Roisin! she ordered herself. *Forget what you've heard and think, woman!*

Inhaling a deep breath through her nose, she exhaled the same way in an attempt to clear her mind and calm her nerves, but also listen to see what these impulsive fools were about. Later, when she was out of this mess, she'd give more thought to what they'd revealed, but now wasn't the time.

This was her first abduction, and yeah, she was in a sticky predicament. She needed to take stock of her surroundings, then get the hell out. Keeping one ear trained on their argument, she went inside herself and reached for the magic to return home. Her cells warmed, but her teleport was aborted before it had begun, telling her she wasn't at full capacity quite yet. The failed effort on her part proved they'd not thought to render her magic useless, just that there was a ward against leaving this particular location. She could work with that.

The coarse material used for the gag was scratchy against Roisin's tender scars, and her first order of business was to loosen the knot locking her jaw in place. She did the same with her blindfold and the ropes around her hands and feet. It required more than a little magic to hold the illusion her bindings were still secure, although she'd hastily disposed of them, and she feared she might not have enough when she needed it later. She prayed to the deity that she could keep it up for a short while until she had the chance to escape.

"What the feck is going on here?" asked a deeper, more commanding voice than the others.

A shiver of recognition ran through Roisin's body as an imposing figure of a man stepped into view. His coloring was the opposite of Carrick's, and yet, the two resembled one another. Perhaps it was the alert expression in his all-seeing eyes or the impression of sharp intelligence he gave off, but she couldn't shake the feeling. She was almost positive they'd met before.

The man was a virtual giant and looked to be about six-and-a-half feet tall. His sheer size gave Roisin pause.

"Our fool cousin thought it would be a brilliant idea to steal away Carrick O'Malley's wife," the woman said with obvious glee in her shrill voice.

In an instant, Roisin recognized Moira. Cian's previous lover. The skank had faked her death and, in the process, had torn his poor heart out. Having met the woman a time or two, Roisin couldn't understand Cian's obsession. Thank Anu, he met Piper and woke up to what real love should be.

All expression dropped from the blond newcomer's face as he slowly turned toward Roisin. "*Christ O'Mighty!* Tell me you weren't so fucking stupid, Seamus."

Roisin couldn't look away from the man's mesmerizing silver stare to see if Seamus felt remorse for his impulsive act.

"Wait! *Wife?*" The stranger spun back around to pin Moira with a glare. "Carrick O'Malley's wife died in that accident you and Seamus engineered," he stated with a silky softness.

"It appears we were all mistaken." Moira shrugged uncaringly and sauntered over to a sideboard and poured herself a glass of wine. "Seamus killed the wrong woman."

"I didn't kill anyone," Seamus denied hotly. Color crept up his neck, and Roisin could practically feel his embarrassment and smell his unease from where she'd been deposited by the hearth.

When the conversation overrode her fear and fully sank into her brain, it registered that she was staring at the people responsible for her sister's death and Aeden's trauma. Fury gave her the strength to sit up and shrug off the illusion of her bonds. Uncaring if she gave herself away, she was intent on hurting them all as they'd hurt her.

With carefully channeled power, she struck out. The gold band of light knocked the wineglass from Moira's hand on its way to wrap around Seamus's thick neck. The sound of the shattering glass was ignored in favor of the gurgling noises he made as he clawed at his throat.

Using the rough stone of the hearth to brace her back, Roisin slowly rose and stalked toward him, throwing one hand up to halt the other woman with an invisible wall should she attempt to save Seamus. A quick glance showed the newcomer wasn't inclined to step in. She met his steady stare, and when he gave a subtle shake of his head, she had a moment's pause. Clearly, he was trying to communicate a message to her, but she'd be buggered if she knew what.

A quick look at Seamus showed bulging eyes and blue-tinged lips. If she didn't release him, he'd strangle to death. The revenge-seeking part of her held no concern, but her conscience was another matter. Could she take a life, regardless of what he'd done?

"Release him, Roisin," the tall, blond man ordered softly. "He's not worth it."

How had he read her conflict? Was it so easily seen in her expression? She'd need to work on her poker face if she intended to outsmart these three.

"*Ronan!*" Seamus gasped and gagged a plea. "*Help... me!*"

Ronan.

The name didn't mean anything to her other than to identify the man with the masterful presence. And from Moira and Seamus's earlier conversation, Roisin immediately understood who was in charge. Perhaps she was exacting her revenge upon the wrong person.

"I'll release him when you remove the wards preventing my teleport home," she replied with a calm she didn't feel.

A small smile played on Ronan's mouth, and respect shone in his admiring gaze. It belatedly occurred to her that he never once avoided looking at her face or reacted negatively to the destroyed half. No, he held nothing but appreciation for her. That, more than anything, jolted her into releasing Seamus.

She ignored the little toadstool as she returned Ronan's frank stare. "I'm leaving, and you'll not stop me."

"I've no desire to prevent you from going, Roisin. But I beg a half hour of your time. We've things to discuss."

CHAPTER 9

*R*onan watched the play of emotions cross Roisin Byrne-O'Malley's interesting face. One half was sheer perfection, the other half grotesquely scarred, thanks to the machinations of Seamus and Moira. Those two never knew when to leave well-enough alone. He thought imprisoning them for a month would've taught them to think first and act second, but Roisin's presence was proof-positive the lesson hadn't sunk into Seamus's pea brain.

The last ten months hadn't been kind to Roisin or her family, and she appeared thinner than a woman of her height should. Still, she was beautiful. Perhaps it was her air of determination or her fury. Feisty women had always held great appeal for Ronan.

"What the bleeding hell do you have to say that I'd care to hear?" she demanded with hands on her hips. "And tell me why I shouldn't bring this pile of rocks down on your worthless arses right now?"

"You and I want the same thing," he replied as he walked to the high table at the far side of the hall. He'd left her a wide berth and a straight line to the exit. The great room was too long, and she'd never beat him to the door, but he wanted her to let down her guard for them to talk. "Seamus, Moira, leave us."

Seamus didn't need to be told twice, and he scrambled away.

Moira, on the other hand, hated to be excluded and gasped her outrage. *"What?"*

"I'm sure I didn't stutter, Cousin. There's no mistakin' what I've said, now is there?"

Red-faced and full of wrath, she stormed toward him.

He faced the threat and lifted a hand to conjure a flaming ball. "Sure, and you have to try me, don't ya?"

Her face paled, but her eyes still burned with hate. Something would need to be done about Moira, and soon. With a sneer and false bravado, she flounced from the room.

Ronan snuffed out the flame and faced Roisin.

"Drink?"

"No." She crossed her arms and looked at him like he was dog shite needing to be scraped from the bottom of her shoe.

"Mind if I have one?"

"If you're after having one, have one. But then say what you have to say. I've a need to get home to my... to get home."

"To your family. You and I can be honest with each other, Roisin O'Malley."

Her cold stare said the Devil would be making ice cream in hell before Ronan would get anything from her lips.

"Will you tell me about tonight's events?" His casualness grated on her last nerve. "How did you come to be in Seamus's care?"

"His *care*? Sure, and that's rich." She snorted and glared. "Are you tryin' to tell me you didn't orchestrate his attack, Ronan— whatever the feck your last name is?"

He hid his twitching lips behind a sip of his whiskey. If she wasn't fit to be tied before, she certainly would be after she heard his surname. As soon as the alcohol settled in his stomach and he had the desire to laugh under control, he casually said, "O'Connor."

She muttered a few choice words as she sunk into the seat closest to her with a wince. "Then you're wrong. We don't want the same thing at all."

"Here, you've not heard it from my lips yet." He toasted her with his glass. "Could be it is."

"But probably it isn't," she snapped. "Get on with it. I'm tired, and my body aches. No thanks to your lot."

Ronan set his tumbler down and crossed to her. Squatting to make his face level with hers, he took her measure and met her wary gaze. "I can ease your pain if you'd let me."

The war between trust and suspicion waged in her turbulent eyes. "And what is it you'll be wanting in return?"

She read him so easily. Only one woman before her ever had: Rebecca Walsh-Thorne. Roisin reminded him of his ex-lover. Although opposite in looks and style, they both had a direct look and don't-fuck-with-me vibe that were fair warning to anyone who paused to take note.

"I want to keep my magic." He surprised himself with the truth as much as he shocked her. Sitting back on his butt, he wrapped his arms around his raised knees and clasped his hands together. Absently, he studied them. Those two large palms of his could conjure mayhem and maim another with ease. Not that he wanted to retain his abilities for those reasons, but he didn't ever want to be vulnerable again. Not like he had been as a child facing his evil-incarnate father. "If the O'Malley family fulfills the prophecy, I lose everything," he confessed, meeting her eyes. "But nothing changes for all of you if they don't."

"And your desire for power was worth this?" She pointed to the ruined side of her face. "Worth the life of my sister?" Her voice rose with every question, but it was the next one that struck Ronan where it hurt. "Worth destroying a small boy and causing him physical injury?"

Ronan was no match for the angry tears racing down her pale cheeks. "I'm sorry, Roisin. More than you'll ever know." When she scoffed her disbelief, he shook his head. "It's the god's-honest truth. Seamus and Moira are madder than March hares and harder to control. The accident was done before I'd ever discovered what they were planning."

She stared at him, and he was certain she saw down to his base layer. Down to where all his childhood fears resided. Down to the secret place where his demons lived. Those fecking demons. They were always telling him he wasn't good enough, clever enough, or brave enough to take what he wanted.

"Look, a prophecy is exactly that, don't ya know. They're unbreakable, and they always come to pass." Roisin actually looked at him with pity, and he wanted to throw up to ease the ache in his belly. "You can't stop it, Ronan O'Connor, no matter how many car accidents or fires you cause."

"Fire?" He clenched his jaw, and he feared he'd crack his damned molars if he wasn't careful. Inhaling and exhaling a long, slow breath, he asked, "*What* fire?"

IF ROISIN DIDN'T KNOW BETTER, SHE'D ACTUALLY BELIEVE RONAN was telling the truth. He certainly seemed surprised by her presence in his beastly castle and by the vandalizing of her cottage.

"Earlier tonight. Someone set fire to my home—with me in it."

Instantaneous anger flooded the man's face, and Roisin leaned back in the chair, fearing Ronan's white-hot rage.

"Regardless of whether it was one of them or not, I'll see to the repairs," he growled.

"Oh, there's no doubt it was Seamus, to be sure. The fecker still has the gravel from my drive on his knees." She glared at him. "And I don't want your help, O'Connor. Any repairs will be done by me or mine." She didn't know where she had the courage to argue, but she'd be damned if she'd take charity from the likes of *him*.

He snorted derisively. "And where will you be finding the funds, huh? It's not as if your family is flush with cash, Roisin."

Embarrassment fired her cheeks, and she lifted her chin. "It doesn't make a blind bit of difference, O'Connor. I'll not take your hand-outs."

He threw up his hands in a gesture of defeat and rose to glare down at her. "Fine. Let the whole fecking building fall in on itself, for all I care."

To make herself feel less small, she stood up and placed her hands on her hips. "I'm going home. You can remove the wards, or I'll reduce your ugly castle to rubble. The choice is yours."

His anger vanished as quickly it appeared, and his silvery eyes sparkled with his amusement. There was something akin to admiration in his gaze as he shook his head. "It's necessary to remove your memory of this conversation first."

A shiver of unease snaked down her spine. It was important she remember tonight, remember all who were a threat to her family, so she could prepare for the coming battle. Good versus evil, so to speak. "No."

"Look, I'm not giving you a choice, Roisin, and it's sorry I am for that. But I can't take the risk of either the O'Malleys or the Thornes coming after me."

She could've made a mad dash for the door, but what would've been the point? At no time in any universe would she be faster or stronger than Ronan O'Connor with his long muscled legs.

But perhaps she was smarter.

"I'll make a pact with you. You keep those jackals away from my son, and I'll keep your secret."

He frowned, and his eyes narrowed on her as he tried to gage her truthfulness.

She tried to portray the picture of innocence and trust.

It wasn't easy.

With a resigned sigh, he shook his head. "I wasn't born yesterday, woman. But I'll do my best to keep those two at bay, all the same. C'mere, and I'll take you home."

He sounded tired, and her heart, that ridiculous organ, turned over in sympathy. Really, she shouldn't feel any. The three of them were responsible for Meg's death and Aeden's suffering, not to mention her own pain. Still, she got the impression he wasn't as evil as the other two, just misguided.

"Thank you." When he nodded and turned away, she touched his arm. "Ronan?"

He glanced down at her hand and froze, expressionless. Then, he raised his eyes to meet hers. She imagined she saw a softening, but in a blink, it was gone, leaving his visage granite hard.

"Be careful of Moira," she said. "Her hatred of you is a living thing."

His smile started slow, becoming wide and engaging, but it didn't reach his eyes. "She's no match for me, Roisin, but you're spot on. She's mad, to be sure." Once again, he shifted to walk away, and again, he turned back as if a thought had occurred to him. "You've a witch among you with the power to stop Moira. Get Piper's family involved if you must, but reinforce your wards, yeah?"

She nodded, and when he offered his hand, she placed hers within his, allowing him to escort her outside. They walked a ways down the lane, with him adjusting his long stride to accommodate her limping gait. By the time they reached the border of the property, her body was aching from head to toe.

"I'm sorry for your pain, Roisin." He tucked one of her wild blond curls behind her ear and rested a hand on her shoulder. An electrical current went through her, and she had a moment's fear.

She'd been a fool to let down her guard!

When he spoke again, his voice was soft and soothing. "Listen carefully. In the back of the O'Malley grimoire, there exists a healing spell. One Anu gifted Carrick's family long ago. You'll need more magic than you currently have, but it's doable if you have the right people, all the same. It should help you and your son by restoring your health."

The sincerity in his voice and the kind expression led her to believe it wasn't a trick; he genuinely wanted to help. His face began to blur, and she struggled to focus. As she swayed, he brought his other hand up to keep her in place.

"What did you do to me?" She tried her damnedest not to panic.

"Nothing lasting."

Her lids grew too heavy to hold open, and Ronan's hypnotic voice drifted to her from far away. "Know this, Roisin Byrne-O'Malley; I don't make war on women or children, and you've suffered long enough for a situation not of your making." She felt a butterfly-soft touch on her brow, and his lips brushed the shell of her ear as he whispered, "You'll forget my involvement in your abduction, remembering only Moira and Seamus. But you'll look for the healing spell after you wake, and when you strengthen your wards, you will add *rochtain a cheadú do* Ronan to the enchantment."

"*Rochtain a cheadú do* Ronan," she repeated dutifully. Though why he'd need to pass through the wards if he intended no harm, she didn't know, and her brain was too fuzzy to solve the puzzle.

"Think of your home, and I'll send you there directly."

"Home," she whispered, picturing the one place she loved the most, the place she could be herself—her herb garden.

He brushed a hand over her forehead. "*Slán abhaile*, now."

CHAPTER 10

*C*arrick was out of his mind with worry. Roisin had disappeared, presumably taken by Seamus to an undisclosed location. An hour and a half later, Piper was still scrying, searching for any sign of Roisin.

Tucked in the corner of the sofa, Aeden hugged a pillow and fought to stay awake. The evidence of his tears was visible on his pale cheeks. How the boy managed to get dirty in the middle of the night was a mystery Carrick wouldn't be solving anytime soon.

"Go to sleep, boyo. When you wake, we'll have your mam back home where she belongs," he told Aeden with a reassuring smile he didn't feel.

"We found her!" Piper shouted and waved him over. Her excitement was contagious, and he smiled when she did. "She just appeared like a blip on a radar. She's in her garden, curled up."

Carrick peered into the mirror and shook his head. He'd checked her entire property and wouldn't have missed her there. How she'd ended up where she was currently would be answered when he fetched her home. After a quick glance Aeden's way, he faced Piper and lowered his voice. "Is she sleeping, or is she hurt, do you know?"

"I can't tell from here, but there's no one else around. That much I know." She placed a hand on his forearm and squeezed. "I'll go get her if you want to wait here with Aeden."

"No. We don't know if it's safe, and I'll not risk your life. Besides, you should be in your bed, resting. If anything happens to you or your babe, Cian will have my hide, he will."

"Go," she said with a light laugh. "I promise, it's all good." She stepped around him and held out her arms to Aeden. "Come on, kiddo. Let's wash that face, or your mom will think I've let you roll in the dirt outside like a little piglet. I doubt that would faze her but for the fact it's the middle of the night."

Once Carrick saw Aeden was receptive to Piper's cajoling, he left to retrieve Roisin.

The instant he saw his wife, he released all the pent-up fear he'd been holding. She was lost to him once, and he didn't believe he could go through that soul-crushing agony again.

He lifted her sleeping form and strode to her cottage. Without a key, he kicked open the door, then settled her on the bed and bundled the covers around her chilled body. Carrick called her name softly as he stroked back her matted blond hair. "Time to wake for me, darlin'."

There was movement behind her lids, but she slumbered on.

"Roisin, I need you to wake up now, pet," he said more firmly, adding a light tap to her unmarred cheek.

Still, she slept, remaining oblivious to him and her surroundings while deepening his concern. Carrick swore under his breath and withdrew his phone to call Piper.

"How is she?"

"I don't know. She's sleeping like she's had one too many at our pub. It's not like her."

"Okay. I'll get Bridget to sit with Aeden. Cian and I will be right there."

"Thanks."

As he waited for the others to arrive, Carrick lit a fire and returned to Roisin's side to watch for signs that she was waking. It reminded him of all the endless hours he'd spent in her hospital room, sitting beside her bed and praying to the Goddess she'd wake alive and well, able to return home with them.

But she hadn't. Not right away, at least.

Her stillness wasn't natural and was too stasis-like. Rage brewed inside him. He'd bet his worthless life that she'd been drugged in some way, shape, or form. If he found the right-bollix who abducted her, he'd tear them limb from limb. Seamus might've been behind taking her, but he didn't possess the brains to do more than that. Someone was pulling that puppet's strings, to be sure.

Piper was the first through the door with Cian hot on her heels. "Still no change?" she asked.

"None."

"Scoot. Let me look at her."

Piper's mother was a skilled surgeon, and it was a given the daughter had picked up a few things along the way. But Carrick was worried they'd need more than modern medicine to wake Roisin. He wasn't certain how he knew, but he'd bet all the income from his entire backlist of books that this was a magical coma of sorts.

"Does this feel like an enchantment to you?" he asked her.

"Yes. There's no dilation of her eyes or other signs to indicate she's consumed anything. But this—" Piper ran a hand along the air above Roisin's torso and the space between her body and Piper's palm crackled with silver light. "—this is from a spell, without question."

Cian shot a sharp glance Carrick's way, then addressed his fiancée. "Sure, and we don't know much about all that, but I've learned enough to understand it's hard to break an enchantment without knowing what spell was used. Is this bigger than you, Piper my love?"

"I'm afraid so." She gave Carrick an apologetic look. "I have the power, but not the skill. If there was a grimoire or something—"

The lid rocked on a decorated box sitting atop a shelf behind them, catching their attention.

They all stared at it, bemused.

The tarps kept out the worst of the weather, and with the windows and doors shut tight, there should be no wind in the house to cause a lid to flutter.

Again, it rocked.

"I think it wants us to check there," Cian said in a stage whisper.

The absurdity caused Carrick to snort. His brother was physically the toughest and likely the wiliest of their family. To see such a clever, capable man tentative in the face of a rattling cardboard lid was amusing to the highest degree. And had Carrick not been so worried about Roisin, he'd have given in to the threatening laughter.

He stretched on his tiptoes and grabbed the box with both hands. Praying it wasn't a rat or some other disgusting creature, he whipped off the top. They all released a collective sigh of relief to find nothing but papers inside.

Carrick immediately recognized all the hand-written notes he'd penned for Roisin over the years, the latest being the one he left on her table after they shared her stew. His heart thunked and turned over in his chest to see one love letter after the other in his barely legible scrawl. Swallowing hard, he put the lid back on the box and set it on the table. With reverence, he ran his fingertips over the finely decorated top.

"Nothing we could use?" Piper asked in a caring, cautious way.

He cleared his throat. "Not that I could see."

The lid rocked back and forth, this time harder than the other times.

They all shared a wary glance before Carrick removed the lid again.

One by one, he gathered the loose papers, unsure what he was searching for but confident he'd feel or sense what he needed. When he got to the bottom of the box, he scratched behind his ear, perplexed by the damned thing's insistence he explore the contents. "I don't understand," he finally said. "I don't know what it's trying to tell us."

Right when he'd have put the papers back inside, the light reflected off a small object in the far corner of the box. Shifting the batch of notes to his left hand, he reached inside with his right and felt around. When his fingers touched the object, he lifted it out, gasping when he understood what he was holding. The Byrne grimoire.

In a blink, it expanded from the size of a dollhouse book to that of a standard-sized spellbook, and the weight of it nearly severed his fingers when thunked to the table. Quickly shoving the hand-written love notes into the box, he put on the lid and set it aside. His fingers itched to open the grimoire, but he feared in doing so, he might open up a world of trouble.

"What do I do, Piper?"

"Obviously, it wanted you to find it. I'd say ask it for the cure you're seeking."

He did.

The leather-bound lid flew open, and the parchment pages of the book whipped back and forth as if a great wind had swept the house. Eventually, it settled, staying open to a specific place. He wasted no time scanning what was written.

"What does it say?" Cian asked, even as he peered over Carrick's shoulder.

The three of them crowded around the book, reading the spell in their own time.

"This looks simple enough," Piper murmured.

"I've no idea where to find these things," Carrick said with a grim sigh.

The doors of the cabinet over the refrigerator flew open, and the contents inside clanked so loudly, he worried the glass would break.

"Aye, we get it," he called out. "Thank you," he added for good measure. He wasn't one to be selfish with gratitude when the magical energy surrounding them was trying to help. After dragging a chair over to the fridge, he climbed up and peered inside the cabinet. He smiled, seeing Roisin's beautifully organized pantry of magical goods. She loved making things pretty, his Ro. Sobering, he swallowed past the thick lump of sadness in his throat. It was probably why she took her disfigurement hard. The loss of what she'd deemed her "beauty" must've been devastating.

Not as devastating as the loss of her son and husband, the little voice in his head countered.

Without a backward glance, he asked Piper to call out the items they'd need.

"One green candle, one purple."

Carrick dutifully withdrew both candles and handed them to Cian.

"See if you can find a pink quartz crystal."

Again, he located it easily enough. "Next?"

"We'll need dried mugwort, wormwood, yarrow, and St. John's Wort, along with a copper bowl and something to grind it all into a powder."

Carrick found it all and again handed the things to a waiting Cian. "Anything else?" When he didn't receive an answer, he looked over his shoulder. "Piper?"

"Is it too much to hope for that she'd have basil oil and charcoal up there?" Skepticism was heavy in her voice, and Carrick chuckled.

"I don't suppose that bleedin' book would lead us this far and not provide all the ingredients, but if need be, can't ya just conjure the rest?"

"The basil oil needs to be prepared at the start of a new moon. It's a process." She shrugged. "But yes, to the charcoal. I could always call my cousin GiGi. She'd definitely have the basil oil."

Carrick rooted around in the cabinet and touched on a medium-size bottle. He squinted into the dark interior in his attempt to read the label. "I wish I had more bleedin' light," he muttered in his irritation.

His cells hummed to life, and instantly, a pale-blue glow filled the space and allowed him to see clearly.

"Holy shitballs!" Piper yelled. "Did you do that?"

"I think so," he admitted with a rueful grin. "It's the third time today something like this has happened. Ro was sure the magic came from me."

Piper turned wide honey eyes to her husband and squealed. "Do you know what this means?"

Cian's gaze darted to Carrick and returned to his fiancée. "No?"

"The O'Malley power is on the verge of returning!" She squealed again and threw herself at Cian, who easily caught her and held her tight.

Once again, Carrick found it difficult to swallow past the build-up of emotion in his throat. Their easy relationship and unwavering love reminded him of what he'd had with Roisin. What he still wanted and would forever want if it was etched into the Fates' design.

"Sure, and can we focus here for a bit. We've a need to wake Ro." He turned back to his basil-oil-finding mission and saw a tall green bottle in the back. "Got ya."

"That's it," Piper said. "Now we put together the ingredients and speak the healing spell."

They worked in unison, crushing up the herbs and measuring them out. Piper conjured the charcoal needed and placed it in the bottom of the copper bowl, then poured a tablespoon of basil oil over the top. Touching her finger to the top of the open bottle, she moved to Roisin's side and made an X on her smooth forehead.

"That should do it. Let's light the candles and put them at the head of the bed."

Cian did the honors as Carrick moved the copper bowl and placed it beside the candles.

"Put a cork pad under that bowl, or Roisin will have your ass," Piper said with a scowl. "I can see you both need to learn about protecting family antiques."

"Now's not the time to be man-bashing, Piper my love. We've been on our own for too long, is all. But luckily, the Unlucky O'Malleys have a beautiful Thorne witch, such as yourself, to turn us from our caveman ways."

Even Carrick laughed at his brother's easy charm and how quickly he diverted Piper from scolding to smiling. "You've always had a way with—"

Cian glared.

Piper laughed.

Carrick shrugged. "Sure, and sometimes I step in it. Ro can attest to it."

"Cian, light the charcoal in the bowl with the purple candle, then replace it to its original position," Piper said as she perused the spell one more time. "I think we're ready. Carrick, sit next to Meg—uh, sorry, Roisin. I still need to wrap my head around the fact she's alive." She waved her hand in dismissal. "Anyway, you sit there and clasp her hand. Cian, you're next to me here. Put your hand on Carrick's shoulder. The idea is to create a current with magic to run through all of us. You're going to pull out whatever is drugging Roisin, take it into yourself, and then pass it along to me."

"*What?* No!" Cian immediately dropped his hand from

Carrick's shoulder. "You're pregnant, and I'll not do anything to harm either of you."

"It won't—which reminds me—" Piper grabbed the basil oil, lifted her shirt, and drew a large X. Her grin had a sheepish quality. "Pregnancy brain and sleep deprivation. I almost forgot the protective oil."

"Jaysus!" Cian gave them both a helpless look. "We can't use Piper for this, Brother. I'm sorry, but I can't allow it."

The loud banging at the cottage door caused Piper to yelp and sent Carrick's heart into overdrive. Damned if it didn't scare him, too.

"Who the hell is *that* at four in the morning?" she asked.

Cian snorted. "Why are you whisperin', darlin'? I think the lights gave us away. Whoever's out there knows we're here, to be sure."

Carrick nodded to Cian to remove the chair from under the knob and open the door. He didn't need to voice caution; his brother was already programmed to take quick action if the need arose. As he swung the door wide, the lights in the house flickered wildly, and the cabinets clapped open and shut as if the cottage was warning of danger.

Releasing Roisin's hand, Carrick rose and placed himself in front of Piper.

"Can I help ya, man?" Cian's tone was hard and forbidding.

"Doubtful, but I can help you."

Piper's shock was evident by her loud gasp. She shoved by Carrick and rushed to the door. "We don't need help from the likes of you," she snarled, raising her hands in preparation to counter an attack.

"I'm not here to fight you, Piper," the giant blond man told her.

Carrick thought that was a fine thing because the fecker was huge, and the light of magic pouring out of him was near blinding.

"Then why are you here?" she growled.

Cian and Piper were shoulder to shoulder, ready to take on the stranger, and although Carrick wanted to help them, he also didn't want to move far from Roisin. He glanced down at his wife's still face and made an abrupt decision. "Let him in."

CHAPTER 11

*R*onan studied the small group and stepped into the cottage when Piper reluctantly moved aside. He had to fight against the rising tide of claustrophobia. The cottage was cramped, and he tended to take up a lot of room. Not only that, but with four other people, in addition to the furniture, the crowded feel was overwhelming and his desire to flee strong. Hopefully, he would be gone before too long and wouldn't be here when the walls closed in on him.

Thanks, da.

He tried to push away the unwelcome thoughts of punishment and small black holes he'd been forced to spend time in. None of that would help Roisin in her condition.

Looking down at her still face, he had a moment of panic. His magic was only meant to remove her memories of him and put her to sleep. He'd never meant to send her into a coma, for feck's sake.

He'd been watching over her since teleporting her to the garden, ready to take action should anyone but her husband come along before she woke. When the others started turning to magic spells they were unfamiliar with to help her, and when

Piper decided the risk to her unborn baby was minimal to wake Roisin, Ronan decided to take matters into his own hands. Sure, the chance of exposure was there, but he'd clean up his own bleeding messes and not let Roisin or her family suffer more than necessary.

"How did you know Roisin needed help?" Piper asked, always suspicious of his motives since his affair with her mother all those years before.

"I didn't," he lied without expression. "The Witch of the Woods makes balms for my old aunt's arthritis. I was simply coming by to leave her a note."

"At this time of the morning?" Cian was skeptical and stepped forward to wrap a protective arm around his mate.

Ronan eyed them with distaste. Not because he didn't want to see them happy, just not happy *together*. They'd fulfilled the first line of that godforsaken prophecy, and although Roisin's words rang true earlier, he would stop the rest if it was possible. His best bet was the third part. For sure, he'd allow no more to be done to Roisin or Aeden.

"Does it matter what time I slip a note through the slot?" he asked, tone dry as dirt. "I figured she'd get it when she woke, and she could call me to pick up whatever she'd whipped up."

"Who's your aunt?" Carrick O'Malley didn't seem any more keen to trust him than the others, but it didn't take a genius to see he was at the end of his rope.

"Millie McL—MacLavery." *Shite!* He'd almost said McLeary, and wouldn't that have given away the fact he was in league with Seamus! Ronan rarely, if ever, made mistakes of that nature, but he was tired from lack of sleep, and this entire situation was scrambling his brain matter like eggs in a frying pan.

Cian's expression hardened, and he shifted into a loose-limbed stance. "Never heard of her."

Ronan recognized the move; Cian was preparing for a fight.

Well, he could ready himself all he wanted because Ronan had no intention of stepping into that trap.

"No? Hmm. Well, that's a riddle for another day. But sure she exists. My mam's sister, or rather, half-sister." Shrugging to show the matter was resolved as far as he was concerned, he faced Carrick. Turning his back on Cian wasn't the smartest move, but Ronan needed to get in and out of here before too long. The walls were already closing in. "What happened to your sister-in-law, man? She looks like she had a bad dose."

"What?" Carrick's expression changed to thundercloud dark.

Ronan gestured to Roisin. "Meg. What's wrong with Meg?"

The other man needed to either acknowledge Roisin as his wife, or he needed to continue with the ruse they'd used to fool everyone since the accident. They'd gotten away with it because Roisin and Meg were nearly identical in looks, with the exception of their hair. But they must've found a way around it to trick so many for so long.

Carrick glanced down at Roisin, and all the love the man felt was in his tortured expression.

"Not Meg then," Ronan said softly. "Roisin."

"Yes." Carrick deflated in front of him, and he sat heavily on the mattress. "Roisin's in some type of magically induced sleep. We don't know who the culprit is, but we need to counteract the spell, all the same."

"I know who I'd pick for the culprit," Piper muttered.

Ignoring her, Ronan squatted by the bed and reached a hand forward. Before touching her, he looked at Carrick. "May I?"

"Are you trying to say you've learned your lesson about touching a married woman?" Piper asked with saccharine sweetness. She accompanied the question with a disbelieving snort. "Right."

Gritting his teeth, Ronan practically growled his frustration. "Aye, Piper Thorne, I have."

Once permission had been given, he held out his hands, palm

down, over Roisin's fair head. The disruption in energy pulled him to the same side as her scarred face.

"Here," he said, gesturing to the spot. "The energy is off. Could be neurotransmitters, could be damage from the accident. She was in a coma if I'm not mistaken?"

"Aye." Carrick watched him with wary eyes. "We were about to perform a spell before you arrived in hopes of helping her."

"Mind if I see it?"

They all remained stubbornly quiet for a minute, sharing concerned glances.

"Or not. I'll leave you to it if you'd rather." Ronan shifted to go, telling himself he shouldn't give a shite. These people would crucify him if they knew he wanted to steal their family magic for his own.

"Wait!" It was Piper who grabbed his arm to prevent him from leaving. Begrudgingly. "Here is what we have."

He read the spell from the Byrne grimoire and cast an eye around the setup. "You didn't create a circle? If you're going to do a proper spell, that's what ya need for safety's sake." He gave her a considering look. She was a Thorne. He'd have thought knowledge like this was standard issue, but maybe not. "I'm surprised you don't know this."

"Listen, Professor Dumbledweeb, I don't go around trying to heal people at every turn. We've family healers for that shit. And besides, some of us don't mind a hard day's work instead of playing at being a Harry Potter wannabe all day long."

He barked an incredulous laugh at her cheeky attitude. "Ya think I don't work, do ya?"

"I don't know anything about you other than you have the morals of an alley cat and prefer another man's wife. I know you don't give a fuck if you leave a girl without a mother."

Tears burned bright in her honey-gold eyes as her body trembled with her building fury, and it bothered him to see Rebecca's daughter so. But Ronan couldn't defend himself against Piper's rightful anger. "Look, I'm not sorry I fell in love with Bec, Piper," he said quietly. "I am sorry you and your da got hurt. But she chose you. And him. And I was a stupid boy at the time. No more than twenty-five and full of piss." He approached her and gazed down into her hate-filled eyes. "It was over two decades past, and I did a lot of growing in that time. I've never again poached another man's wife. It's a firm rule for me now, it is."

She compressed her lips and shifted her attention to the floor.

"I'm sorry you were hurt," he said again. "I've no way to prove it. But I'd like to help Roisin if that's all right with you."

She lifted her chin and met his calm gaze. He imagined he saw a lessening of her anger, but time would tell. With an abrupt nod, she stepped away from him. "For the record, I know about casting a circle. This entry didn't mention one was required." She shrugged. "I thought it might be like smaller magical spells and wouldn't need a circle."

"Fair enough. But for future spells, you may want to assume you need a protection circle, yeah?" He gestured to the bed. "Each of you grab a corner. We need to move it out from the wall."

CARRICK IMMEDIATELY JUMPED INTO ACTION. "DON'T SCRAPE THE wood floor, or Roisin will kill us all when she wakes."

Ronan chuckled.

Carrick didn't know what to make of the man. His timing was suspect, and Piper certainly didn't trust the guy, with good reason. But looking a gift horse in the mouth wasn't smart. Although if history was to be a lesson, the Trojan-horse incident certainly encouraged caution.

Roisin would've laughed and said she was no beauty like Helen of Troy was reported to be, but Carrick would beg to differ. To him, she was the most beautiful woman he'd ever encountered. And all the Helens in the world combined would never measure up to one Roisin.

He and Cian stood back while Ronan and Piper cast the circle. They repositioned the candles and copper bowl, then Ronan stepped in to work the spell, preventing Piper from risking herself and her baby on an unknown enchantment.

Roisin didn't respond immediately, and they all shared a concerned look.

"Maybe I should get GiGi or Alastair?" Piper chewed on her nail as Cian brewed a pot of tea.

With a hearty yawn and a rub of his hands over his face, Ronan was the one to urge them to be patient. "Her mind needs to knit back together. Give it a little time."

"What's considered a little, or for that matter, a lot?" Carrick asked.

A small smile twisted the other man's mouth. "I'll stick around and let you know when you should worry. How's that?"

With a sharp nod, Carrick sat on the bed beside Roisin. He stroked her wild hair back from her temple. "Ro, this is too similar to the time spent after the accident. I'm going to need you to wake, pet. Save me the heart failure."

"Why hide who she was?" Ronan asked softly.

What exactly it was about the man that inspired confidences, Carrick didn't know, but he couldn't be cagey when the guy was only trying to help. "A number of reasons. Mainly because Aeden was terrified when he first saw her face. He believed he was looking at a ghost, and he screamed his fecking head off whenever he came within a foot of her." He closed his eyes against the painful memories. "Ro also told us someone was in the road right before it happened. Though she never said who or why, I have the feeling she suspects and was worried about bringing trouble to our door. It was easier to let the world believe she was Meg for her own peace of mind." Carrick grimaced. "Here, if I'm being honest, I thought the person was someone she dreamed up. No witnesses came forward. But we couldn't dismiss somebody had taken her to hospital."

"That's the reason for the rumor 'Meg' couldn't remember the entire thing," Ronan concluded with a nod. "Makes sense to hide what she knew."

"Yeah, for all the good it did us. She was abducted tonight by Seamus McLeary—or we think she was."

"You don't know?"

Carrick shrugged. "He tried to use my head as a sliotar earlier. Ro disappeared shortly after and was gone for hours. We found her in the garden, like this."

Ronan's mouth tightened as if he were fighting anger, but he nodded slowly. "I'll see her healed, O'Malley. I'll promise that."

"And how can you make such a promise?" Cian asked as he handed off a cup of tea to Carrick and turned to Ronan. "And why would you involve yourself?"

Both great points. They all faced Ronan, awaiting his answer.

"I suppose I feel I owe you all." His silvery gaze touched on Piper before settling on Roisin. "And I despise men who make war on women and children."

Something flashed in the man's quicksilver eyes, and Carrick got the impression Ronan wasn't being exactly truthful. "Yeah, and what did you say your given name was?"

Eyes as hard as steel, Ronan smiled congenially. "I didn't."

CHAPTER 12

*R*oisin registered the voices around her. One, in particular, teased her mind and tried to kickstart her memories. But the harder she tried to recall, the more elusive that bit of knowledge remained. Her head ached like the devil, but she would create a magical remedy when she woke.

"She's coming 'round," the stranger said.

And Roisin opened her eyes to stare straight into the worried depths of Carrick's.

"Welcome back, pet," he said with a tender smile.

She frowned and glanced around, noting she was in her cottage. "Why am I here? I thought we brought Aeden home—Aeden!" She tried to sit up, but Carrick placed a hand on her shoulder and held her in place.

"He's fine, Ro. He's with Bridget."

Piper touched a hand to Carrick's back and smiled down at Roisin. "I'll call Bridget and check on him. Be right back." She left the cottage with Cian right behind her.

A tall, well-built blond man in the corner shifted and came into the light. His expression was carefully blank as if he were holding himself in check. The tickling started again in her brain.

It was as if something was trying to pick off a bandage or scab to let the information bleed out. "Do I know you?"

Satisfaction flashed in his eerie eyes but just as quickly disappeared as warm concern replaced it. Unease crept through at the dark alleys of her mind, skulking ever closer.

The man would've made an excellent actor.

"I'm sad you don't remember me," he said with an easy smile. "I've been by a time or two to pick up a balm for my aunt." When she would've opened her mouth to deny any knowledge, he waved a hand in dismissal. "No need to worry about any of that right now, Mrs. O'Malley. Sure, and I'll pop back by another time. She has enough to tide her over for a few more days."

She'd definitely have remembered him had he stopped by to pick up anything for his aunt. He wasn't someone easily forgotten. Even knowing he was lying, Roisin couldn't bring herself to call him on it in her tired state.

She nodded. "Tell your aunt I'm happy enough to make her another batch when she's ready."

His smile widened, and her heart fluttered at the beauty of his face. If she weren't married, and here she couldn't say she was happily anything anymore, she might've followed through on her interest.

Or perhaps not.

His larger-than-life presence dominated, and likely any woman he set his sights on would be overwhelmed by all that animal magnetism and intensity.

"See ya around, Roisin O'Malley. Take care of that boy of yours, yeah?"

Again, an elusive memory tickled her.

She turned toward Carrick, conscious of his troubled regard.

"Thank you for your help, Ronan," he said, purposely clasping his hands together instead of offering one to shake. "Ro will be coming home to stay after she wakes more fully. If you've something you need, you can visit the pub and ask for her there."

Roisin released a relieved breath. There was a comfort in knowing she'd be under her husband's watchful eye. The Ronans of the world were like predatory birds, ready to swoop down on the less-suspecting smaller animals and snatch them up in their talons. But under Carrick's guard, she felt safer.

If she paused to think about it—and here she didn't want to—she would surely be embarrassed that she was doing her gender, as a whole, a disservice. Strong, brave, and independent women existed and were to be celebrated, but Roisin couldn't help that she loved the protective feel of a man's arms around her.

Ronan's open smile dissolved into a small, wry twist of his lips. "Understood."

No one spoke until he left.

"You don't remember him, Ro?" There was suspicion in Carrick's tone, and it annoyed her to hear it.

"No."

He watched her, doing a slow sweep of her face, eyes dipping to her lips as if he suspected they spouted lies. "Convenient that he showed up when he did."

"Isn't it, though?"

His distrust rankled. She'd given him no reason for it. Well, not that he was aware of. She hadn't told him the full details of the accident. True, she'd confessed someone had been in the road, but no more than that, because she hadn't known anything else. Back then, she certainly hadn't told him she suspected the incident was on purpose. And because she'd been sleeping since her recent abduction, she hadn't had time to tell him she now believed it was Seamus who orchestrated the accident. She just wished she could recall all the details of that day. Who was their rescuer?

"What happened tonight, Roisin? You were gone for hours."

Lying down made her feel vulnerable, so she eased into a sitting position. Knowing his head would explode if she confessed to putting herself in Seamus's path to gain answers, she lied. "I couldn't sleep and went outside to clear my head. Seamus McLeary came round to the back garden and grabbed me. I'd no idea he had the ability to teleport."

Carrick jerked, his eyes flaring wide in his surprise. "He can?"

"Aye. Took me to…" The memory wasn't clear. She had the vague impression of a large hearth and being tied, but she didn't recollect much more than that. "I don't know where he took me. It's gone." Panicked, she gripped his wrist. "Why can't I remember, Carrick?"

"I don't know, love." His suspicion of earlier was gone and in its place was concern for her. "We'll find out, though. Never you worry."

"I hate that I'm unable to account for the time!"

"And I hate that Seamus can teleport," he replied grimly. "We have to let the others know."

Roisin rubbed her temples, wishing the evening wasn't fuzzy. There was something about Ronan. An elusive thought. Could be she really had met him when he'd come to fetch an elixir, but it was doubtful. Why, she couldn't say, but something was definitely off. "Please take me home, Carrick."

CARRICK'S HEART FILLED TO HEAR ROISIN SAY THOSE WORDS. HAD she meant them as they sounded? It remained to be seen, but still, he was elated. The feeling lasted for the span of a breath but disappeared in the face of his unease about Ronan. The man was too everything; too big, too powerful—*too handsome by far.* And Carrick didn't care for the way the fecker watched his wife, as if he were invested in her welfare. The timing was far too suspect, but if the guy did have a soft spot for Roisin, he'd see she didn't come to harm. For now, Carrick would shove aside his pride and take whatever help the man offered if it protected Roisin and Aeden.

Cian and Piper returned as Roisin rose to her feet. His brother's warm, appreciative smile wasn't feigned. Cian had always adored Roisin.

"Ah, Ro!" he said. "Sure, and it does my heart good to see you alive and well."

"You didn't think that when you believed I was Meg," she said archly.

He winced, then flushed. "Well, aye. I believed you were out to snare Carrick with your wiles. I was only looking out for your man."

Roisin's mock indignation disappeared, and she opened her arms in invitation.

Cian hugged her tight, and Carrick's envy snapped and snarled underneath the surface like an untamed wolf. But there was no room for that jealousy here, not for his brother, who was crazy for his new mate. Roisin's disappearance only served to make Carrick more determined than ever to rebuild what they'd lost.

"Ro, you met Piper a few months back, but I'd like to properly introduce you to my fiancée." Cian drew his love forward and stood beside Carrick while the two women summed each other up.

Roisin lifted her chin, but her instinctive desire to cover the damaged half of her face was evident in the way her hand started toward her cheek then dropped. Lacing her fingers together, she smiled but didn't quite meet Piper's direct gaze.

Again, Carrick's heart hurt for her. There was no reason for her embarrassment or shame. Her scars were a badge of courage and resilience; a testament to how tough and determined she was to survive. She should be proud, not ashamed.

"It's a pleasure to finally meet you, Roisin," Piper said with a sweet smile. "I've heard wonderful things about you from your family." With a teasing grin and a thumb toward Cian's direction, she said, "I think this one has been secretly in love with you for a while."

"Sure, and he did try to get me to rid myself of Carrick so we could run away together," Roisin said with a wink and a twist of her lips. The smile never reached her eyes, though, and her sadness sat on her shoulders like a cloak.

Piper's melodious laugh eased the tension in the room. "Sounds like him." With a glance in their direction, she nodded toward the door. "I'd like to talk to Roisin in private, fellas. Mind taking a hike?"

Carrick approached Roisin, and cupping her neck to lift her face to his, he dropped a light kiss on her soft, pillowy lips. "I'll not be far, Ro. Call out if you need me."

"It's doubtful I'll be fighting with Piper unless it's over Cian, but she's welcome to him. The man gads about too much for my likin'." Her soft smile warmed his insides. "You've been the one for me since I'd first set eyes on you, Carrick. You know that."

"Aye, but I've a need to earn your trust and love again." His tone was gruffer than he'd intended, likely due to the overabundance of strong emotions swirling about in his chest. Only his Ro was able to call them up. "When Seamus took you tonight, I about went mad. I don't know that my wits have returned."

She stroked the exposed skin at his throat. "He did us a favor, all the same. He showed us we're what matters. This." She gestured between them.

Carrick's heart began to pound at what he believed was her way of saying she wanted to try again. "You'll always matter."

"Go on with you now," she ordered.

He stole another kiss from her delectable lips and left her to it.

As he stood in the damp morning air with Cian, he silently thanked Anu for Roisin's return.

"What do you suppose they have to talk about in there?" His brother nodded toward the house and blew into his cupped hands. "What's so fecking important we couldn't do this back at the inn, where we wouldn't be freezing our bollocks off?"

Carrick laughed, surprised he could after such an eventful night, and clapped Cian on the back. "The cold is no more than we deserve. Could be they're exchanging recipes. Could be they've sent us out to suffer. But we'll not complain because we have two of the best women in Ireland, and we're grateful for it."

"Sure, and you have to be all logical and shite," Cian grumbled. But a hint of a smile curled his lips, and he never stopped staring at the cottage door.

"You're whipped," Carrick teased.

His brother snorted and raised a brow. "Why do you think that large blond fecker decided to visit when he did?"

"Ronan?"

"Yeah."

"Don't know. Not sure I care."

"The timing was suspect, and Piper hates him." Cian's expression hardened. "I trust her instincts, Brother, and I'll thank you to do the same."

"If you think I'd trust the man as far as I can throw him, you'd be wrong. But he helped Ro, and I can't forget that either."

Cian gave him a nod, and whatever else he might've said was cut off as the cottage door opened.

They'd need to meet later today, after they all got sleep, to discuss what happened and how to prevent another attack of its like.

CHAPTER 13

The O'Malleys aren't a superstitious lot—
Oh, who am I kidding? They're Irish, so of course they are. That's
why this chapter has been omitted.

CHAPTER 14

*A*eden nearly severed Roisin's spine with the strength of his hug, but she didn't complain. It had been too long since she'd received uninhibited affection from her son, and she'd never again take for granted one moment of one day, nor the love he offered.

With a gentle hand, she brushed back his thick blond hair. "It's alright, *mo stór*. I'm fine and back where I belong."

He squeezed tighter.

Roisin met Carrick's gaze and gave him a watery smile. Blinking rapidly, she fought the tears blurring her vision. When he shifted forward, she feared his intent was to usher Aeden away, so she shook her head and held her son tighter. But Carrick didn't do as she expected, and instead, he squatted down beside Aeden and rubbed his shoulder.

"Your mam is tired, Aeden. How about we all snuggle down in bed to sleep together? You're welcome to stay with us tonight."

Roisin felt the movement of Aeden's head against her stomach, and she drew back slightly to cup his pointy little chin. "But first, I'll conjure a bite to eat, yeah?"

His smile filled her heart to overflowing.

"Apple tart with custard, or has your favorite changed?"

He shook his head and held up an index finger. She assumed he meant the first option was the right one.

"Apple tart with custard it is," she declared. "And we'll be heathens and eat it in bed with a cuppa tea."

His happy grin was the balm her wounded soul needed.

Thirty minutes later, the remains of their tart were nothing but a spattering of crumbs, and Aeden was sprawled between Carrick and Roisin, his head again resting on her stomach with his legs carelessly thrown across his da's torso. His was the sleep of contented, safe children, secure in the knowledge of love.

"You should get sleep, too, Ro," Carrick said in a low voice.

"I can't stop watching him," she whispered. "He's grown a foot, at least."

Her husband chuckled. "Only about two inches. But he goes through pants faster than I can replace them."

They shared a smile.

"I missed this," she said as she lightly drew a heart on Aeden's pajama-clad chest.

He shifted and struck out with his foot.

Carrick winced and captured both spindly legs within the circle of his arms. "You missed having your spleen relocated by his hard little heel then?"

She laughed. "Not that, to be sure. But this—the three of us, spending lazy days with each other and enough apple tart to make us sick."

Carrick's expression was sad and guilt-ridden.

She could hear his throat work as he swallowed. "Please don't, Carrick. Don't shoulder the blame for what you thought best."

"Last night, you weren't so forgiving."

"I was tired and angry *and* hurt," she confessed. "It felt like you'd once again decided what was right for us without asking." She entwined her fingers with his. "Here, yeah, you have to stop doing that, Carrick. I've a mind of my own."

"It's sorry I am for it, Ro." He raised their joined hands and kissed her knuckles. "I'll not do it again."

"Pfft. You say that now, but I'll give it a week."

He chuckled, and she felt the rumbling sound to her womb. The man could win over the Devil if he'd a mind to.

Carrick's attention shifted to Aeden. "Do you think the elixir you made will help his throat?"

"I'm hopeful, but I'm also not opposed to speaking with a witch who knows more about healing than I do."

In the farthest recesses of her mind, a memory was trying to surface. Something having to do with the back of the O'Malley grimoire. She shrugged it off because she couldn't recall what it was she was supposed to remember. And yes, she was praying the elixir would work, but the Goddess might have something else planned for their son's future.

"Did you know Anu speaks through him, Carrick?" she asked in a whisper. Why, she wasn't certain. Perhaps she feared mischievous deities or spirits might overhear and interfere.

Carrick looked up in surprise. "Still?"

"That's what he indicated last night. Said she directed him to the cottage."

"Sure, it explains a lot," he murmured.

"Is he psychic, then?" She didn't want him to be. Therein lies the path to madness for a witch. But maybe Aeden would be lucky because the O'Malleys had no true power. She felt a piercing pain in her frontal lobe and sucked in a breath as she grabbed her head.

"Ro!" Carrick moved Aeden's legs, then hurried around to her side of the bed. Leaning over her, one knee on the mattress, he gently touched her cheek. "What is it?"

The discomfort receded, and as she looked into Carrick's caring eyes, she had the burning desire to kiss him. The only thing stopping her was Aeden's presence in their bed. Well, that and the fact she wasn't convinced she was the model bedmate with her spastic back and ruined face. How anyone could be attracted to her scarred body was a mystery.

But an answering fire started and burned boldly in his gaze. A small, sexy smile tugged at his lips, as if he understood exactly where her mind had gone. Her body hummed as he lowered his head toward hers, and as she lifted her chin to meet his lips, she eagerly embraced the anticipation, almost laughing at the butterflies dancing in her belly. After all these years, Carrick still made her feel like a girl in the first bloom of love.

Aeden moaned and rolled in his sleep, his arm reaching out to punch Roisin in the side. Agitation was clear on his scrunched-up face, and sweat beaded his brow.

"Carrick," she said in a low, warning tone.

But he'd already noticed the beginning of Aeden's nightmare and swore under his breath. "Ro, could you...?" He nodded toward the living room, and she felt her heart drop into her toes.

It didn't take a genius IQ to know he was worried her face would terrorize their son should he wake and see her. But if she walked away—*hid* away—she'd be falling back into the vicious cycle of letting Carrick decide what was best for them all. Especially when her instinct was to remain and comfort her son.

"No, Carrick. Not this time. I'll stay here, for Aeden."

Surprise and a healthy respect for her response showed on his face, but overall, he didn't look convinced it was the best option.

"I'm done hiding," she snapped.

"All right. We'll deal with things as they happen and not borrow trouble," he readily agreed.

CARRICK RETURNED TO HIS SIDE OF THE BED, SETTLED INTO THE mattress, and gently shook Aeden's shoulder as Roisin smoothed back the hair from their son's sweaty forehead. "Aeden, wake up now. That's a good lad."

Locked in the night terror, Aeden's limbs stiffened, and his mouth opened in a silent scream. He was frozen in place as he waited for whatever demons haunted him to strike.

Hating his ineffectualness in waking or comforting Aeden, Carrick huffed his frustration. "You're stronger than the dream, Aeden. Wake now. Follow my voice."

"Aeden," Roisin called in an achingly sweet voice. "Come now. Wake for your mam."

Her encouragement did the trick, and his head angled toward her as his body lost its rigidness. His thick lashes fluttered, and though it seemed like a lifetime, he finally opened his eyes to stare up at Roisin. "Mam?" he croaked.

"I'm here," she assured him. "I'm here, *mo stór.* I'll never leave ya again." She kissed his forehead. "And I'll never be giving you apple tart and custard this close to bedtime if it brings on bad dreams."

Aeden snuggled into her, with his head upon her breast. "Love you," he whispered fiercely.

"And I love you. You'll always hold my heart. You'll remember that, won't you?"

He nodded.

Carrick hated himself at that moment. All the wasted months he spent believing Ro's presence would make this situation worse culminated to shame him. Yes, he had his reasons, but looking at them now, seeing the two of them as they should be, he understood his reasoning had been flawed.

"I'll get him some water," he said gruffly.

He didn't miss her sharp look, but he compressed his lips and shook his head, hoping she'd understand he needed a moment to compose himself. When he got to the kitchen, he stared unseeing out the window at their wooded back garden. He'd failed to protect his family tonight, and once again, Roisin paid the price. He was determined it wouldn't happen again. If need be, he'd seek out Ronan, the Aether, a unicorn, or any bleeding magical being on this godforsaken island if he had to, but he *would* protect his family from future harm. He'd also have a day of reck-oning, and Seamus would pay for what he'd done. If he didn't confess to what he knew, Carrick would take it out of his arse, inch by inch, if need be.

Shaking his head, he put aside their problem for another day. He poured a glass of water and grabbed the elixir Roisin had sent him home with the day before. Had it really been less than twenty-four hours? It seemed as if he'd aged a lifetime in the last ten.

When he returned to the bedroom, it was to find mother and son snuggled together, almost asleep.

His heart hiccupped.

Leaning against the doorjamb, he watched them. His beloved wife and their boy. Yes, he loved his siblings, but no one meant more to him than the two people in that bed. He'd die for them. Take a life for them. Do whatever it took to ensure their happiness.

And he'd grovel, too. He had a lot of making up to do—to both of them.

Earlier, he'd caught a glimpse of Roisin's former self, and it made him believe they had a chance, albeit slim, to restore what they once had. She'd have to get past her need to hide from him. To understand he didn't give a feck about the scars marring her body. Those marks were external and had nothing to do with the beautiful woman she was on the inside. Somehow, he'd make her see she was still desirable to him.

Her lashes fluttered, and she lifted sleepy lids to find him watching her. The slow, welcoming smile made his heart beat faster—just as it always had, and just as it always would.

"What took you so long?" she asked, barely above a whisper.

Carrick crossed to her and sat on the edge of the bed. He set down the potion and water glass on the nightstand before he answered. "I wanted to give you two alone time. You need to reinforce your bond." When her brows lifted and she said nothing more, he shrugged and grinned sheepishly. "And I might've been a bit overcome. It wasn't manly to cry in front of you earlier, and I feared twice in one night would send you fleeing."

"You're an eejit, Carrick O'Malley, but you're my eejit." She lifted a hand to cup his jaw. "Lock up and come to bed. You need sleep, too. I'll keep watch."

"How did you know it was my intent to stay awake?"

"Because I know you." She blinked as if fighting tears. "I'd forgotten for a bit, but tonight reminded me of who you are."

"That I'm worthless at protecting my family?" He hadn't meant to say it, and his neck burned from embarrassment. Scratching behind his ear, he shook his head. "Forget I said it. It's likely I'm more tired than I thought."

She entwined her fingers with his. "You aren't worthless." Her gaze dropped to their joined hands. "And you didn't fail to protect me, Carrick." She took a breath and exhaled on a long sigh. "I put myself in harm's way on purpose tonight."

"What?"

"When Seamus ran outside, I teleported out to confront him." Her grip tightened. "He was the one in the road that day. I didn't remember until I saw him tonight, but I'm positive it was him."

"Ro! What were you thinking? If that's true, then he's half-mad, and he doesn't care who he hurts." Carrick pressed her hand to his chest above his heart. "Promise me you'll never do that again."

She scrunched her face and shook her head. "Aye, I won't, but I wanted to see who else might be involved."

"Well, for sure, Moira."

"Yeah, she was there… but I think someone else was too, but I can't remember who." She frowned and shook her head. "It's teasing my brain, like I should know, but when I try to recall, I get a headache for my troubles."

"Sure, it sounds like another spell cast on you. I'm getting awfully tired of that witch playing fast and loose with your health."

"Me, too." She grimaced and tilted her chin toward the door. "Make certain we're all secure and come lie with us. I've had all the sleep I'm likely to get tonight."

CHAPTER 15

$\mathcal{A}$s Carrick held her in his arms and as she in turn held Aeden, Roisin wondered if she might be dreaming. If perhaps she'd gone over the edge of reality into a fantasy state where she didn't know what was the truth anymore—*and she didn't care*. In this bed were the only two people she'd ever need to make her complete. Her husband and her son. She needed them like the air she breathed.

Tonight had proven one thing: she'd do whatever it took to keep their family whole. And if that meant killing Seamus and Moira, then that's what she'd do. But what really disturbed her peace of mind was the shadowy third figure. Seamus wasn't intelligent enough to be a mastermind, and Moira, who had given in to madness, was prone to impulse. There *had* to be another. There just had to be.

Ronan's handsome visage flashed in front of her mind's eye. That penetrating silver gaze had seen and categorized too much. She could definitely see him as a leader; however, he'd helped them tonight. He had shown up, performed the ceremony, and stayed until the magic worked. Would someone determined to hurt them do something so out of character?

"Know this, Roisin Byrne-O'Malley; I don't make war on women or children, and you've suffered long enough for a situation not of your making."

Who had said it to her? Ronan? It sounded like his voice inside her head. But if so, when? Certainly not tonight, yet she couldn't recall a time when they may have met before. And if they had, why say something of that nature?

Carrick's arm tightened around her, and he nuzzled her neck. "You're thinking too hard, Ro. I can feel your turmoil, and it's keeping me awake," he murmured.

His comment was odd, and she shifted to look at him. "What do you mean by that?"

He blinked. "I'm not sure. What did I say?"

"You said you could feel my turmoil, and it's keeping you awake."

He blinked again, and the sleepy confusion left his face. "Yeah, like a buzzing in my brain."

Barely comprehending what he was saying, she eased away from Aeden and slowly sat up. "Are you saying you feel my thoughts in your own mind?"

"For the last minute or two, yeah."

"But not now?"

He went still, as if he were thinking about it. Finally, he shook his head. "No. Just before I woke, I felt it, though."

What had she been thinking about before he spoke? She thought back and settled on Ronan. Pulling his face up in her mind's eye, she once again tried to recall when they'd first met.

Carrick pressed fingertips to his forehead and rubbed. "The buzzing started again. Do you think I'm havin' a stroke?"

Releasing the image of Ronan, she asked, "What about now?"

"It's gone." Carrick sat up. "What the hell, Ro?"

"I think I know who is behind our woes. The third in that dastardly trio that includes Seamus and Moira," she told him grimly.

"Tell me."

"Our visitor at the cottage. Ronan."

Carrick stared at her as if she'd lost her bloody mind, and likely she had. Her supposition was mad, and yet, how else could she explain the magical buzz he was feeling, other than a stroke as he'd suspected?

With a scrub of his palms down his face, he stood and held out a hand to help her up, then led her down the hallway to the kitchen. After filling the kettle and turning it on, he leaned back against the counter and crossed his arms. "Explain."

"I hear him in my head. It's like a conversation we've had; him telling me he doesn't make war on women and children."

"And you don't remember meeting him before tonight, yeah?"

"No."

Carrick nodded slowly and turned away to make their tea. As she watched, he prepared it exactly as she liked, and she had to smile at the old familiarity between them. He placed the mug in front of her and raised his brows in question.

"This. Us. The easy rhythm we've fallen back into just by the simple act of having tea." She shrugged and picked up her mug, unsure how to explain it in a way that made sense. But she didn't have to, because Carrick being Carrick already discerned what she was trying to say. Sitting across from her, he clasped her hand in one of his as he sipped from his cup. A sweet warmth filled her, and she silently thanked Anu for giving her back a large portion of what she'd lost.

"Look, I'm not saying you're wrong about Ronan, but he seemed invested in helping you recover tonight. Why would he do that if he was behind all our woes?"

She didn't have a plausible explanation. Every road she went down was a dead end. "Do you think he was *too* invested?"

Pausing with his mug halfway to his lips, Carrick frowned. "Now that you mention it, yeah."

"I thought so, too. I'm positive I've never seen him before. Did he ever say his aunt's name?"

"Millie MacLavery."

"Never heard of her."

Carrick snorted a laugh. "I told him the same thing. Sure, and he thought he could cod us."

Oddly, she found herself grinning. "I can't see him pulling the wool over on you or Cian."

"I'd have made a pact with the Devil himself if I thought it would wake you tonight, Ro. That's the god's honest truth." The chair creaked as he leaned back. "And strangely enough, I didn't think he was codding me when it came to the concern he felt. It's why I asked if you knew him. His worry for you was more than that of a stranger."

"If I've met him before, I can't recall, and that's bothersome."

"I'll have Cian reach out to his contacts to see what they can find. And you can talk to Piper, see what she knows about him. It should be plenty, seeing how he shagged her mother."

"I can't believe he played the maggot, and the Thornes let him live to tell the tale." She sipped her tea and thought of Ronan. He was a charmer, and the power radiating off of him was impressive and awe-inspiring. The entire package was attractive, yet he seemed lonely, too. As if he were in a self-imposed isolation of sorts. She couldn't say why she got that impression, but it stuck with her all the same.

"Yeah, I've met Hoyt Thorne. To hear him talk, you wouldn't believe he's as clever as he is. But after watching him in action, you'll change your thinkin' soon enough." Carrick gave her a half-smile. "And of course, there's Alastair Thorne, who I'd never cross swords with. The man is lethal. But Ronan…" And here, her husband shook his head. "For sure, Ronan has a certain somethin', and I think it's a powerful attraction for women and men alike."

Roisin nodded. She couldn't argue with Carrick's assessment.

Ronan *did* have a certain something, and it was hard to ignore. "It makes him dangerous."

"It does. He could easily influence others, I'm thinkin'."

"Did you get the feeling he was sad, Carrick? That underneath it all, he was lonely?"

"I'm afraid I didn't give him that much thought, pet. All my attention and worry was for you."

ROISIN'S OBSESSION WITH RONAN WAS WORRISOME. SHE SEEMED fixated on figuring the man out, and Carrick didn't want that much of her attention devoted to another guy. He leaned forward, and careful to avoid touching her scarred side for fear of her shying away, he caressed her unmarred jawline. "Let it go for now, Ro. You've had one major thing after another over the last day. Give your mind a break now."

"You mean stop thinking about another man," she said with an arch look.

"That, too." He chuckled and pressed a kiss to her lips. "Sure, and I'm the only man you need to obsess over."

She sandwiched his face between her palms and looked deeply into his eyes. "And I've obsessed plenty for the last nine months. Jaysus, I missed you, Carrick." Her voice broke on his name, and she pressed her lips together, blinking rapidly. "I missed moments like these; the two of us at the table after Aeden falls asleep, sitting and drinking tea or sharing a glass of wine. I felt totally lost without you."

He couldn't speak. All the words he wanted to say, the love he felt but couldn't express, were bottled in his throat behind a thick lump of self-hatred. Instead, he knelt between her legs and buried his head in her chest as she hugged him in a death grip. Tears burned the back of his lids, and he tried his damnedest not to let them fall. He'd cried buckets since the accident, more than a grown man should.

When he could speak, he drew back and said, "When souls were created, ours were carved from one mold, Ro. The Goddess divided it in two, giving one half to you and the other to me. We're only whole when we're together."

Her love burned fierce as she stared at him, and her fingertips traced the lines of his face as if memorizing each of his features. "Yes."

Releasing a breath he hadn't been aware of holding, Carrick helped her stand and rested his forehead against hers. "We're stronger together. You, Aeden, and me. A unit." He swallowed hard. "Never leave me, Roisin. I'm not sure I could take it a second time."

"I thought it was you who didn't want me anymore," she whispered. "That I was broken and useless to you. To Aeden."

"No! Jaysus! You're the glue that keeps us all together. Here, Aeden and I were living half-lives without you." He tilted her chin up and gently traced her scars. "I can't tell you enough how these don't matter to me, Ro, other than they break my heart because they cause you pain."

"Do you think Aeden will be okay?"

"He's our son. He's got your cleverness and steely resolve."

"And your kindness of heart."

"And his own tough little spirit."

She smiled through her tears. "Then he'll be okay."

"Yeah. I think he'll be okay. Now that we have you back, that is." And because he couldn't help himself, couldn't go another minute without tasting her love, Carrick kissed her. When she didn't pull away but instead returned his passion, kiss for kiss, he felt lighter. Happier. "I want to make love with you more than I want to breathe," he growled, trailing his fingers across the flat plane of her abdomen.

"Too bad there's a child in our bed," she laughed and followed it with a low moan as he dipped his hand beneath the waistband of her pajama bottoms and touched her. It thrilled him to find her wet and ready, even as it frustrated the feck out of him.

"We can use the spare room upstairs," he said and hoped like hell she'd take him up on it.

"Ye—"

Aeden's terrorized scream rent the air.

"Stay here!" Carrick ordered as he dashed for the bedroom. Static began in the tips of his fingers, and by the time he reached the bedroom, blue sparks were dancing in the palms of his hands. But as he skidded to a halt inside the door, it registered this was only another of Aeden's night terrors and not an enemy attack.

Carrick shook his hands to dispel the building magic and climbed onto the bed, drawing his son into his tight embrace. "It's okay, Aeden. It's okay. Da's got you. I'm here."

"Mam!" Aeden's eyes were wide and staring at some distant horror only he could see. "No!"

It hurt to hear his strained cry, and Carrick knew from experience, Aeden would wake with his throat on fire for his efforts.

Roisin joined them on the bed and stroked the sweat-damp hair from Aeden's face. "I'm here, *mo stór*. I'm right here." Fat droplets dripped from the outer corners of Aeden's eyes and rolled into his hairline at the temples. She continued to smooth back his hair as she rained butterfly kisses on his face. "I'm here."

Slowly, second by agonizing second, Aeden's body relaxed and softened, and he blinked, coming back to himself. Carrick felt the exact moment when Aeden recognized them as his little body lost its rigidity, and he breathed his relief.

"Mam?" Aeden croaked, grabbing his neck.

"I'm here," she assured him with a trembling smile. She'd positioned her face to only allow Aeden to glimpse the undamaged half, and Carrick wanted to assure her again neither of them cared anymore about the scars. But he couldn't speak for Aeden, and he didn't know how their boy would react waking from yet another nightmare.

Aeden hugged Carrick briefly before drawing back and reaching for Roisin. The peace on their son's face as he cuddled into her embrace and curled his fingers into Ro's corkscrew curls stabbed Carrick right in the fucking heart. Not for reasons of jealousy, but once again, he understood what a colossal mistake he'd made in keeping them apart. Who knows how much sooner Aeden would've recovered? And Roisin, too. He'd not wanted to cause her undo stress or tax her strength, but might she have healed sooner with the love of her family?

Carrick's self-hatred was all-consuming.

"Seamus and Moira want to hurt us, Mam," Aeden signed.

Roisin compressed her lips and hugged him tighter.

Carrick met her worried gaze over the top of their son's head. He shook his head, silently promising that those two monsters would never get close to either of them again.

CHAPTER 16

*T*he morning was relatively quiet, but Roisin still kept her family within eyesight until it was time to reinforce the wards. She approached Piper to help with the spell for both the cottage and the home she shared with Carrick and Aeden. If anyone with ill intent set foot on their property, they'd be alerted to trouble and be able to react accordingly.

The two women met inside the study at the Black Cat Inn, and Piper immediately hugged her. Last night at the cottage, she had requested private time with Roisin so they could be properly introduced without the men. Piper hadn't judged her for staying away from her family, and she'd promised to fill Roisin in on all the things she'd missed about Aeden's life in the interim. Other than with Bridget, Roisin had never felt such an instant friendship with another woman. Piper had also assured her she'd find a way to help Aeden heal completely, cementing Roisin's adoration for the woman.

"I fell in love with the ceremony room the moment I saw it," Piper said, as Roisin ran her hand under the lowest shelf in search of the lever to open the secret door. "Hidden behind a bookcase! How freaking cool is that?"

Roisin smiled as the door swung outward. "Sure, and it was the same for me. I was excited by the discovery the first time Carrick showed it to me, and I practically lived down here for the first months after."

As they traversed down the stairs, the lights flared to life, illuminating the way. And as they entered the cavernous chamber under the inn, the wall sconces flared, and the dancing flame revealed a ten-foot-wide pentacle on the stone floor. The moment the two of them stepped into the circle, the runes on the altar's wooden base woke and pulsed with a low light.

"It awes me every time I see this," Piper said with a light laugh. "It's like this house is alive."

"I've always thought so."

"It makes sense since it's on a ley line."

They worked quietly together; Roisin setting the candles on the exterior points of the pentacle as Piper thumbed through the O'Malley grimoire to find the spell needed to protect the combined estates.

"It's difficult to believe you were able to open that bleeding thing. I've only known it to wake once when we were looking for one of Granny O'Malley's recipes for brew." Roisin shook her head in wonder.

"I believe it was because of the prophecy." Piper shrugged and continued to peruse the pages. "We never tried it, but I'd lay odds Aeden could open it now since his is the next line of the riddle."

Roisin joined Piper at the altar. She'd not given much thought to the prophecy other than Piper and Cian's part. "Who do you think the One is going to be?"

"You? Carrick? Not sure, but it will be someone he cares about." She paused to consider. "We know the first section was for Cian and me. We know the second is for Aeden, as the only blond son born into the O'Malley family. And we know the third section probably pertains to Bridget and Ruairí O'Connor. Those two can't keep their eyes off each other, even though she still considers him the enemy."

"So if we are to base it on acts of love, it would need to be someone Aeden cared for more than his own life," Roisin concluded with a frown. "If that is the case, it's likely Carrick or myself. He doesn't know anyone outside our family." She hated the idea of her son putting himself in danger's path for any of them. When it came down to it, she'd rather sacrifice her life for Aeden's or Carrick's, and without question, her husband would feel the same way. "It's always been my understanding that prophecies can't be stopped once in motion. Can they?"

"I don't believe so, no."

Her heart hurt to think about it, but the more she did, the more the answer became clear. She'd beg the Aether to step in to protect her son. Like Carrick, she'd sell her soul to the very Devil if it meant keeping her family safe.

"Let's boost these wards and worry about it after," Piper said softly. "The rest we'll figure out as we go along."

"What if I can't save him?" Roisin asked hoarsely. "Everything Carrick and I did has been for Aeden's sake. I stayed away, believing someone was targeting me," she confessed to what she'd never told anyone.

Piper jerked in place, and her eyes flew wide. "Carrick never told me."

"He doesn't know. I kept it to myself." She focused on the floor at her feet. "I have shadowy memories of the accident. Of Seamus in the road, and then a stranger saving us. But I still can't remember it all." She met Piper's concerned gaze. "What if I've wasted time I could've spent with Aeden, and I lose him anyway?"

Her throat was raw and achy with the tears she refused to cry. She had to firm her resolve. Had to be stronger and smarter than she'd been until now.

"You won't, Roisin. I promise you, you won't. My family will be on call, and we'll never let Aeden out of our sight. Fuck this prophecy. That precious boy is too important to us all."

Piper's fierceness helped to ease the building dread, and Roisin impulsively hugged her. "Thank you for taking care of him when I couldn't. Here, I owe you a debt of gratitude I can never repay."

"He's easy to love, Roisin. He's such a wonderful little boy."

Pulling back, she inhaled and exhaled a cleansing breath. "He's a gift from the Goddess." Glancing down at the grimoire, Roisin noticed it was glowing brightly. "Is that normal when you're around?"

"It is when I connect with anyone in this family. When Cian and I touch it together, the light can be blinding. It's more muted for just me." Piper grinned and bumped her shoulder against Roisin's. "I guess our newly formed friendship makes it happy."

"Then it's glad I am that you like me," she replied with a warm smile. "And I'm grateful you don't think I'm a toe rag for staying away from my son this long."

"You had your reasons, Roisin. It's not for me to judge what you did for the love of your child."

"I don't think Cian could've chosen a more perfect partner, Piper Thorne."

"I agree. Piper is the moon to me stars," Cian said from behind them.

They spun around and found him sprawled on the bottom step, legs straight out in front of him and ankles crossed as he leaned back on his elbows. A wide grin took up half his striking face.

Thickening his accent, he added, "Me lucky charm, to be sure."

"When did you get here, player?" Piper scowled.

His grin widened, and his eyes lit with wicked amusement. "Calm your temper, Piper me love. I'm a trained spy, remember? I'm able to sneak up on many an unsuspecting target."

Roisin laughed as Piper rolled her eyes.

"Yeah, James Bond has nothing on you," Piper said dryly. "Now I know why this finicky book lit up. It loves you best."

He climbed to his feet and sauntered over to them. Wrapping an arm around his fiancée, he buried his face in the crook of her neck. "Sure, and can I help it that I'm pleasing to the eyes with a personality to match? The book knows I'm the stuff of legends."

Piper struggled not to laugh as she looked at Roisin. "What can I do? He's incorrigible."

"I've always thought so."

Cian kissed Piper's smiling mouth in a sweet, slow manner, then repeated the action, lingering a little longer the second time. "How long will this take? It's your nap time, darlin'. I'm positive you need to spend the afternoon in bed."

His wicked leer caused her to lose her fight with laughter. "You're ridiculous, and it's a good thing I love you."

"Aye, I think we've established that." After kissing Piper's temple, he faced Roisin. His easy-going expression disappeared. "How are you feeling after last night?"

"I'm fine," she assured him with a half-smile. "No ill effects."

"You had us all mighty worried, Ro. Carrick was ready to slay dragons to bring you back."

She grinned. "Who doesn't love a man willing to slay dragons on her behalf?"

Cutting a side look toward Piper, he said, "Or a woman."

The soft glow emanating from them spoke of their unbreakable bond, and Roisin was a little envious of their newfound love. She didn't desire Cian for herself, but she missed the excitement of dating and connecting for the first time. The unexpected thrill of it all and the flutters in the pit of her stomach. She still experienced something similar with Carrick, but not to the level that Cian and Piper probably did in the throes of their budding relationship. Roisin's bond with her husband was solid but for their recent bump in the road. Steadfast. But only when he left her those endearing notes in random places was she transported back to a time when those butterflies first took root in her belly.

"What has you so sad, Ro?" Cian's eyes were kind and melted more of the coldness encasing her heart.

"Not sad. More like nostalgic." Standing on the tips of her toes, she kissed his cheek. "Seeing you both together makes me wish I could go back to the beginning with Carrick. To the days we couldn't keep our hands off each other and we snuck away to enjoy a *nap*."

"I seem to remember you were doing that up until last year." Her brother-in-law gave her a wink but sobered again. "You'll get it back, love. Carrick will see to that."

As she was struck by an onslaught of tears, she turned away on the pretense of studying the open grimoire.

"You will, Ro," Cian said from behind her. His warmth against her back, as he hugged her from behind and rested his chin on her shoulder, was welcome against her sudden chill. "You and Aeden are his reason for living."

"Yeah. So he says." She couldn't prevent the small edge of bitterness from creeping into her words. Was she still cross about the separation? Perhaps. She thought she'd let that go last night, but maybe she still held residual anger. With the help of the Goddess and time, she hoped it would subside.

With great care, Cian turned her to face him. "You doubt it?"

Her shame colored her cheeks. "No. Not truly. Don't mind me."

"When you wouldn't wake up last night, I saw the man struggle to retain his sanity." He tucked a lock of her hair behind her ear. "In the months you'd been staying at the cottage, he was a caricature of his old self, Ro. And he never looked at another woman." Cian shook his head slowly. "It's why I reacted so badly when I thought you were Meg, the night I caught you sneaking onto the property." He gave a low snort. "He came alive again, and it infuriated me that your sister might be the one to do that. In my mind, I thought it should always be you."

"Thank you," she whispered past her dry throat. "I needed the reminder." A movement by the stairs caught her notice. Carrick stood there, an unbearable sadness in his eyes, and Roisin had to close hers to shut out his pain, or she'd lose her fight with the sobs building in her chest.

When she had herself under control, she lifted her lids in time to see him exchanging places with Cian.

"It's okay that you still have doubts, Ro," Carrick said quietly. "But know this; I'll spend the rest of our days putting those doubts to rest. Not one hour of one day will go by that I won't prove my love for you."

"Oh, Carrick." She wrapped her arms around his waist and pressed her forehead against the hard wall of his chest. "I'm sorry."

"No, love. I'm the one who's sorry. I played the proper fool, but I'll make it right."

She lifted her face to gaze up at him, and his sweet sincerity almost broke her heart. "You already have."

"Not completely, but I will."

She pressed her scarred cheek against his chest and looked at Cian and Piper. She almost laughed when she saw the other woman wiping away tears. Here *she* had been struggling against breaking down, yet Piper had no problem letting her true feelings show.

It took Roisin a long minute or two before she could force herself to break their embrace—in Carrick's arms was where she could live forever—but she eventually pulled back. She had a job to do, and the wards weren't going to strengthen themselves.

"Where's Aeden?" she asked him.

"Directly above us with Bridget and Hoyt watching over him."

"My dad won't let anything happen to him, Roisin," Piper said with firm conviction.

"Right." Roisin nodded toward the lit candles, now burned a third of the way down. "We should finish this before we've no wick left, yeah?"

Carrick smiled, and in his warm gaze, she saw his understanding of her uncomfortableness. Never had she liked being the center of attention.

"Can we help, or will we be a hindrance?"

"You both seem to have a small amount of power..." She looked at Piper, who nodded her agreement.

"The more, the merrier, I always say."

Cian snorted. "Sure, and that's not what you say when I mention—*oomph!*" Hamming it up, he bent double from Piper's elbow to his stomach and caused the rest of them to laugh.

"Take your place over there, you *eejit*," Piper said, her amusement still heavy in her voice.

"Now, Piper me love, I'll not have ya callin' me names in front of others," he warned with a wicked gleam. "Tonight, you'll get a proper spank—"

She covered his mouth with a horrified sputter. "Shut it!"

Laughing, he drew her hand from his face and kissed her. "You're beautiful when you're scarlet, darlin'." As she growled, he danced backward out of striking distance. "No more messin' about," he scolded as if she were the one being the fool. "We've a job to do."

"I'm going to kill him," Piper muttered in an aside to Roisin. "Dead as a doornail."

"And I'll help dispose of the body," Roisin told her. "It's the least I can do for your kindness to Aeden."

"I already adore you."

Laughing, Roisin bumped Piper's shoulder just as the other woman had done to her earlier. "The feeling is mutual."

"Feckin' hell, Cian!" Carrick punched his brother on his bicep. "Look what you've gone and done. You've got them ganging up on us, and we've lost the balance of power."

"Sure, and don't blame me that you can't keep your woman under control. I've no troub—"

"Don't finish that line if you ever want a taste of my lucky charms again," Piper warned.

"Sound advice," Carrick added.

His brother opened his mouth to retort, but Piper narrowed her eyes.

Cian clammed up and mimed locking up his lips.

She nodded her satisfaction. "Good boy."

For Roisin, the teasing seemed foreign. She hadn't had much of it in the months she'd been separated from the O'Malleys, but she remembered how quick they were to laugh or rib each other. Piper fit in well with their group, and Cian was happy in a way he'd never truly been before. If nothing else, Roisin was grateful to Piper for adding the missing element this family needed.

They were inside the circle when her head began to throb. A random thought came to Roisin that she should add a line to the spell for the wards, but she couldn't quite recall what it was until Piper spoke the first part.

A high-pitched ringing started in her ears, and though she couldn't hear her own voice, she said, "*Rochtain a cheadú do* Ronan." A small sharp stab in the front right side of her head distracted her from all the gasps.

"*What?*" Carrick's shock couldn't be plainer.

She looked from one to the other, not sure why he was bothered. "Why are you upset?"

"You exempted Ronan from our spell." Piper's worried gaze darted between the brothers and settled back on Roisin. "Why?"

"I didn't do that!"

"Yeah, Ro, you did." Carrick couldn't leave his position in the circle to cross to her, not with the spell incomplete, but he watched her as if he were afraid she would faint at any moment. "Can we restart from the top?"

Piper nodded and spoke the written spell from the top.

The high-pitching ringing started again, and Roisin grabbed her head a second time as the pain pierced the frontal lobe. She felt her lips moving but couldn't hear the words she spoke. "*Rochtain a cheadú do* Ronan."

"You did it again." Carrick was white-faced. Sweat beaded his brow and his body practically vibrated, making his desire to cross to her was obvious.

"That sonofabitch!" Piper's expression turned livid. "He's somehow brainwashed her to give him safe passage through our wards!"

Roisin was growing angry on her own behalf. "I don't understand what you're talking about."

"Ro, you've included a line in the spell to allow Ronan entry to our homes," Cian said. He looked more concerned than upset. "You said, '*Rochtain a cheadú do* Ronan.'"

"No! I wouldn't do that!" She looked wildly around. "I wouldn't!"

"Piper, end this." Carrick never removed his furious stare from Roisin and appeared about to come out of his skin.

"Goddess hear our plea,
assist us in our time of need
and reverse the words we said unto thee.
As you will, so mote it be."

The candles' flames flared higher and extinguished on their own. Anxiety pounded in Roisin's chest, and she wanted to physically stop Piper from talking. For the third time in as many minutes, the ringing in her ears became all consuming. This time, Roisin clenched her jaw and refused to speak. When the spell was finished, the noise in her head stopped. Drained, Roisin dropped to her knees, and Carrick dove toward her. He got there just as darkness claimed her.

CHAPTER 17

"*W*hat do you want to do?" Piper asked.

Carrick didn't know how to answer her; he had no easy solution. And as he stared down at his wife's still visage, he wondered what the hell else Ronan had done to her. Had they made a mistake when they allowed the man to conduct the spell at the cottage? Had he woven an enchantment into it, like a hacker building a backdoor into a computer program?

It was possible Carrick's writer's imagination was getting the better of him, and he was seeing villains where none existed. However, Roisin had spoken Ronan's name in conjunction with the words to give the man a free pass through their wards. She'd either been victim to Ronan's magic, or she was in league with the guy.

"I don't know," he finally said in answer to Piper's question. "Cian?"

His brother grimaced and shook his head. "She can't be allowed to participate in any ceremonies, Brother. Not if a possible enemy has swayed her to his side."

"He hasn't," Carrick said, positive in his heart of hearts Roisin was a victim. "She'd never betray us willingly."

"Sure, and she might be doing this unwillingly, but either way, we can't risk it, Carrick."

"Yeah, I know." Shifting his burden, he rose to his feet. "I'll send down Hoyt and Bridget. Perhaps they can lend you the magic Roisin can't."

Piper nodded and shot a worried glance toward Cian.

"As soon as she wakes, we'll go see the Aether. I'll see if he can undo the damage Ronan has done," Carrick said heavily. "She shouldn't have to deal with one more thing."

From his spot beneath an ancient oak tree, Ronan stared at the Aether's grand house. Gothic in nature, it radiated a very hands-off vibe. The square turrets added to the castle-like impression and made one believe an army of soldiers could appear at any given moment to defend the inhabitants. The only welcoming features were the sprawling steps that led up to large double doors, with their large urns filled with flowers, and the well-manicured lawn.

"Why are you watching the house?"

A young voice almost scared him out of his skin. The Aether would have the best protection imaginable and a strong sense of presence, and Ronan hadn't expected anyone but Damian to find him hanging about. Years ago, he had been granted permission to come here if needed. He'd only been working up the courage to approach the house to confess his sins to his friend and ask for a potential solution.

Still, who would've thought a small child would be wandering the grounds?

"And who are you, wee beastie?" he asked with a warm smile as he willed his heartbeat to return to normal.

"Beastie," she replied promptly. "Or that's what Papa calls me."

One look at those large obsidian eyes, and he knew exactly

who her father was. "I didn't know your da had a faerie child roamin' the grounds."

She giggled, and Ronan lost his heart.

Her eyes twinkled up at him, and she did that enchanting little dance young children do when they put their hands behind their back and rock their shoulders. "You talk funny."

"Do I, now?" He purposely thickened his accent. "Sure, and maybe it's you, ya wee wild beastie, who be the one talkin' funny."

Again, she giggled, and he chuckled at the sound. Damn, but she was precious.

In the blink of an eye, she became serious. "I'm sorry your papa was mean to you, Ronan."

The blood in his veins turned to ice, and his heart thudded painfully. "How do you know my name? And how do you know about my father?"

"I'm the Oracle. Or I will be," she said with a small shrug of one shoulder.

An Oracle. A chill swept him. Sure, everyone knew what they were—all-seeing witches with the power to predict the future and recall a person's past—but he'd never met one. They were legendary, like King Arthur's Merlin. It stood to reason Damian Dethridge's bloodline would produce a witch of her caliber. Ronan wondered if the girl had the powers of an Aether, like her da and her gran before her.

"I do," she said simply.

He didn't bother to hide his confusion. "You do what?"

"Have power like Papa's and like my grandmother used to."

For a moment, Ronan froze in horror, but he forced himself to take a deep breath and relax. The child wasn't a threat. "Did ya just read my mind, wee wild beastie?" he asked with a casualness he didn't feel.

The girl tilted her head and watched him for five long heartbeats before she laughed. "I did, but I can't right now. You're good at hiding your thoughts. But don't worry, Ronan. I won't tell your secrets." She gave him a sly look. "Or I won't if you promise not to tell Papa I was out here."

"So not only are you the Oracle, you're a bloody con artist to boot," he retorted.

Her unrestrained laughter held pure joy, and Ronan found himself laughing with her.

As she watched him, her delight faded, and sadness filled her eyes. "I'm sorry your papa was mean to you," she said again.

"It was a long time ago, sweet. I'm a mighty warlock now. He can't hurt me." Or at least he couldn't while he maintained the O'Malley magic. But every day, Ronan felt that power slipping through his fingers and his abilities faltering a little bit more.

"You can't stop the prophecy, you know. But you can save the Golden Son when he sacrifices for the One."

Her solemn words tore at his heart. She knew his future, and all he had to do was ask, yet part of him didn't want to know.

Once again, she tilted her head as she watched him. "The Fates have a plan, and you can fight it, or you can accept it. Accepting is better."

"And that plan, is it that I should be powerless?" He sounded as if he had a frog trapped in his throat, but his own fear was beginning to strangle him. If he lost what magic he had, his father could return.

"You don't truly want the answer to that, my friend," Damian Dethridge said from behind him. "And little girls with big mouths eventually find themselves in a boatload of hot water."

Ronan's pulse had been pounding so loudly in his ears, he'd missed the Aether's approach. He didn't turn right away, instead keeping his focus on Damian's daughter. Any sign—a nod or a shake of her head—would do. But her gaze locked on her father, and her face filled with chagrin.

Dropping her head, she swung a foot back and forth, stirring the grass by the root of the tree with the tip of her bare toes. "I'm sorry, Papa."

"Doubtful," Damian said with a laugh. "Go find your mother, Beastie. Ronan and I must talk."

A mischievous grin curled her lips, and she gave Ronan the type of flirty look that only a manipulative seven-year-old girl could. "Save the Golden Son," she ordered in a stage whisper.

Before he could respond, she was off and running, her dirty bare feet flying across the expanse of lawn as she headed toward the house.

"Here, I don't envy you when she becomes a teenager, Dethridge."

"For over two hundred years, I never had one strand of grey. Now, I feel them sprouting on my head daily." Damian held out a hand. "It's good to see you again, O'Connor."

"You, too, my friend. And if I didn't know you had a wild child gadding about, it's been way too long."

"For safety's sake, Beastie isn't common knowledge."

"You really call her Beastie?" Ronan laughed. "That's solid craic. And not a soul will hear about her from my lips," he promised.

"Now, how about we get to why you're here? As delightful as this visit has already been, I'm not a fool to believe you're here because you missed me."

Damian Dethridge was smaller than Ronan by at least six inches. Dressed in a grey shirt and black trousers that probably cost more than most people's vehicle payment, the Aether was the picture of class. His black hair was always stylishly cut and his face freshly shaved, lending to the air of elegance.

"I've come to dump my problems at your door, man. And I hope you'll take mercy on me. I need advice and likely backup should the Thornes and O'Malleys decide to retaliate."

"You started a war?"

The dangerous Aether took the place of his life-long friend, and Ronan had a moment's pause. "Not intentionally," he finally said. "But I fear that's where this is headed if we don't stop it, and soon."

DAMIAN DETHRIDGE HAD BEEN MANY THINGS IN HIS LIFE, BUT NO one could ever consider him a fool. Although he hated to get in the middle of warring families, it was essentially his job as the Aether to do so and to keep the magical community balanced as a whole.

From his study window, he had watched as Ronan worked up the courage to approach the house, only to have Sabrina seek the man out before he could drum up his nerve. Knowing Ronan wouldn't be a threat to his daughter, Damian had taken his time joining them, hoping Beastie's unique brand of charm could put his friend at ease before he reached them. He should've known better than to think his daughter could keep her predictions to herself.

"Tell me, O'Connor. Who is the Golden Son? Alastair Thorne?"

"No. It's from the O'Malley prophecy."

Ronan ran a hand through his hair and looked out over the vast expanse of the Dethridge estate. Damian had a sense the man didn't see anything.

"What's going on, Ronan?" Though his voice was velvety soft, it was lined with steel. "I need to know if I'm to help."

Seeming older than his forty-plus years, his friend faced him, and his haggard expression spoke volumes. "I'd never make war on women and children, but apparently my family has no qualms about it."

Fury coursed through Damian. He hated conflict as a whole, and it was shit like grudges and wars that made his life difficult. After two centuries, all he wanted was a peaceful existence with his small family. Yet trouble always came knocking on his door.

"Who was hurt in their war?" His tone was deadly, and Ronan took a step back, rubbing his neck and looking wary.

"Can you rein it in, man? That anger shite ain't comfortable."

Damian made a concerted effort to contain his emotions. He was well aware how other people could feel his more powerful emotions like a slap to the face. It stung them when the tentacles of his magic reached out and struck.

"I ask again, O'Connor. Who was hurt in their war?"

"First, let me quote you the prophecy." Clearing his throat, Ronan continued. "It starts with, *When the mighty Thorne pricks the heart of the Frozen, the end shall start in motion.* And to the best of my understandin', that part was fulfilled when Piper Thorne saved Cian O'Malley a few months back."

Damian nodded absently. Later, he'd confirm with the O'Malleys what went on, but for now, he'd accept Ronan's story at face value. "The next line?"

"It states, *When the Golden Son sacrifices for the One, only then can the curse be undone.*"

"Who is the Golden Son, and who is the One?"

"I don't know who the One is, but I'm right certain the Golden Son is Aeden O'Malley. He's the only true blond-haired *wean* born into his clan."

"So if we interpret the prophecy in the literal sense, and who the hell knows for sure with a prophecy handed down from the gods, young Aeden will risk his life for another. The key is to find out exactly who that is."

"Aye."

"What's the next line?"

"*When the Enemy at the Gate is welcomed by the Keeper of the Sword, all that is lost shall be restored.*"

"Ah. Well, we know one of your family possesses the sword. It's what started the O'Malley/O'Connor feud to begin with. Who holds it?"

"I do."

Damian felt surprise for the first time in a long while. Usually, like all the other Aethers before him, he caught glimpses of the future and could read a person's mind if their thoughts were loud or emotional enough.

Ronan's were more challenging to decipher than most because he kept his cards close to his chest and tended to be reserved. The man had an overabundance of charisma, but rarely did his teasing smile reach his eyes. Most couldn't see the heavy weight Ronan carried on his shoulders, but Damian could.

"And the Enemy at the Gate?"

"Don't know." Ronan grimaced. "If I had to guess, I'd say an O'Malley. The Sword of Goibhniu is rightfully theirs, and they could be considered my enemy, all the same."

Most people tried to apply literal translations to a prophecy, but by and large, it wasn't that simple. For instance, Ronan might view the O'Malleys as the enemy at the gate, but they would definitely consider him the same. So there was no way the title could be applied to either without closer inspection of the situation. The more pressing matter was identifying the One and being on hand for Aeden O'Malley should the boy truly be required to sacrifice his life for another. Damian wouldn't allow a child to die on his watch unless the Fates required it. Even then, he'd balk and try to find a way around it.

Clasping his hands behind his back, he watched Ronan carefully as he asked, "So why not give it back and save everyone the headache?"

"Can I do that? Can I bypass the prophecy and simply hand the fecking thing back?"

Ronan actually sounded hopeful, and Damian was pleasantly surprised by his reaction. "Doubtful. Once these things start, they need to play out."

"That's just grand," Ronan muttered, rubbing the back of his neck.

Before him was a man in turmoil, and Damian found it difficult to say no and send him on his way. Whatever had happened in the past, Ronan was remorseful, that much Damian could determine.

"I'll help you." He chuckled at his friend's gobsmacked expression. "Provided you tell me what's happened to date and what plan you have cooking in that head of yours." He held up a hand when Ronan would've spoken. "Over a drink. I have the feeling I'm going to need it."

CHAPTER 18

*O*nce they were firmly ensconced in the study, Damian handed Ronan a tumbler of scotch and sat across from him. As he sipped the proffered drink, Ronan thought about what he needed to say. Better to start from the beginning and tell the whole of it, or the Aether would sense the omission. There was a distinct chance he could refuse to help.

Downing the last of the alcohol for courage, Ronan began his tale.

"As you know, my father was a power-mad, abusive bastard." He couldn't meet Damian's eyes. Even to this day, he felt shamed by his helplessness.

"Yes, and he's locked in a Witches' Council stronghold somewhere, preferably never to be heard from again, if I remember correctly."

"Anu willin'," Ronan muttered. "His siblings were just as evil as he was, and they all created twisted little feckers to follow in their footsteps. Seamus McLeary and Moira Doyle being two of them. If any survived that aren't as warped as their parents, they've long since hied off to parts unknown."

"What do Seamus and Moira have to do with this? I'm assuming this is where the conversation is headed."

"Yes. When our ancestor took the sword—and let's be clear here, I know he was a thievin' bastard and that the Sword of Goibhniu truly belongs to the O'Malleys—we acquired their power with it. Combined with the O'Connors' magic, it made them strong. Nearly impossible for standard witches to defeat outright, with the exception of the Thornes. Over time, that magic became diluted, but the madness it brought with it, *that* grew stronger." Ronan's voice was as grim as his feelings on the matter. The O'Malleys would've been within their rights to kill his entire family, and likely they should've.

"You're not crazy."

The Aether's assessment brought Ronan up short. He met Damian's considering gaze and, for a brief moment, felt hope. But just as quickly, it faded. "I may not be as mad as the rest of them, but for sure, I'm a right bastard. Make no mistake about that."

"That remains to be seen." With a wave of his hand, Damian refilled Ronan's drink. "Go on. Tell me the worst of it. That's why you're here."

Lifting the tumbler, Ronan took a long, slow sip of his scotch, allowing the smooth taste to wash over him even as the alcohol warmed the path from his throat to his belly. It was the best form of fortification—and courage.

"I don't know how or why my family originally learned of prophecy, but we've always known about it. Prior to seven years ago, it seemed like a myth. Like it might never come to pass. Then Aeden O'Malley was born."

"The Golden Son."

"Aye. But the plotting began long before that. A just-in-case plan, if you will."

"Who is the mastermind?"

"Initially, my father, but he went and got on the wrong side of the right person. As you know, he's rotting in a Council jail cell. The only place that would make me happier is in a grave on the far side of the world."

"But you took over for him." It wasn't a question. Damian had either read Ronan's mind, or he surmised that Ronan was the only one of their clan clever enough to carry it out.

"I did. Not because I gave a shite about the sword or the magic, but because without it, I could potentially be weak." And Ronan hated to be perceived as anything but fearless and embodying strength. "Also because I thought I could do damage control."

"Damage control?" Damian stilled, and his face lost all expression, and Ronan got the impression the man was waiting for him to misstep with his next words.

"Yeah. If left on their own, Moira and Seamus would simply wipe out the O'Malleys and be done with it. Sure, and I figured if I assumed command, they'd have to listen to me, and the collateral damage would be nil."

"But they didn't."

"Nah. It's like wrangling cats if I'm honest. They get it in their mind to do a thing without thinkin' of the consequences. They're bleeding fools."

"What did they do?"

"Moira convinced Seamus I wanted him to take out the Byrne sisters. I got there too late to stop it."

"What happened?"

"I was across the pond on business, and Moira, that silver-tongued snake in the grass, convinced Seamus to remove the women's powers and make their deaths, along with Aeden's, look like an accident. She'd assumed by removing the one boy who could make the prophecy come true and the woman who had the potential to birth another blond *wean*, that the O'Connors would keep the O'Malley magic forever."

Damian sighed heavily. "That's not how prophecies work."

"Here, and I know that now, after speakin' with Roisin O'Malley, but none of us knew it then."

"You're not innocent in all of this, O'Connor." He smiled wryly when Ronan would've prevaricated. "I wasn't born yesterday, my friend."

Ronan snorted and swallowed more of his drink. "I'm not. The beginning of my part of the plan was to send Moira to seduce Cian O'Malley. I thought if she could break his heart, he'd swear off love. But in my foolishness, I made him the Frozen."

"Ah." Damian smiled, and in his eyes was genuine amusement. "He met and fell for Piper Thorne."

"Aye."

"Had you not worked out the mighty Thorne was one of my family at that point?"

"Prior to her arrival, no."

Damian nodded. "And let me guess. She met with some unfortunate incidents while in your country." At Ronan's nod, he asked, "Your doing?"

The casual question was anything but, and the anger brewing beneath the Aether's surface could be felt. Damian Dethridge was a man to whom family was all-important. And it wasn't widely known, but he was a Thorne both by blood and adoption. Over two hundred years ago, when he was still a small boy, his distant cousin Nathanial Thorne saved his life and brought him home to America to live, providing protection until the boy became a man and could take care of himself as well as his legacy as the mediator of good and evil.

"Of a sort," Ronan acknowledged, prepared for whatever punishment the Aether cared to mete out. "Piper is the daughter of an ex-lover. I'd tried to protect her, but Moira and Seamus had other ideas. I blame myself. I should've known better than to trust either of them to take care of the problem without attempting to murder the girl."

Damian abruptly rose and strode to the French doors to stare out at the landscape of his home. He seemed preoccupied with something in the distance, but then he stilled and shut his eyes.

Unsure whether to move or speak, Ronan remained where he was and kept quiet.

"Naiveté was your crime, O'Connor. You aren't to blame for that."

"So why do I feel such guilt?" he asked roughly.

Turning to face him, Damian smiled sadly. "It's who you are as a person. Men like you and me, we feel all the world's troubles. It's woven into our DNA. Not only do we attract the evil, we feel terrible when we're forced to take extreme measures to end it."

"I don't deserve to be held to your level, Dethridge. I'm not a pimple on your arse, to be sure."

With a short bark of laughter, Damian returned and placed a hand on his shoulder. "You're wrong. You're a far better man than you believe you are." He held out his hand for the empty tumbler. "It's time for you to make yourself scarce. I've company to see to."

"But you don't know why I came."

"Don't I? They're here now, seeking what you would have me fix."

"They?"

"The O'Malleys."

"Feck!" Ronan jumped up, his heart beginning to pound hard. "They can't know I'm part of this. Please, don't tell them."

Damian cocked his head, similar to how his small daughter had done, and studied him. "I'll not lie if they ask, but otherwise, your secret is safe with me."

"Will you heal her? Roisin?"

"If that is what is requested of me."

"If you do, if you heal her and the boyo, I'll be in your debt. And if you call, I'll come, no questions asked."

With a grin and a hearty slap on his back, Damian said, "You're too nice to be a dastardly mastermind."

"Yeah, I've a soft spot for innocents."

"As soon as I let them in the front door, you can leave through—"

Sabrina's sweet voice drifted to them. "My Papa is in there with Ronan."

Ronan swore under his breath as Damian sighed.

"So much for escape. I suppose you'll have to face the music, O'Connor."

CARRICK MANEUVERED HIS BODY IN FRONT OF ROISIN AND AEDEN as soon as Damian's daughter shoved open the door to the study. Roisin's claim that she believed Ronan to be the head of the troublesome trio had stuck with him, and he couldn't shake the sick feeling that she was right. Too many things were off about this entire situation.

The second his gaze connected with Ronan's, Carrick knew the truth. The other man couldn't hide his dismay fast enough.

"We shouldn't have come without an invitation," he said with a slight nod in respect to the Aether, inching his small family backward toward the door. "We'll just be headin' home now."

"Don't be ridiculous, Mr. O'Malley," Damian Dethridge said smoothly. "You've traveled all this way. Come in."

Of all the people in the room, only the girl and her father looked at ease. Expectant, even.

Carrick's instinct told him to scoop up his family and get the hell out of there, but one didn't dismiss a direct invitation from the Aether.

Next to him, Roisin gasped when she saw Damian for the first time. A side glance showed she was utterly enthralled. And a check of his son showed Aeden was similarly affected by the daughter. It stood to reason they would be; not only was the Aether the most handsome person imaginable, but his unlimited power also drew unsuspecting witches like a moth to a flame.

Like his Enchantress mother before him, Damian Dethridge could seduce with a mere look. Apparently, his daughter would inherit the trait.

The little girl hadn't moved far from Aeden and stared at him with similar fascination.

"I can't see you," she said in awe. "What are you?"

Aeden frowned and looked up at Carrick, then back at the girl.

"He doesn't understand the question," Roisin said softly. "He's our son."

"What's your name?" the pint-sized girl asked.

Aeden's frown deepened.

"His name is Aeden," Carrick told her, placing a hand on his son's shoulder and giving it a slight squeeze.

"Aeden." The girl said the name as if she were testing it out. Inching closer to him, she peered up into his too-serious face. Suddenly, she smiled, and the sunniness radiating from her warmed their small group. Carrick found himself smiling despite himself. "I'm Sabrina, but Papa calls me Beastie."

Carrick exchanged a look with Roisin and opened his mouth to tell the girl that Aeden had difficulty speaking when Sabrina reached out and touched their son's throat.

"Ah." Locking eyes with Aeden, she took his hand in hers and tugged him toward the Aether. "Papa can fix it. He can fix anything," she said with the confidence of a young child who adored their parent.

Carrick surged forward at the same time Aeden tugged away and ran back to him.

"Beastie." With a stern look, Damian said, "While I appreciate your faith in me, you can't go around offering my services without first understanding the situation."

Her expression crumpled, and she half-turned from him to face Aeden. "But he's in pain, Papa. We need to fix him."

It appeared Damian was no match for the tears welling in his daughter's eyes, and he rushed to her, squatting to take her in his arms. "Hush now, my love. We'll help him, but it has to be his choice. Do you understand?"

She nodded, all her worried attention on Aeden.

Carrick looked down at his son, only to see him peeking back at Sabrina. Curiosity was replacing his fear.

"We came to see if you could provide a cure for Aeden's throat," Roisin said. She cast a wary glance at Ronan but squared her shoulders. "And help us with another matter best discussed in private."

Damian rose to his feet, leaving a hand resting atop his daughter's dark head. "Why haven't you asked if I can heal you as well?" The question was softly spoken and not intended to mock. The kindness in his eyes was disarming. There was no pity, just compassion.

After clearing her throat and shooting a nervous glance around the room, Roisin said, "It would be presumptuous."

Carrick's heart began to hammer. He wanted nothing more than for Ro to be happy and healthy, and now, the moment was at hand. If the Aether could make her emotionally and physically whole once more, her pain a thing of the past, perhaps they could get back what they'd had.

Hooking his pinky with hers, he gave a small tug, enough to propel her farther into the room.

"First things first. I believe introductions are in order. As you've likely already suspected, I'm Damian Dethridge. And the statue on the other side of the room, trying to blend in with the wood paneling, is Ronan O'Connor."

Roisin moaned and grabbed her forehead. As she swayed, Carrick caught her. "Ro? What's happening?"

Damian growled low in his throat, and the air in the room became heavy. "Unless I miss my guess, she's been spelled to react adversely to the name." He shifted to face Ronan. "Care to explain?"

"Not to react adversely, but to forget the name altogether." Redness crept up Ronan's neck, and he crossed his arms over his chest, lifting his chin defiantly. "Something misfired in her brain."

The man reminded Carrick of Aeden when his son was scared but trying not to show it. His anger toward Ronan was muted by the odd feeling of compassion he felt. Part of him wanted to rearrange the guy's beautiful features, and the other part wanted to offer sympathy for whatever he was going through.

Carrick shot a look at Damian only to find the Aether watching *him* in return. There was a bemused look on his face, as if he could read Carrick's thoughts and was surprised by them.

"I can, and I am," Damian said.

The blood drained from Carrick's face. "You can read my thoughts?"

Ronan snorted from his spot across the room, but everyone ignored him.

Damian nodded. "Some, yes. As well as your conflicted energy."

The urge to flee and never return was overwhelming. "Are you friends? You and Ronan *O'Connor*?" It took a concerted effort not to sneer the name. Carrick wasn't sure he'd succeeded.

"We are." Amusement danced in the Aether's obsidian eyes. "And now you're wondering if you can trust me not to betray you. The simple answer is yes. I'm the balance between good and evil, Mr. O'Malley. I don't choose sides without extenuating circumstances."

"And is this one of those times?"

"No."

CHAPTER 19

*S*abrina was different from any other child Aeden had ever met. More like *him*. Like maybe she could speak to Anu, too. And as weird as it made him feel, he wanted to be Sabrina's friend. With no little fear in his heart, he left the protection of Da and Mam and walked to where she stood next to her father.

If the Aether could read thoughts like he'd told Da, then maybe he could understand what Aeden needed without him having to struggle to say it.

When he was next to Sabrina, she held out her hand, and without any hesitation, he took it. Aeden didn't really like girls, couldn't say if they were pretty or not; they were *girls* and irritating most days. But with her strange dark eyes and black hair, she was pretty in the way his mam had once been, in the way that she stood out from all the others. He wanted to stare at her forever. Wanted to feel the warmth from her magical light every day.

She looked up at her da. "Papa, I think he wants you to fix his throat."

Afraid to ask for what he really wanted, Aeden dropped his eyes to the floor.

The Aether knelt in front of him and tipped up his chin. "Is that true, Aeden?"

"Can you truly read minds?" he asked silently.

"Yes, I really can." When the Aether smiled, all Aeden's fear disappeared, and he wanted to fling himself in the man's arms like he did with Da when he needed a hug.

"Does it drain your magic to help people, like it does Mam's?"

"No. Mine is unlimited, for the most part."

"Will you make Mam's pain go away?"

"And what about you?"

Aeden shrugged. He felt he was being selfish asking anything for himself when Mam needed help the most. His throat didn't hurt unless he tried to speak.

Once again, the Aether smiled, settling a hand on Aeden's shoulder. "It speaks well of you that you want me to help your mother first."

Mam gasped. "No! I—"

The Aether turned his easy smile on her. "No need to fear, Mrs. O'Malley. All will be well. I'll see to it." He rose to his feet and trailed a finger down Sabrina's upturned nose. "Why don't you take Aeden to your room and show him your toys? I need to speak with his parents and Ronan."

A pout formed on her mouth, but her father lifted a brow and gave her a don't-even-think-about-it look. The same kind Mam had always given Aeden when he was about to argue a point.

"But—"

"Beastie, there will be no debate. Go on now."

She huffed out a breath and was a little rough when she grabbed Aeden's hand. "Come on."

Looking to his parents for permission, he halted Sabrina's forward movement.

"It's okay, Aeden," Da said. "I'll come get you in a bit."

He smiled at Da and allowed Sabrina to lead him from the room.

Once they were in the main hallway, she put her finger to her lips and gestured to the front door. "Papa doesn't like me to go outside when he's not watching, but he worries too much. I want to show you the bird's nest I found."

Because Aeden couldn't see why it would be wrong to look at a nest, he silently agreed and followed her outside.

As the children left the terrace, Moira smiled. Recently, she'd blackmailed an ex-lover into putting a trace on Ronan's phone, so she always knew where he was. It allowed her to be on par with him instead of always one step behind. She didn't dare set foot on the Aether's land. She didn't want to alert him to her presence, but she could certainly scry and attach the magic to Ronan, so no one knew she was watching.

She'd only seen the Aether one time, but the man certainly made an impression, and the girl looked exactly like him in miniature form. There was no mistaking the child was his. Rumor had it, if you could kill an Aether, you could capture their abilities for your own.

The girl might not be as powerful as her father, but hers would be enough for Moira to defeat Ronan when the time came. And she hoped it came soon. She was tired of his orders and stupid rules. No war on women and children, pfft! *Fool!*

If she didn't know better, she'd think he didn't want to keep what they already possessed. However, now she had the opportunity to have both: Aether and O'Malley magic. She only needed to convince Seamus, the pea-brained eejit, to help her tempt the children past the wards. It shouldn't be hard in either case; little brats tended to wander where they weren't supposed to in direct defiance of their parents.

With a wave of her hand over her scrying mirror, the Dethridge estate expanded to view the surrounding area. *Her supernatural version of Google Maps.* She laughed aloud. No one understood her or her humor, but she didn't need them to. Soon enough, she would be the new Enchantress, taking powers from other witches' and warlocks' as she saw fit. With the Aether's and O'Malleys' magic, she'd be unstoppable.

THE INSTANT SABRINA STEPPED ONTO THE GROUNDS OF THE estate, she felt the evil intent brush against her like icy fingers along hot skin. Image after image came to her, and with it, the Fates' design. Her instinct was to run inside and find Papa, but if she did, the Sisters of Fate wouldn't be happy with her. As the only Oracle, her visions became clearer and stronger every day; millions of possibilities for every presented situation floated about in her brain until she could isolate a solution to a problem. This time, however, she could only see two possible outcomes to the upcoming attack. In one, she died. In another, Aeden did.

She shot him a sideways look. The difference depended on his courage. As the Golden Son, he needed to sacrifice for the One— for her. If he didn't, the prophecy wouldn't come to pass, and any magic his family had begun to reclaim would revert back to Ronan.

And for the first time, she understood why Papa scolded her for telling the future. If she told Aeden about the evil woman's plan, he could possibly run for the safety of his parents instead of staying out here, where he needed to be to satisfy the Fates.

Butterflies began to dance in her belly. She didn't want to mess this up. "Do you like birds?" she asked to distract herself.

He shrugged, his expression neither caring nor uncaring.

She frowned and stopped walking and turned, so they stood face-to-face. Wanting to do something nice for him, to make up for the sacrifice he would make, she said, "I don't need Papa to fix your throat. I can do it now if you want."

He thought it over as he stared at something beyond her shoulder, and the wait was irritating. He should answer her since she was trying to do something nice for him.

"Well?" she demanded.

With a suddenness that stole her breath, he grinned, and she knew she couldn't let him die for her. His soul was too beautiful, and it made her heart beat faster just to look at him.

"We have to go back to the house." She reached for his hand, but he backed away and shook his head. "Aeden, if you don't come back with me, I'll be very cross."

He must not have understood about her ability because he laughed. Noiseless, except for a whisper of his breath, he charmed her with the sound. Still, she balled her hands and glared. She couldn't let him see she liked him or his laugh, or that she found him interesting. If he doubted she meant business and they didn't return soon, they would be past the point of rescue.

"I can teleport us, you know." The challenge in her tone only made him laugh harder—so she shoved him. "You're not very clever, are you?"

He stopped laughing, but his eyes twinkled with humor, and she had the impression he was very clever indeed. She wished she could read him like she could others. The fact she couldn't was confusing.

"Anu," he croaked. "Stay here."

"You talk to a goddess?" Maybe he was harder to read because he was tuned into the deities. That would make more sense if his brain was on another plane of time and not here on this level.

He nodded and did something with his hands. The gestures

were fast, and Sabrina had a hard time following the movement. The longer she watched him, the clearer what he was trying to sign to her became. He repeated the sentences again and again until she grasped his special language, and by the time he was done, she had absorbed his knowledge of sign language. It seemed Aeden was far smarter than she'd given him credit for.

"Anu said we need to be here, at this moment. She said not to be afraid," he signed.

Nodding, she gave him a curious look. "How did you guess I would learn your language?"

He grinned again. "Anu."

Sabrina didn't necessarily like that someone knew more than she did. She was to be the Oracle. The All-Seeing One. Nobody should be able to know more than her, especially not a boy. And it was as if he understood his knowledge bothered her and thought it funny.

"Did she tell you what would happen if we stay here?" she demanded.

"No. But she said not to be afraid." His hands stopped moving, and he shifted closer to her. He was slightly taller, and he ducked to meet her eyes. The color of his irises shifted from the greenest grass to the darker shade of moss, and she could tell he wasn't going to tease her anymore. He was deadly serious. "Protect you," he whispered. "Always."

She couldn't stop the tears welling in her eyes, and she felt like a big baby when they poured down her cheeks. "I don't want you to be hurt."

He hugged her, and it felt nice. Not like Papa's strong hugs, but close. The idea came to her that she could save him another way; no one had indicated she couldn't. Holding tight, she mentally formed a protection spell and wove it into his dormant magic, fusing the two so it could never be separated without the help of another Aether. When Aeden needed it, it would be there for him.

She should've asked permission first, but she liked this boy too much. The feelings were cemented when he drew back and wiped her cheeks for her.

"Will you be my forever friend, Aeden?"

He smiled and nodded. "Always."

CHAPTER 20

"*I* don't trust my daughter to do as she's told, so I'd like to keep this discussion short and sweet." Damian crossed to the sideboard and poured himself another drink, then turned slightly to offer the room's other occupants one. When they all declined with a shake of the head, he capped the decanter and returned to the center of the room.

On one side, Ronan stood, ill at ease but seemingly ready to face the conflict head on.

On the other, Roisin and Carrick eyed Ronan as if they'd like to tear his throat out.

These situations and the boiling emotions that accompanied them were what Damian usually tried to avoid. However, when unexpected people showed up on his doorstep, he had no choice but to mediate. With a heavy sigh and a hearty sip of his drink, he sank into a leather club chair and crossed his legs, studying the other three.

Ronan was in the wrong, yet his motives were understandable; acquire power by any means possible to protect himself against the thread of deranged family members.

This, Damian understood. He'd been there in the early days

when his Enchantress mother had lost her fight and succumbed to the Darkness, trying to kill thousands to amass the entire magical community's power. It had taken members of the Six—the original six families descended from the gods and goddesses, who resided on both sides of the veil—as well as two deities to stop her the first time, and it had taken Damian, full-grown and fearful for his daughter's life, the second.

But the old saying *two wrongs didn't make a right* came into play here. Ronan would need to find a way to rectify what he'd done to the O'Malley family.

Speaking of the O'Malleys...

Carrick was growing more restless and angry by the second, and Damian needed to nip this one in the bud if he didn't want the war to progress.

"In the good old days, we'd resolve this conflict by marrying off your children and making a pact," he said casually. "Too bad Ronan doesn't have a daughter."

They all looked at him as if he were mad.

Again, he sighed. No one but Alastair Thorne ever seemed to get his humor.

"Since that isn't an option, what do you propose?" Damian wasn't above tossing the mess back into their laps. With enough motivation, they'd resolve their difference. He only hoped he didn't need to resort to threats to get it done.

"Well, I, for one, would like to hear why you cursed me to begin with," Roisin said to Ronan. "What did I ever do to you?"

Real regret flashed across Ronan's face. "You've done nothing, Roisin Byrne, and it's sorry I am you were pulled into the O'Connor-O'Malley war."

"She *is* an O'Malley," Carrick ground out. "And don't forget it again. She'll not be taken in by the likes of *you*, to be sure."

A small smile twisted Damian's lips as he watched the scene play out. He'd seriously underestimated Carrick O'Malley's gumption.

"Please explain to Mr. and Mrs. O'Malley what you told me earlier, Ronan," Damian suggested. "I think it's important they understand you weren't malicious in your dealings."

Carrick shot him a sharp glance but immediately refocused on Ronan. "Sure, and be quick about it, man."

"We should sit for this. It isn't a short explanation." Ronan plopped into the matching club chair and dropped his head back against the leather. "Please." He nodded toward the loveseat.

The couple exchanged a wary look but eventually sat down.

Ronan proceeded to tell them about his desire for power to protect against his father, how Seamus had attacked the sisters and Aeden that long-ago day in the road, and how he—Ronan— found out about it too late but did what he could to save her and Aeden by taking them to hospital. He ended with the explanation of Seamus's second attack and abduction of Roisin.

"I erased her memory of her time in my home." Ronan leaned forward, resting his elbows on his knees and clasping his hands together. "I watched over her until you found her in the garden, but when she didn't wake right away, I got worried and came to help."

"And the brainwashing?" Carrick demanded coldly. "What about that?"

"I never intended to sneak into your home if that's what you're askin', O'Malley." Ronan's voice had turned hard, as did his expression. "I merely intended it so if I got wind of Moira or Seamus plannin' another attack, I could show up and stop them. If I'm trapped on the outside, I can't rightly help now, can I?"

"If the wards do their job, Moira and Seamus can't get inside," Roisin retorted.

Ronan softened as he met her gaze, and Damian couldn't help but wonder if his friend was sporting a crush on another man's woman. It wouldn't be the first time, and it would likely get him killed this time around. Carrick O'Malley looked to be feral when it came to his wife.

"But they've managed it before, haven't they?" Ronan said gently. "I've told your family once, and I'll state it again, I don't make war on women or children."

Roisin blew out a frustrated breath and looked at her husband. "I believe him."

"Damned if I don't as well," Carrick said with a whole lot of resentment. "He's made a complete *haymes* of this, all the same."

"You have a decision to make," Damian told the O'Malleys.

Carrick's brows shot up. "Whether to kill and bury him or let him leave here alive?"

"Okay, you have two decisions to make," Damian returned smoothly.

Ronan snorted and shook his head. "The only thing they need to decide right now is whether or not to have you heal what I made a right bag of."

Damian met Roisin's worried eyes. "Will you trust me to fix it?"

Roisin turned over the question in her mind. *Would she?* So far, Damian Dethridge had been a proper host, seemingly kind and caring. More importantly, he'd treated her son with respect and made him feel comfortable. Ronan watched her with an odd expression, wariness mixed with deep regret. It was disconcerting to learn he'd rescued her more than once.

The warmth of Carrick's hand gave her the strength she needed, and she nodded her agreement. "Yes, please."

"Okay. Sit back and let me examine you." Shifting to rise, Damian placed his drink on the coffee table and gestured toward the French doors. "Gentlemen, if you'd be so kind as to step outside. I'd like to limit distractions."

Ronan climbed to his feet, but Carrick remained seated.

"I'll stay with my wife." His tone held no compromise.

"Carrick," she said softly, stroking the back of his hand. "It's all right. You should probably check on Aeden."

"He should be fine with Sabrina," Damian assured her.

Ronan half-turned from where he waited at the terrace doors. "Did you not direct them to play upstairs?"

Roisin almost laughed when the Aether swore and stalked toward him.

"That little beastie will be the death of me," Damian ground out.

Joining him, Roisin and Carrick peered out the window in time to see Aeden hug Sabrina and wipe the tears from her eyes. Her heart caught in her throat at the sight, and she squeezed her husband's hand. "He's made a friend, Carrick!"

"Aye," he said roughly, his voice thick with emotion. More than once, he'd voiced worry over Aeden's self-imposed isolation. To see him exit his cocoon was heartening. "Ro, before—" he gestured to Damian "—I'd like to have a word. About Aeden."

Understanding dawned. She nodded and squeezed his hand, then went outside when Ronan opened the door for her. Waiting until the door clicked behind her, she faced Ronan on the patio. "I can't say I'm happy with you for taking my memories, but I owe you a debt of gratitude for saving us from the wreck and then me from Seamus and Moira at your castle." She gave him a half-smile. "Thank you, Ronan."

"I can't apologize enough for what you and your son were put through, Roisin, but I'll do what I can to make sure nothing else happens to either of you."

Her heart began to pound uncomfortably in her chest. "And Carrick?"

The long, silent moments as Ronan gazed out at the children were agonizing. Finally, he looked down at her. "And Carrick."

She hadn't been aware of holding her breath until it whooshed out, and she was forced to take another.

His lips twitched as if he knew he'd tortured her with his

silence, but his eyes were sad when he said, "After speaking to both you and Damian, I've come to realize that bleedin' prophecy was always going to come to pass. The O'Malleys will have no more trouble from me." His mouth tightened into a grim line a second before he said, "But I can't speak for Moira and Seamus, mind. They're as mad as hatters when it comes to this situation, and as unpredictable. I'll do what I can to mitigate their actions, but stay alert to their special brand of mischief, yeah?"

She worried her lip and glanced at the children. Sabrina was making up for Aeden's standard silence by happily chatting away. "I'll murder anyone who hurts my son."

"Sure, and you tried to kill Seamus in my home. Wet his pants, he did." Ronan gave a wicked little laugh. "The little shite deserved it, no doubt, but I couldn't let that be on your conscious."

"And what about you, Ronan O'Connor? Do you have death on your conscious?"

"Aye. Your sister's." He looked so guilt-ridden, Roisin's heart would've ached for him had he not been instrumental in Meg's demise. "I should've guessed at Moira and Seamus's plan or hired a surveillance team to keep me informed of their whereabouts. It's sorry I am for your loss, Roisin. And I won't ask your forgiveness because I don't deserve it."

"But I'm giving it to you anyway," she said softly, placing a hand on his folded arms. "Maybe Meg's death is partially your fault, but you've sworn time and again, you don't make war on women and children. You've also saved my life and that of my son. I might be a fool, but I trust you to hold to your promise."

"I believe yours might be the most lovely soul I've ever encountered, Roisin Byrne-O'Malley. I hope Carrick realizes what a treasure he has in you."

"You've not seen me with bedhead and morning breath. You'd change your thinking right enough."

He laughed and shook his head. With a wink and an appreciative grin, he said, "If I was after stealin' you away, neither of those things would make a difference."

Flustered by the wicked gleam in his silvery gaze, she looked toward the French doors.

"Your husband and Damian still seem to be in deep conversation. Would you care to walk with me?"

She gave him a considering side glance. "You're an endearing rogue, and I'm afraid you'll distract me from my mission here today."

He chuckled. "If only all women were as honest as you! Come, I promise not to seduce you."

"More's the pity," she muttered under her breath.

Obviously, he had the hearing of a bat, and again, he laughed. "Don't tempt me with lines like that, love. I'm mending my ways and have sworn off other men's wives."

"Sure, and I'd not be unfaithful to Carrick, but a woman can fantasize, Ronan O'Connor."

"Scarlett is your mam, Roisin O'Malley! And my cheeks are close to matching from all those grand compliments of yours."

She enjoyed their flirty banter. Odd, since he'd technically been the unknown enemy to her family all this time. But she wasn't lying when she'd called him endearing. Men like Ronan could rule the world if they'd a mind to. She only hoped they didn't find themselves on opposite sides again in the future. She'd meant what she said about murdering anyone who would harm her family. This time, she'd be ruthless.

CHAPTER 21

"*N*o."

"You're a fucking *planc*, Seamus McLeary!"

"Call me what you will, Moira, but I'll not hurt that boy again." Seamus guzzled more of his pint. "I'm of a mind to listen to Ronan." Not to mention he still felt the noose of Roisin O'Malley's magic around his damned neck and his eyes bulging from his head. That spot of retaliation hadn't been pleasant.

"Ronan's gone soft," Moira snapped. The "like you" was implied.

She wasn't wrong. Other than curtailing the two of them, Ronan seemed distracted most days, moodily staring at his phone's screen or off into space while nursing his tumbler of whiskey.

"If we want the O'Malleys' magic, we need to take it for ourselves. The boy is unguarded and ripe for the plucking." Her voice turned wheedling, but she couldn't hide the calculation in her cold blue eyes. "And there's another prize to be won if you've the bollocks."

Curiosity got the better of him, and he spun on his stool to face her. "What prize?"

"The Aether has a child."

Seamus's sphincter contracted, and he stared at her in horror. *"Are you mad?"* What was he saying? Of course she was!

Her hand shot out, and she dug her nails in his throat as she squeezed. "If ya call me mad again, I'll finish what Roisin O'Malley started," she snarled.

Spittle gathered on the sides of her mouth, and with her eyes narrowed in warning, Moira looked as dangerous as a pit viper.

He tried to nod his assent.

Releasing him with a hard shove, Moira grabbed his Guinness and took a hearty sip before slapping the mug back on the counter.

"If you'd a brain in your oversized head, Seamus, you'd know I have a foolproof plan."

"Sure, and you always do," he readily agreed. Inside, his stomach was a ball of knots. Moira's "foolproof plans" never failed to end with Seamus mired in shite. "Out with it. I might as well know what will be the death of me."

"The children are wandering on the estate—alone. Not an adult to be seen."

"And you want we should kidnap them?" Doubt was heavy in his tone, but he couldn't suspend his disbelief that Aeden O'Malley's mam and da would be far, considering.

"No. I want we should kill them and take their power."

Seamus's life flashed before his eyes. If he attacked a child of the Aether, he wouldn't live to tell the tale. If he didn't, Moira would murder him on the spot. To put it simply, Seamus was fucked. When he remained quiet, silently assuring Meghan Byrne he'd be seeing her beautiful face very soon, Moira outlined her ridiculous plan. Sure, and it was genius in its simplicity, but it was stupid all the same. They'd never succeed, and they certainly wouldn't live to tell the tale of their attempt.

As she rattled on, he slowly sipped his drink, savoring every drop. If it was to be his last, he'd damned well enjoy it.

"We've got to act now, Seamus. We've a small window of opportunity here."

"Aye."

He considered attacking Moira. Chances were he was physically stronger, but she was rabid and had a powerful hate in addition to madness on her side. Magically, she'd defeat him in a fecking heartbeat. Moira knew blood spells and enough black magic to shrivel a man's bollocks and make him bleed out his eyes. He'd writhe in pain on the floor as she stood over him, cackling in that ear-deafening way she had.

"To be clear, I'll stab the girl," she said, and there was no mistaking the command in her voice.

"If you do, you get all her power?" He needed it clarified. Because if he could get to the child first, he'd take her life just to be stronger than Moira and have a fighting chance against Damian Dethridge when the girl's da came calling.

"Yes. Your job is to kill the boy."

Seamus nodded absently. Would he need the O'Malley magic if he had the power of an Aether? He could afford to let Aeden live if that were the case. It only briefly occurred to him to wonder if he could handle the bulk of those abilities.

Meg's smiling face appeared in his mind's eye. She'd always treated her nephew abysmally, but when no one was looking, she had gazed at the boy with longing. As if she wished he was hers. She probably had if she loved Carrick O'Malley as much as she'd claimed. Her longing stuck with Seamus, as did the horror of the scene he'd created when he overturned their vehicle.

If he could, he'd save the boy. But ultimately, it would be his life or the children's, and he wasn't fool enough to believe in sacrifice. Seamus was out for himself in this. His survival would be the deciding factor in whether to kill Aeden O'Malley or not.

Sabrina was inundated with images, and her heartbeat was painfully fast as she processed them. "I don't like this plan," she signed to Aeden, who was too calm for her liking.

"It will work," he signed in return. "Come on."

He led her away from the tree where Ronan and his mam were talking, and he took the path toward the secret garden where her grandmother's body once rested in an enchanted sleep. The place no longer held her, and the cracked tomb was now overgrown with flowers, making it a pretty spot to play.

Sabrina recalled her beautiful grandmother. Not as she'd been when the Darkness had claimed her body for itself, but how she'd been in the waiting area of the Otherworld. She'd been sweet and loving, full of remorse for her actions. That's what the waiting area was designed for; it was a place for people to work through their rights and wrongs. And if they were ultimately good-hearted, they could stay in the extraordinary world Isis had created. But if they weren't, if evil remained in their heart and soul, they would go to hell.

She wished her grandmother was here to ask so Sabrina would know what she should do. Papa would "protect her from herself," as he liked to say, but Grandmother would encourage her to make her own choices, she was sure. However, Isolde de Thorne was now in the black pit of the Netherworld, keeping guard over the Darkness. Someday she'd return when Sabrina needed her the most, but not yet.

As Sabrina and Aeden got close to the rose garden, she glanced back along the trail and kept thoughts of Papa out of her head. He was dialed into her, and if he felt her indecision or fear, he'd come, and Aeden's plan would be ruined.

"Aeden!" Roisin's worried voice reached them just as they arrived at the garden gate.

"We should go back," Sabrina whispered in a raw, scratchy voice, glancing around at the darkening shadows. "I think we were wrong," she croaked out.

"Wrong about what?" asked a cool voice.

She spun around and saw a petite red-haired woman approach. Behind her, looking like he wanted to be anywhere but where he was, a nervous red-haired man followed. His shirt was wet in the armpit area, and sweat beaded on his forehead.

Sabrina knew a moment of fear. Yes, she had a lot of magic, but she was a young Aether, not as powerful as she would be when she grew up. And the ability she was using to keep up appearances and the invisible protection bubble was taking a large part of her magic. Deciding it was time to teleport home, she reached for Aeden's hand, but he'd moved to stand between her and the red-haired woman—just outside of Sabrina's magic barrier.

"You must be Damian's daughter," the woman purred. All her attention was on Aeden disguised as Sabrina.

He gave a sharp nod and lifted his chin.

"Excellent." The woman laughed and grabbed his arm. "Seamus, get the other brat. Be quick about it."

Seamus focused on Sabrina, who was glamoured to look like Aeden, and as he approached, he withdrew a knife from behind his back. He was only halfway to her when he grabbed Aeden from Moira's clutches and held the blade's tip to his throat.

"If anyone's to have the tiny Aether's magic, it be me, Moira."

"Go!" Aeden screamed with his newly repaired voice.

Seamus sliced his throat.

Moira screamed her rage.

And Sabrina froze in shock as Seamus dumped Aeden's skinny little body on the ground.

With both hands clamped on his opened throat and as the blood oozed through his fingers, Aeden shot her one last pleading look. His thoughts came to her clearly for the first time since meeting him.

Go, Beastie. Go get your da.

. . .

MOIRA GASPED IN SHOCK AS THE GLAMOUR SURROUNDING THE child at their feet dissolved, revealing the scrawny form of Aeden O'Malley. She met Seamus's stunned gaze for a split second before she ran for the girl behind him. She had a chance now that the child was frozen in her fear. But before she took two steps, the Aether's daughter was gone.

The wind around them picked up, and a bellow of anguish carried on the current.

Moira spun back around to see Roisin O'Malley running for all she was worth through a copse of trees. The anguish on her face was either from the pain of her damaged body having to move so quickly or from witnessing her son's attack. Probably both. Moira took a grim pleasure in the sight.

Ronan's long legs ate up the ground, out-pacing Roisin by far.

He was almost upon them when Moira had the idea to protect herself. Instinctively, she recognized the greater threat. Rushing to Aeden's dying body, she dipped her hands in the fresh blood and twirled in a circle.

"I bind thee, Roisin Byrne-O'Malley, from harming me," she shouted as she ran to the closest tree and drew ancient ruins on the bark to protect herself. Blood magic was the most effective against a powerful witch like Roisin. It was how Seamus had stolen her power to begin with.

But Roisin went straight for Seamus, who still held the dripping knife, and the absolute rage on her face told Moira, no binding would stop her this time.

Hands in the air, Roisin threw glowing gold ropes in his direction, and Seamus, dumbfounded she could hold him, turned to look at Moira. She saw the second he registered what she had known all along. By killing Aeden O'Malley, he'd not made the O'Connor clan stronger; he'd made them all weaker. It was why Moira had wanted the girl's power before he killed the boy—to mitigate the loss of the O'Malley magic when that part of the prophecy was fulfilled.

The Golden Son had indeed sacrificed for the One.

RONAN CRASHED TO HIS KNEES NEXT TO AEDEN, A HARSH CRY escaping him. He pressed his palms flat over the gaping wound on the boy's neck and directed all his fading O'Malley magic into Aeden's severed throat. As he worked, he imagined the flesh knitting and the lost blood returning to the child's body. With a mind for dirt, bacteria, and possible infection, he isolated these things and drew them out.

Dull, near lifeless eyes locked with his, and Ronan wanted to beg Aeden's forgiveness for not killing Moira and Seamus when he had the chance.

"I'm sorry," he repeated over and over again. "I'm so sorry, Aeden."

As Ronan grew weaker, the child's skin fused together. With one last push of his receding magic, he sealed the boy's wound, releasing a harsh breath.

Aeden raised a shaky hand, and his dirty, blood-drenched fingers brushed Ronan's cheek, just below his eye. "Don't cry, Mr. Ronan," he said in a hoarse voice. "The Aether will make it right."

Ronan hadn't realized it was the salt of his own tears burning his eyes until that second. He hadn't cried since he was a small boy, roughly Aeden's age. After swiping at the moisture, he stared in surprise at the wetness on the back of his hand. His wry smile disappeared the instant Aeden's eyes grew round and focused on something behind him.

Moira!

For the length of time it took Ronan to heal Aeden, he'd forgotten about that treacherous bitch.

He rolled at the exact moment she struck, and the blazing hot pain from her knife cut a trail across the skin on his back.

Leave it to that hellcat to have the sharpest fucking blade on earth!

He had little magic left to fight her, but he was a damned sight stronger and trained in physical combat thanks to his over-bearing monster of a father. This was the one woman he'd gladly make war with.

As she charged a second time, the knife poised to strike, Ronan drew up his legs and thrust out toward her stomach. She flew backward into Seamus and lost her weapon. Simultaneously, Moira and Roisin dove for it, with Roisin marginally beating her out.

Ronan rolled to his feet, intent on helping Roisin, but as he rose, the ground shook, and a deafening rumble echoed in the evening sky. He struggled to maintain his balance.

The Aether had arrived.

CHAPTER 22

*R*oisin braced her legs against the rolling ground beneath her feet, and when she had her balance, she looked around and discovered Moira was gone. Apparently, that vicious wagon teleported away to save her worthless arse. Any retaliation against that black-hearted bitch would need to wait, but Roisin could—*and would*—take another chess piece off the board in the meantime.

The earthquake didn't alter Roisin's intent or shock her into forgetting what Seamus McLeary had done to her son. The time was at hand to make him pay for all his past sins, and the Goddess could sort it out when he made it to the Otherworld's waiting room. With any luck, the scaldy bastard would go straight to hell.

Seamus was still tied in place by her magical ropes, and his eyes flared wide like a wild horse trapped in a pen. From the sweat pouring down his face and the paleness of his skin, it was easy to see he understood he was about to take his last breath. Staggering toward him, she looked him square in the eye.

"Roisin, don't." Damian's voice held barely suppressed anger and an unmistakable warning.

But he was too late. Roisin was done being a victim. She'd become a mother tiger protecting her young: vicious, deadly, uncontrollable. With no hesitation or remorse, she held the knife to Seamus's throat. "You'll feel what he felt, but no one will save you. And when you're gone, no one will mourn your loss. After everyone breathes a sigh of relief, they will forget you ever existed."

His lower lip trembled, and tears welled in his eyes. "It's sorry I am—"

She plunged the knife into the side of his neck and dragged the razor-sharp blade sideways.

The gurgling sound he made sickened her, and she knew she'd remember the horror of what she'd done for the rest of her days. But she'd never regret it. Not once.

Tossing the knife away, she recalled the magical ropes holding him in place. Dropping to her knees alongside Seamus's body, she emptied the contents of her stomach. She didn't move until all his blood stopped its rapid exodus from the artery she'd severed and the light died from his terrified eyes.

Part of her was afraid to turn around. Afraid to see the disgust and horror in the men's eyes. In her son's eyes. So she remained where she was.

Thin arms encircled her from behind, and she gripped them hard, sobbing her anguish that she'd not been there in time to save Aeden when he needed her the most. Once again, it had fallen to another to help him, and although it had gutted her not to act, she'd instinctively known Ronan could and would save him where she didn't have the type of magic to do it. "I'm sorry, *mo stór*," she cried. "I'm so sorry, my darlin' boy."

His little arms squeezed her tighter, and a distant part of her brain registered his strength, surprising in his diminutive form. Shifting and turning their bodies so his back was to Seamus and she was facing Aeden, she remained kneeling in front of him. She ran her fingers over his sticky, blood-stained neck, feeling for any trace of the wound.

"Seems we owe Mr. O'Connor a world of debt, don't we?" she said. Her voice was shaky, and she couldn't stop the copious amount of tears pouring down. Aeden's sweet face was blurred, and she continuously blinked to try to see him clearly, to assure herself he was whole and healthy.

"He's a good man," Aeden whispered, as if he were imparting a secret, and it registered on her that he could speak without any apparent pain. "He just doesn't know it, Mam."

"I quite agree," she whispered back. Pulling him close, she sat back on her heels and rocked her son in her arms. "I love you, *mo stór*. More than my own life, I love you." She choked down another sob. "No one will ever hurt you again," she said fiercely. "No one."

"I know."

He patted her back like she was the one needing comfort. And perhaps she was. The horror of seeing her son drop to the ground, clutching his sliced throat, would haunt her, leaving her with nightmares for as long as she lived.

Drawing on what was left of her courage, she looked up at Damian Dethridge. His expression was impassive, giving nothing away.

"It needed to be done," she said, and there was defiance in her tone. She might be punished, but she'd do it all over again.

"Yes," he replied. "It did. But I'd have saved you the trauma and done it for you."

Heavy emotion clogged her throat, and all she could do was nod.

"Go from this place, Roisin," Ronan said gently from behind her. "Take Aeden and go. I'll clean up the mess my family made."

"Moira used blood magic. I can't stop her if she comes for him again," she croaked out.

"You won't need to. I'll neutralize her spell," Damian said. He hiked up his slacks and squatted beside them. With a hand on the top of Aeden's head, he smiled. "If I'm not mistaken, Beastie wove protection into his DNA. Even had Ronan not gotten to him in time, Aeden wouldn't have crossed to the Otherworld. He'd have held on until help arrived."

"Then I owe your daughter more than I can ever repay," Roisin said gruffly.

"And I owe your son for sacrificing for her, so we're even."

"Thank you for charging to the rescue."

He chuckled, but there was a weary sound to it. "I did nothing but chase Moira away. You and Ronan were the ones who saved the day."

"Mr. Ronan needs to be healed," Aeden said. "She cut his back."

Roisin gasped. She'd forgotten Moira had attacked Ronan. Setting Aeden on his feet, she struggled to rise and cast Damian a grateful look when he helped her.

"I'll take care of him," he assured her. "Teleport to my home. Your husband will be beside himself. I left him guarding my family."

"But he has no pow—"

"He does," Ronan said, fatigue heavy in his voice. "I felt my own draining, and Seamus couldn't break your magic."

"The prophecy!" She looked down at Aeden. "*Sabrina* was the One?"

He nodded, a secretive smile on his beloved face.

"Why didn't you tell me... never you mind. I suppose I can reason that out on my own. If you had, I'd never have let you out of my sight, and none of this would've come to pass."

His smile widened, but there was still the hint of worry in his eyes.

"We'll be fine, *mo stór*," she whispered, crushing him to her again.

"I know, Mam."

She nodded, although he couldn't see. "Hold tight."

After Roisin and Aeden teleported for Damian's home, Ronan released a relieved sigh and sat back on his arse, hanging his head and dangling his hands between his upraised knees. "I think I adore that woman."

Damian chuckled. "She's magnificent."

"Wouldn't it have been grand to have a mother like her?"

Neither of them had been blessed in the parent department, and Ronan was always amazed how they'd turned out to be vastly different men. Granted, Damian had a better start for the first five years of his life with a mother and father who adored him until the Evil had taken hold of them. Three years into his hell, at eight years old, Damian had been rescued by Nathanial Thorne and adopted into his mother's side of the family.

Ronan, on the other hand, had dealt with an uncaring mother and a monster for a father until his mother eventually died, and Ronan found a way to have his father incarcerated.

"You've turned out just fine, my friend." Damian turned from him and kicked Seamus's lifeless leg. "Your parents were worse than his, and you wouldn't dream of attacking a child. In fact, you saved Aeden—twice."

Ronan nodded. "But how much of this was my doing?" His throat felt thick, and his gut churned. "I fed into their insanity—his and Moira's. They initially did my bidding, and I've created Frankenstein's monster."

"Circumstances created those monsters, O'Connor. Not you." Damian held up a hand when he would've argued. "Granted, you were the puppeteer in the early days, but it seems to me you've been trying to keep them in check since you woke up to what was right and wrong."

"Yeah." Still, he felt regret when he looked at Seamus's ghastly wound and pale face frozen in horror. "If one of them could've been swayed back from the dark side, I thought it would be him," Ronan said quietly.

"The Fates have a design, and there is no altering its course without penalty."

"Aye." Making a study of his stained hands and flexing his stiff fingers, he asked the question heavy on his mind. "I'm weak now. The bulk of my abilities are gone. Who will fight Moira when she returns?"

"I can't see that far ahead."

He sighed and closed his eyes. "I'm knackered, man. My life has been one fecking struggle after another." Meeting Damian's impenetrable stare, he asked, "How do you do it? I feel ancient at forty-two, and you've lived two centuries longer than me."

Damian stared off into the distance, his thoughtful gaze seemingly focused on the garden gate next to them. "I had a job to do." He shrugged one shoulder and sighed. "I still do. My main goal was always to keep the Darkness at bay and to keep the balance for our kind." His smile held a bittersweet quality. "Then, I met Vivian. Of course, I don't have time to grow bored now that Beastie has come along and we've another on the way."

"Sure, and you've a full-time job protecting that one." Ronan snorted. "She'll lead you on a merry chase. Goddess help ya if you have another just like her."

"Sabrina's already led me on that merry chase. And yes, it's a full-time job. One I wouldn't trade for anything in the world."

The fierce love for his daughter shone brightly in Damian's eyes.

"You're a changed man since she came along. More tolerant in some ways, less in others," Ronan said.

"Yes. I've needed to be. She's helped to breathe life in these old bones of mine, but it can be trying, too." He grinned. "But enough about all that. Let's get you healed and burn this body."

"Burn it?" A shudder ran through Ronan. Roisin's words came back to him. *"And when you're gone, no one will mourn your loss. And*

after everyone breathes a sigh of relief, they will forget you ever existed."
Would he end up the same as Seamus? Dead by someone's hand,
left to rot or be burned and never mourned?

"Ronan."

He jerked his head up. The understanding in Damian's face
caused his heart to spasm. Shuttering his deeper emotions, he
said, "Yeah, let's do this."

Standing and drawing his shirt over his head, he hissed in
pain. The fucking cut hurt like a mother. It felt as if it was
burning through his spine and seeping into his bloodstream.

"Shit."

He twisted to face his friend. "I don't like your tone, man.
Sure, and that sounds like we have a problem."

"We do." Damian whipped out his phone and took a picture of
Ronan's back, then showed the image to him. "See that network
of black lines?"

Dread started to build in Ronan's chest, nearly suffocating
him. "Here, I'm not going to like this, am I?"

"Not in the least," Damian replied, his mouth set in a grim
line. "Apparently Moira cursed the knife she used. It's going to
take a little more than a simple healing spell to remove the
poison from your system."

"Bleedin' bitch!"

"I couldn't have said it better myself. Wait there." Damian
walked a circle around Seamus's still form, and with every step,
the grass beneath his feet leached of color and shriveled, creating
a ten-inch-wide border.

"Neat party trick," Ronan quipped.

"Isn't it, though." Damian didn't spare him a glance as he
called on the element of fire and created an eighteen-inch ball of
flame between outstretched hands. "Shield your eyes; this will be
bright."

After Ronan averted his head, he heard a loud whoosh and a

pop. Turning back, he saw Damian staring coldly at the blazing body from outside the circle he'd created.

"Right, if I haven't already said this, remind me not to get on your bad side, yeah?"

Damian's smile never reached his eyes. "I think you're clever enough to know that already, O'Connor." He shifted away from the fire and gestured to the knife by Ronan's feet. "Throw it in. It has the blood of powerful witches, yours included. You don't want that in the wrong hands."

Bending wasn't comfortable, and with each movement, Ronan's body made known its agony. He could only assume it was the work of Moira's curse. He'd rip her heart out with his bare hands if he had to, but that was one monster he intended to stop. After he tossed the knife in the fire, he swayed on his feet. "Sure, and I don't want to seem like a newborn *wean*, but I don't think I can make it back to your home on my own steam." So saying, his knees went out from under him.

Strong arms broke his fall, and he frowned across at Damian. A wry smile played on the Aether's lips, and he nodded to someone behind Ronan. A glance up showed a grim-faced Carrick O'Malley.

"You helped my son, O'Connor. The least I can do is see you healed."

"You'd be best served leaving me to rot, O'Malley, but I thank you all the same."

Darkness descended.

CHAPTER 23

*T*he instant Roisin and Aeden returned to the estate, Carrick had wrapped them in his arms and held on for dear life. His fecking sanity about deserted him when Damian ordered him to stay behind, and seeing Aeden with blood staining his neck, shirt, and hands, Carrick couldn't believe he'd almost lost his son a second time.

"Will you go make sure Seamus is dead?" Roisin had asked after briefly relaying what had happened. There was a frantic quality to her. As if she didn't trust the truth she'd seen.

He looked to Vivian and Sabrina. Not for permission, but for assurance they'd be safe without him. The mini-Aether's knowing obsidian eyes gave him the guarantee he needed. When he would've run for the door, the girl stopped him with a tug of his sleeve.

She leaned in as if imparting a great secret. "Teleport."

Frowning down at her, he felt the tingling start in his cells, the heat building to almost burning. In a flash of cobalt light, he was standing by a cove of trees behind Ronan, facing an unsurprised Aether in front of a bonfire.

Carrick was in time to witness Ronan sway on his feet after

tossing a knife into the blaze, and he rushed to catch the over-sized plonker before the man imitated a felled tree.

Ronan wasn't wrong when he'd said Carrick would be best served letting him rot, but his sense of justice wouldn't let him ignore the man's pain, nor what he'd done to save Roisin and Aeden.

"I've got ya, man. S'okay."

That eerie silver gaze measured Carrick's sincerity for the span of two slow heartbeats, then Ronan nodded as his eyes rolled back in his head.

"Fecker's heavy," Carrick muttered as his legs almost buckled under the dead weight. "Sure, and a hand here wouldn't be remiss, Dethridge."

"Your dormant magic is waiting for you to use it, Mr. O'Malley." He crossed to them. "Even children know this game. Watch."

With a hand beneath Ronan's wide shoulder, he said, "Light as a feather, stiff as a board. Rise in the name of the Goddess."

The air crackled around them as Ronan's big body stiffened, with his arms folded across his chest. The wind picked up around them and lifted him parallel to the ground, essentially causing him to float with only the support of the Aether's hand beneath him.

"You can do this, too," Damian assured him with a half-smile. "Put your hands beneath his back and say the words."

As instructed, Carrick placed his hands palm up under Ronan's airborne body and said, "Light as a feather, stiff as a board. Rise in the name of the Goddess."

He was gobsmacked when the Aether nodded at him like he was a clever pupil and stepped back, leaving Ronan's body in the air.

"Well done, Mr. O'Malley. Now, think about my garden at the bottom of the terrace. Close your eyes and visualize an open area where you might land safely. It's important before you teleport, that you send a magical feeler when you picture the spot in your mind's eye. That will be for your safety and the safety of those around you."

"I'll never understand how teleportation is possible."

"It's a matter of manipulating time and space. When we have downtime, I'll explain, but for now, you need to get Ronan back to my home while I finish here." Without another word, Damian strolled off toward the inferno within the circle, leaving Carrick to his own devices.

"What do I do with him when I get there?" Carrick hollered after his retreating back.

"Make him comfortable. I'll be there when I can."

Placing his arms more firmly under Ronan, Carrick closed his eyes and visualized the garden as he remembered it. He focused on the empty expanse of lawn close to the bottom of the stone steps and envisioned himself standing there. Through this process, his cells began to warm, just as they did earlier when Sabrina sent him to this location. At the moment of intense burning, he felt the shift in the wind, and as quickly as his body heated, it began to cool.

He opened his eyes and gaped at the building in front of him, unable to wrap his mind around the fact he'd teleported on his own. "I can't fecking believe it," he said aloud. "I did it."

Ronan stirred, and his pain-filled gaze met Carrick's. "It's unimaginably freeing, isn't it? If anyone deserved to have their abilities return, O'Malley, it's you."

"I understand better why you wanted to keep them." Carrick couldn't prevent his underlying anger spilling out at how the man had gone about it. "But you had to know it was wrong, all the same, and especially when it hurt innocents."

"Someday, I'll tell you the story of my father, and maybe you'll understand. I don't expect you to forgive." He hissed in a breath. "Look, I can manage the stairs if you've a mind to give me a shoulder to lean on."

Ronan's skin was flushed, and whether it was from the

embarrassment of being held like a child or the resulting fever from poisoning, Carrick didn't know. Still, he couldn't help getting a little of his own back. "Shhh, just you rest. No one will think you more of a *lagú* than you are."

Scarlet color surged up Ronan's neck and into his cheeks, telling Carrick the other flushing had been illness-related. He felt a twinge of guilt when Ronan rolled and dumped himself on the ground with a grunt and a few choice swear words.

"Jaysus, man. I was havin' the craic. No need to injure yourself over a spot of fun."

"Feck off, O'Malley."

But Ronan didn't refuse the offer of a hand up or the support when Carrick wedged his shoulder under the guy's arm to add support as they ascended the stairs.

The double doors opened as they reached the midway point, and Roisin limped out to position herself under Ronan's other arm. Together, they managed to get him inside and settled on the sofa.

"Damian said he'd be back soon, and I don't know what else to do for him," Carrick told her as Ronan's eyes rolled back in his head and unconsciousness claimed him.

The man had been sweating like a sinner in church, and his skin coloring fluctuated between grey and flushed.

"I'm worried about him, Ro."

"I'll clean the wound, but I'll need you to make an antiseptic paste for me." She turned her attention to Vivian, who was entering with a tea tray. "Do you have herbs for healing in your garden, Mrs. Dethridge?"

"Call me Vivian. And yes. Damian also keeps a store in the pantry. Tell me what you need."

"Marshmallow and gotu kola to make an ointment, but I'll start with slippery elm bark as a poultice after the first cleaning." With a glance at her hands, Roisin grimaced. "Of course, I'll need to clean up again, and if you have iodopovidone, that would be grand."

"I've got just the thing. Come with me."

Carrick watched the women leave and couldn't help notice the differences between the two.

Vivian looked like what he'd imagined a high-end porcelain doll would. Her cool blond hair was nearly white, as one would envision an angel's to be if they existed. Her elegant clothing consisted of a long-sleeved maternity blouse buttoned to the collar and slacks, with wide legs that floated around her ankles when she walked. She wore flirty high heels, even in her own home, leaving him to wonder if either of the Dethridges ever dressed down or relaxed. When Ro was pregnant, she'd always complained about her feet hurting, so it was hard to believe Vivian Dethridge preferred heels at this point of her pregnancy.

Roisin, on the other hand, was earthy and bold. Her golden blond curls flowed midway down her back. At any given time, she would shove the mass of hair impatiently away from her face when she wasn't remembering to hide her scars. Her clothing reflected her laid-back nature, and she preferred jeans and a thick jumper most days.

But the one area that they were the same was their core strength. Vivian had been ready to go to war with Damian over the attempt on their child's life. When the Aether had ordered her to stay behind, her mouth had tightened in frustration, and the strain was there in her icy blue eyes. In the duration, she'd barely spoken to Carrick other than to offer refreshments or scold Sabrina for her recklessness right before dragging the distraught girl into a hug.

And Roisin, well, she hadn't had time to tell him the complete story of what had happened, but he knew she'd been in the thick of things before returning with Aeden. Now, she was using the last of her strength to help the man responsible for their woes.

"Ya look ready to murder something… or someone," Ronan said. "If it's me, I'll not hold it against ya."

"Shut up, ya tool." Carrick touched the back of his hand to Ronan's brow and frowned. "You're burning up, man. What was on that knife?"

Ronan groaned as he shifted to his side and tucked the pillow into the crook of his neck. "If I had to guess, the same thing Moira poisoned your brother with."

"Jaysus! I should've guessed that was what was causing your problems." Whipping out his phone, Carrick placed a call. "Piper, I need ya to listen to me. Can you remember the recipe you used on Cian when you removed the poison and your mother injected the antidote?"

"Not off the top of my head. That day was absolutely insane, but I'm sure my mother made notes in her medical journal, and I can grab the spell from your family's grimoire.

"Could you get your mother here? I know it's an ask, but I think Moira is up to her old tricks. She cut Ronan across the back, and he's in a bad way."

There was a long pause on the other end of the line.

"I can't guarantee she'll come, but I'll try. Where's 'here'?"

"The Dethridge estate." He glanced down at Ronan, who was fighting to stay alert. "And I don't need to tell ya to hurry, do I?"

"No. I'm well aware of how fast that toxin works. See you soon." Before disconnecting, she said, "Oh! And Carrick? Don't let anyone touch the wound without gloves."

He looked down at one of his hands, covered in Ronan's blood. "Right. Bring enough for two doses, yeah?"

"*Shit!*"

CHAPTER 24

$\mathcal{T}$he wait for help was maddening and went against Roisin's healing nature. It hadn't helped that she'd overheard the tail-end of Carrick's phone call with Piper and realized he'd probably absorbed some of the deadly toxin through his own skin. By performing magic and speeding up his cells, he would've accelerated the effect.

Roisin limped back and forth, trying to pace off her anxiety, as Carrick casually sat and sipped tea in one of the leather club chairs.

Vivian had helped prepare the poultice but then left to keep an eye on Aeden and Sabrina, who were resting in the girl's bedroom.

"What's taking so bloody long?" Roisin snapped.

"They'll be here soon, pet." Her husband's calm assurance irritated the feck out of her.

She stomped to where he half-reclined, hands on her hips, and glared down at him. "You'd think a man with your brains would know better than to expose himself to poison. But did you? No! Always the fecking hero, ya are!"

His brows shot up, and his tired eyes lit with humor. "There's my Ro. Always salty when she's worried about those she loves."

"Of course I love you, ya eejit." She growled and would've gripped his beloved face between her hands to kiss him if she wasn't worried about potential harm to herself. Her knowledge of Moira's poison was scarce, and she blamed herself for not learning more about it when she'd heard Cian had first been attacked. "And if you die on me, I'll be so cross I'll not mourn you. Not for one second of one day."

He tried to hide his grin behind a sip of tea. "I'll be grand, Ro."

"You don't know that!"

"Actually, I do. The Aether would never have let me touch Ronan if there was a chance I'd become infected."

She frowned and dropped her arms to her sides. Sure, and he was right. Damian had the ability to see the immediate future, and he had no reason to jeopardize Carrick's life. Plopping down in the chair next to him, she compressed her lips against a relieved sob and nodded absently.

"It'll be all right, love," he said. "You'll see."

"How can you be so certain, Carrick? This is so far beyond our skills and understanding..." Roisin shook her head and locked her attention on Ronan. He'd worsened in the last little while. "And I'll be gutted if he dies."

"Are you growing fond of him, then?"

She couldn't miss the sullenness in her husband's tone, and she shot him a weary smile. "You've had me from the first day of primary school, and you still question my commitment?"

Carrick straightened in his chair and set the empty cup and saucer on the table beside him. "What can I say? He's a handsome man. I can only imagine he'd get any woman he set his sights on."

She opened her mouth to respond, but there was a commotion behind her. When she peered over her shoulder, she saw Piper and her mother, Rebecca Walsh-Thorne, the talented world-renowned surgeon—and Ronan's ex-lover—had arrived.

Rebecca shot Ronan a sour look and responded to Carrick's comment. "I'm living proof of that."

"Cut yourself a break, Mom." Piper gave her mother a warm smile. "The guy looks like he'd earn millions modeling underwear."

"Oh, he definitely could," Rebecca said with an appreciative sigh.

Her daughter scowled. "We just ventured into TMI territory."

Roisin laughed and stood up to greet the newcomers. Holding out her hand to shake the doctor's, she said, "I'm Roisin O'Malley."

"Rebecca Thorne, and you know Piper, of course." Approaching Ronan, she stared down at him and jolted the instant he opened his eyes to stare back. "I heard your vicious bitch of a cousin infected you, Mr. O'Connor," she said coolly.

With her upswept dark hair and carefully made-up chocolate-colored eyes, she was a striking woman. She complimented Ronan's blond good looks, and it was easy to see why they'd been attracted to each other to begin with.

A wry smile curled his lips. "That's the way it's to be then, Bec?"

"Yes. I'm here to save your life and nothing more." Color stained Rebecca's cheeks. "And don't get any ideas. Hoyt chose to stay behind because he didn't want to be tempted to undo all my hard work."

"Aye." He struggled to sit up, and Carrick joined Rebecca in helping him. "I'm grateful he resisted the urge to finish me off."

Roisin edged closer to the doctor. "I don't want to hurry your reunion, to be sure, but those odd black lines have crept up to his neck."

Rebecca's sharp gaze dropped to Ronan's throat and narrowed. "I don't recall that happening to Cian. Piper, do you?"

"No. This could be a new side effect," her daughter said. "Does this mean I can't stab him through the heart with a syringe?"

Turning green and looking about to pass out again, Ronan attempted to stand, only to be held back by Carrick.

"Sure, and tell me I've died and gone to hell. It's why I'm surrounded by the lot of you, willing to torture me while my veins are on fire," Ronan muttered as he swiped his forearm across his forehead.

"Can he have water?" Roisin asked, well aware he was burning up and hoping that the fluids might ease his suffering to a small degree.

Rebecca shook her head as she checked his vital signs. "I want to know what we are dealing with before he has anything, but you and our hostess can set up a room for him to be comfortable. An en suite bathroom with a tub might be useful. We probably need to ice him down until we can get this fever under control."

"Where the devil is Dethridge?" Carrick muttered. "Shouldn't he have been back by now?"

"I'll go see if I can find him." Piper was heading for the hallway when Damian appeared outside the French doors. "Wait! He's here now."

DAMIAN TOOK ONE LOOK AT RONAN AND SWORE UNDER HIS breath. He'd waited too long. The poison was coursing through his friend's entire body, destroying everything it touched, and it was a wonder Ronan had survived this long.

Approaching Rebecca, he asked, "What have you given Ronan so far?"

"Nothing. I was afraid to until I drew blood and had an idea of what it is."

"Good. If you'll please stand back, I want to examine his wound." To Ronan, Damian said, "Move to the floor and rest on your stomach."

The others in the room winced as Ronan lurched upright and screamed his agony.

Damian caught him as he tumbled forward, and he grunted under the unexpected weight. With the help of Carrick, they positioned Ronan face down on the floor. "O'Connor, I'm going to put you into a temporary stasis and suspend your body's functions. Don't fight it. I won't let you die."

Ronan gave Rebecca one last long look and shut his eyes, cradling his head on his forearms. "Do what you will. I'm too knackered to fight."

"It will be okay, my friend."

"Sure, and I wish I believed ya. But I'll keep the Devil company until you decide if I'm worth bringin' back."

"He's always been dramatic," Rebecca said.

She knelt on one side of Ronan, directly across from Damian. Her hand twitched, and he could read her emotions without difficulty. Despite her cool façade, she still cared for her ex-lover. While Damian had never loved anyone to the extent he loved Vivian, he'd been around for over two centuries, and he understood human emotions were complicated to the extreme. Although Rebecca loved her husband, she and Hoyt had been going through difficulties in their relationship around the time Ronan arrived on the scene. Young Ronan O'Connor, handsome and mesmerizing fella that he was, had swept her off her feet and straight into a torrid affair. But ultimately, Rebecca returned to Hoyt and their young daughter, Piper.

Ronan had never fully recovered from his broken heart, and after confessing to the affair, he never spoke of Rebecca again to Damian.

Vivian entered the room with a second tray of tea—her go-to for stressful situations—and Damian met her worried stare head-on. In the early days of their relationship, before Sabrina had come along, they'd entertained Ronan in their home multiple times. As his friend, she was invested in his welfare, too.

"He'll be okay, Viv," Damian assured her. "He's too stubborn to die."

Her wan smile told him she knew what he was trying to do. His assurance wasn't just for her; it was for everyone present. With two fingertips on each of Ronan's temples, Damian probed the other man's mind and was happy to discover the poison hadn't invaded the brainstem yet. Finding the section of the brain responsible for sleep, the Aether focused all his attention there and sent Ronan into what constituted as a medical coma.

Inside the mind, Damian could feel the toxin knocking on the door to the brain. Ronan didn't have much time, and although Damian hated to do it, he needed to drop a truth bomb. Viv was going to fight him. However, Ronan was too far gone for Damian's magic alone. The toxin was practically traveling at the speed of light, and Ronan would be dead within a half-hour if Damian didn't do something quickly.

"I need Beastie, Viv."

Her hand flew to her mouth, and her worry increased tenfold. "Damian—"

"I'm here, Papa."

He shook his head and snorted softly. Of course she was. Sabrina Dethridge was all-seeing and full of mischief. What she couldn't learn with her gifts, she did with her endless curiosity by spying on those around her.

"Come, Beastie. You and I are going to perform a magic trick to heal Mr. Ronan."

Unsurprisingly, Roisin was the first to object. As the mother of a young child, her mama bear quickly came out of hibernation in situations like these.

"Ro." Carrick moved to place an arm around her shoulders. "He knows what he's doin'."

"But the poison! If she becomes infected—"

Leaning in, he gave her a gentle kiss. "He knows what he's doin'," he repeated. "Now come, let's give them room."

"Actually, I need everyone's help," Damian said smoothly. "It will take all seven of us." He paused to look at Vivian and Piper, standing side by side. One fair, one dark, both expectant mothers with their hands cradling their bellies. Vivian was much farther along, and he had a moment's pause. Did he risk the unborn? What were the chances it would affect them?

He met Sabrina's steady gaze and silently asked her his unspoken questions.

"No harm to them, Papa."

"Are you up for this, Beastie? You and I will need to take this black magic into us before it can be bound and destroyed."

"Will it hurt?"

"A little, like a bee sting, but you are stronger than the threat."

He didn't believe in lying to her. As a future Aether and supreme power for the witch community, she'd need all the knowledge she could gain between now and then. He wouldn't be around forever, and with her constant high jinks, death by heart attack was likely to happen for him sooner rather than later.

She bit her lip and nodded. Damian wouldn't have said it was possible to adore her more than he did, but her bravery made his love for her swell. Already he was proud of her. When she grew into her potential, she'd be incredible—and unstoppable. The threat to her as an adult would be minimal.

"Let's prepare a circle." He rose and lifted his arms, then closed his eyes and concentrated on pushing the furniture to the far corners of the room. When he lifted his lids, it was to find Sabrina conjuring candles and placing each one in a large circle as she went. A pleased smile curled his lips. "Well done, my love. Okay, everyone enter the protective circle and join hands. Beastie, you'll be here, next to me, and Piper will be on your right. Vivian, here on my left. The rest of you can take any spot."

Once they were in position, he said, "Sabrina and I will work the toxin free of Ronan's bloodstream. We only need the rest of you as a conduit for the remaining magic we need. It will initially feel like we are trying to pull your power from you due to the strength of our spell, but I promise you won't lose any of your natural-born abilities."

A few of them shared wary glances, but Damian understood their fears, and he'd let them come to the decision whether to help on their own. Most of them knew about his mother's reign of terror and how she'd stolen the magic of others under one guise or another. She'd been a trusted servant of good and the overall balance until the day she'd been infected by the Darkness. Then she'd become a machine of destruction, consuming and amassing power to grow stronger, killing anyone standing in her way.

Damian was a risk to their very lives should he turn like she had. But he'd banished the Darkness last year, and he'd hoped they would remember he was doing this to save a life, not take it.

One by one, they came to the same conclusion and nodded their assent.

"Excellent." He gave the group a reassuring smile. "Let's get started."

He didn't need spells like a standard witch; everything he intended could be done by manipulating time, energy, and molecules. Taking a deep breath, he became one mind with Sabrina. Starting from the left, he drew what he needed through their physical connection as his daughter did the same. They created a live conduit, and the energy swirled through each of them, pulling from their cells and sending that magic through the seven-person chain. As the bulk of it impacted Damian, he closed his eyes and used his inner vision to search out the black magic within Ronan's body. He rode the bloodstream, dodging the poisonous sludge that tried to cling to him like a drowning man to a life preserver.

Moira had done her job well when she created this particular weapon. Her spell had created the type of parasite that killed its host in order to survive.

"It lives in his lungs, Papa."

191

Damian changed directions and dove through the tissue into the chamber of Ronan's left lung. When he got there, he discovered a tar-like substance coating the walls. It was a wonder the man could breathe.

"Anu said that in the Netherworld, you cut off the Darkness from all magic to kill it. This is like that." Aeden's hesitant voice almost jerked Damian out of the spell when it reached him, but he managed to hold on.

He understood the concept—cut off the power supply.

Ronan would hate him when he woke, but he needed to be made into a regular mortal if he was to survive.

CHAPTER 25

$\mathcal{I}$n the corner of the room on the large comfy sofa, Carrick cuddled his sleeping wife and son as he watched his unconscious enemy. The Aether had conjured an extra-large mattress after the spell concluded and covered Ronan with a thick, down comforter. In the hour or so since the ceremony, he hadn't moved so much as an inch, and Carrick worried what the final outcome would be.

Having sent Piper home to Cian earlier, Rebecca was curled up in a club chair, reading a medical book. As if she sensed his attention, she looked up and met Carrick's considering gaze.

"What is it you'd like to know, Mr. O'Malley?"

"Do you still love him?"

She sighed and closed her book. Before answering, she took a sip of wine, and he had the feeling she needed the fortification. "I care about him, yes. Love? No." Setting the book aside, she sat forward, and her sad eyes dropped to where Ronan slept. "I'm in love with my husband. I always have been. But a stressful job, a small child, an emotionally distant husband, and endless loneliness all made me vulnerable to Ronan's fun-loving personality at the time." She smiled, and her look held a margin of tenderness. "He made me feel treasured when I was ignored at home."

"Is he a good man, do ya think?"

"I believe so." She nodded and looked at Carrick again. "Deep down, he has a moral compass. It's a little skewed at times, like all of ours can be if the circumstances are right. But he doesn't desire to hurt anyone."

"How do you know?"

"We had many hours to talk, him and I. Confidences were shared. You can't fake the kind of genuineness he showed me." She sipped her wine as she considered her next words. "Ronan didn't set out to steal me from Hoyt. I walked away from my husband first. A separation, if you will. Piper still holds resentment because she keeps her father on a pedestal, but no one person is perfect. No marriage, for that matter."

"I'm prying, to be sure, but why did you decide to return to Hoyt?"

"Love. His contrition. My daughter." Rebecca shrugged and smiled. "Realizing I didn't want to go through life without them. And Hoyt forgave me for my indiscretion. He recognized he'd kept his cards too close to his chest and failed to tell me he loved me and to listen when I needed him to. Throwing away years of marriage isn't an easy thing."

Carrick glanced down at Roisin and smoothed back her wild mane of hair. "I think we can all be guilty of stupidity now and again," he said softly. "But if your Hoyt's feelings are anything like mine for my family, he adored the feck out of you."

Roisin snuggled closer and smiled in her sleep as if she heard his words and embraced them.

"The O'Malleys have a reputation for being unlucky, but I'm here to tell you that you are all fortunate indeed. Today could've gone a lot differently, and you have a wonderful family." Rebecca crossed to Ronan and knelt to feel his brow. "If you want to go home, I'll watch over him."

"No. I promised Damian I'd stay while he and his family rested. I'll keep watch in case Moira decides to strike again."

"She'd be a fool to."

"Aye, but it's just like her to try."

She rose to her feet. "Would you like me to call my husband for backup? Not many want to deal with a formidable Thorne."

"I'm happy if you can keep him on speed dial, but I'm too wired to sleep."

"Ah, yes. The return of your magic. It does that." She picked up her wineglass then headed to the French doors to stare out at the expansive gardens. "The constant hum of power coursing through your veins can take time to get used to, but I've no doubt you'll adapt soon."

Turning to face him, she said, "You're finding it hard to hate Ronan, and you want to be sure your trust isn't misplaced. So in answer to your original question, there is a lot to admire about him. At heart, I believe he's a good man."

"He keeps saying he doesn't make war on women and children, but they're both the first to suffer in a war." He brushed his fingers over Roisin's scarred cheek. "My wife and child almost died because of his machinations."

Rebecca frowned down into her wine. "I don't know the circumstances surrounding their accident, but I can tell you, it's no fault of Ronan's. He doesn't have it in him to hurt them."

Against his better judgment, Carrick believed her, and he'd developed a grudging admiration for the man. Still, he'd be unwise to trust him. Especially now that O'Connor's power was gone. The man would be highly motivated to get it back.

"I thank you for your honesty, Dr. Walsh. You've given me a lot to mull over."

"Of course." She drained her glass and set it on the sideboard. "Don't think too harshly of him. His life until now hasn't been easy. The affection he gained from our relationship was probably the first he'd ever encountered in his life. It's a wonder he isn't a bitter bastard."

"Who said I'm not?" Ronan asked in a raspy voice.

"Ah, it wakes," Rebecca quipped. "Are you done being a lazy lay-about?"

"I seem to recall you liked when we lazed about, Bec," he countered.

She flushed and cleared her throat. "Stop, or I'll call Hoyt to nurse you back to health. I can promise, you won't like him for a caregiver."

"A fate worse than death, to be sure." Ronan yawned and rolled onto his back with only the slightest wince. "Should I feel like a newborn babe?"

Carrick met Rebecca's worried gaze, then eased his family off him to stand. "I'll tell him."

Folding one arm over his eyes, Ronan sighed. "You don't need to, O'Malley. I know my magic is gone."

"How?"

"It's like a lost limb, and my body aches to have it back. Like an itch where it was amputated."

"I'm sorry, man," Carrick said as he looked down on Ronan's covered face. "Truly."

Lifting his arm, Ronan's tired gaze focused on him. "Now why would you be?"

"I've been without magic my entire life, never believin' I'd ever have it." He glanced at his sleeping family and shrugged. "It's not that I didn't envy those who possessed it, but I shoved down my feelings and concentrated on other things." He squatted beside Ronan and placed a hand on his bare shoulder. "To have it, to be used to relying on it for everything... yeah, the loss has to be painful."

"If my da ever gets free of his prison, you'll need to be prepared, Carrick." Ronan's eyes were haunted. "He'll have felt the drain due to the first two parts of the prophecy coming to pass, and he'll want it back. The man's ruthless, to be sure, and I won't be around to stop him."

"Where will you be?"

"Likely dead if Moira has her way. But you heed my words, yeah? Stay alert."

Carrick watched him for signs of falsehood and only saw a world-weary truth. "I promise."

"That's grand. Now, go away and let me sleep." Ronan released a jaw-cracking yawn.

RONAN CLOSED HIS EYES, HALF WISHING DAMIAN WOULD'VE LET him die. His life would alter drastically from this moment on. No conjuring the things he needed, no swaying the stock market to fund his extravagances. Hell, he'd need to learn a trade to feed and clothe himself. For sure, he'd never afford the upkeep of his family's estate. But the loss of that rubble wouldn't be a hardship. He'd always hated the place, with the exception of the ocean view.

He had enough money in his account to keep him in comfort for a time—*if* Moira hadn't found a way to get to it first. If he returned home, the probability was high that his guards and staff would be under her control—the poor buggers.

Sensing Carrick's stare, he pretended another yawn. Yeah, and he was too stressed to sleep, but the other man didn't need to know that.

"Whatever you need, Ronan, you'll have," Carrick promised him softly.

Throat tight, he opened his eyes and met the man's compassionate green gaze. "You're too nice for your own good, O'Malley. It will be your downfall, just as my soft heart was mine."

"What's life without kindness? The lessons in my books teach that to small children, and it's my belief that, as adults, we should've already learned it."

"I'll be the first to tell ya; kindness was never allowed in my world. Remember that when dealing with Moira or my father. They'll murder you where you stand, and your family will be causalities, too. Never give them a chance to get close." His gaze bore into Carrick's as he tried to get his point across. "*Never.* If you see them, kill them. No mercy, yeah?" Carrick studied him, and Ronan sensed an underlying pity. He wanted to shake the man and beat some sense into him. "*No mercy,* O'Malley. Promise it."

"He promises," Roisin said from the sofa. "As do I."

"Ro—"

"No, Carrick." Impatiently, she shoved back her hair as she sat up. "Look, you didn't see Moira's madness, but I did. She was gleeful." Roisin gestured toward Ronan without looking at him. "If his father is as bad or worse than Moira, we should be gnashing our teeth and losing sleep."

Rebecca, who had remained silent since he woke, moved to stand at Ronan's feet. She, too, stared at Carrick and ignored him. "Your wife is correct, Mr. O'Malley. Speak to Alastair or Damian. They'll set you up with someone at the Witches' Council who you can talk to. Perhaps be on a call list for early alerts should the senior O'Connor escape."

Carrick held up a hand. "I'll do what it takes to protect my family, and I'll study what I need to so I can use what's been gifted to me."

"That's all I ask," Ronan said.

"Okay, all of you, time to let our patient rest." Rebecca retrieved her medical bag and returned. "I want to check your vitals."

THROUGHOUT THE PROCESS, BOTH DOCTOR AND PATIENT WERE stoic and avoided meeting each others' eyes, leaving Roisin to wonder if she'd have been the same way with Carrick had they not resolved their differences. She squeezed the hand cradling hers, and her husband kissed her temple.

"I feel sad for them," she said, for his hearing alone. "I think she really cared for him and was torn between him and her family."

"Sure, and it's hard to believe hers is the only love he's ever known," Carrick replied just as quietly.

"Should we set him up with Bridget, do ya think?"

He chuckled. "Only if you want to see a giant of a man terrified. Dealing with my sister would probably make him take a flying leap off a short pier."

Roisin swatted his arm as she giggled. "She isn't that bad."

"I'll let my sister make her own decisions, all the same, thanks. That way it'll save us from her temper."

"Good point. Anyway, she's still in love with Ruairí."

Her comment caused Carrick to jerk sideways and stare down at her. "What?"

"Sure, and isn't it as obvious as the nose on your pretty face?" she said pertly. It was easy to tell when her knowing look got under his skin, and she couldn't resist a grin.

"I wondered at times, and yeah, I knew they were attracted to each other, but not that she loved him." He shook his head. "How long have you been party to that information, woman?"

"Since I caught them snogging behind the pub."

He shifted and glared. "When?"

"She was fifteen or so." She scoffed at his indignation. "Oh, give over, Carrick. Not one O'Malley is a saint, with the exception of that one." Roisin gestured to Aeden. "I recall a time or two when you and I—"

Clamping a hand over her mouth, he shot a sharp glance their son's way, checking that he was still asleep. "Shhh, or there will be no controlling him when he's that age."

A smile curled her mouth beneath his palm, and he moved his hand to replace it with a tender kiss.

"It didn't turn out too badly for us." She gazed up at him with all the love in her heart. "Did it?"

"No, pet, it turned out just grand."

She cuddled into him and looked back at Ronan only to find the man watching them with a hint of a smile and a whole lot of sadness. Yes, she'd find him someone to make him happy. He deserved a second chance for giving Aeden back to her.

CHAPTER 26

*D*amian joined their group, and after checking on Ronan, he approached Roisin. "You came to me to heal your son, but obviously, Beastie did that outside earlier. Now, I offer you the choice. Do you wish me to reverse the damages done by the accident, or are you prepared to go on as you are?"

She looked at Carrick.

"I know what I'd choose, Ro, but you need to decide what is best for you."

Worrying her lip, she stared into Damian's patient eyes as she debated what she wanted. It should be a simple matter to have all her pain taken away, but she doubted it would be without penalty. There was always a balance or trade necessary.

"There's no cost to you," Damian assured her as if she'd spoken the words aloud. "You've gone over and above for everyone, and this is your reward, should you choose it."

She touched her scarred cheek, tracing the tangle of scars to her blind eye. "And my magic? Will it be completely restored? No drain after performing a spell like I currently have?"

"You will be whole once more."

Again, she looked at Carrick. What she was seeking from him, she wasn't certain, but when he leaned in and gently cradled her face, she saw his fierce love but not the pity she expected. His gaze roved over the scars, studying them in their entirety.

"Sure, and I've said it before, but they've never bothered me or turned me off, Ro. That was always your issue, never mine. Remove them or keep them; it's up to you. I'll love you and desire you the same either way."

"I don't want to keep them," she whispered past her aching throat.

"Then let the Aether help you. But do it for yourself, love, and no one else, yeah?"

With a careful, butterfly-soft touch, he brushed away the tears she didn't know were flowing.

"There's nothing to fear, Mrs. O'Malley," Damian said. He held out his hand, and peace settled in her heart when she placed hers in his. "I won't lie to you. The initial removal will burn like hell, but once I'm done and the marks fade, so will the pain. Your scars will never return."

"Do we do this here?"

"It might be best in my study. That way, if you cry out, your husband isn't tempted to rearrange all of my perfect features," he said dryly.

She laughed as he intended, and the last of her tension vanished.

Her gaze touched on Ronan, and he gave her a smile and an encouraging nod as if to say, "You go, girl!"

More and more, she found herself softening toward him.

As they entered the study, she faced Damian. "Will you ever give Ronan his abilities back?"

"If I do it now, he risks a reoccurrence of today's illness. I can't guarantee there isn't residual black magic in his cells at the moment. But when the time is right, I'll confer with the Fates and his goddess to see what can be done."

"I should hate him for what he set in motion, but I don't," she confessed.

"He did something wrong for what he considered was the right reason. It's hard to hate a man like that."

"He's your good friend, yeah?"

Damian took a long time to answer, and Roisin got the impression he was weighing his words.

"I've known him a long time. Twenty-four years, if I remember correctly, but we fell out of touch when I found out Vivian was pregnant." He poured her a glass of wine and handed it to her. "I ended a lot of friendships to protect Sabrina. She's too young to fight off those who would try to steal her power. It was better if the world didn't know she existed."

"And you didn't trust Ronan not to be one of those people?"

"I can't afford to trust anyone. It puts me at a distinct disadvantage if I'm wrong about a person's true motives. But I do regret not being there for Ronan when he needed my counsel."

It was a terrible way to live, not trusting friends. Roisin had dealt with isolation this year, and she hated almost every minute of it. "Then it's sorry I am that you need to live the way you do."

"I'm content, and Sabrina is a well-adjusted child for what she is."

"She and Aeden are friends, and should she ever want a play-date, you've only to call, and I'll bring him to her." He smiled, and under the full force of that beauty, she forgot to breathe. "Sure, and now I see why you don't whip that thing out more than you do. It's lethal."

She basked in the loveliness of his unrestrained laughter.

"You're good for my ego, Mrs. O'Malley."

"I'll bet you say that to every woman who gapes at you. For sure, you must have them lining up. Tell your wife that I said she could make money off the deal." She sipped her wine to calm her nerves for what was coming. "I suppose we should get on with this."

"There's a gift I'd like to give you along with the total restoration of your magic and the healing of your body. From one parent to another." He removed the glass from her trembling fingers and took her hand to lead her to a nearby chair.

"What gift?"

"The gift of premonition, for you to be prepared against any future attacks."

"How does it work?"

"When I knit your neurotransmitters, I'll wake up a new section of your brain." He squatted in front of her, tilted her chin to expose her marred cheek to the light, and began studying the ruined side of her face. "It will be like an early warning system if there is intent to harm you."

"That's useful. And would there be any side effects?"

"Not a one."

"Then I'd be grateful."

He gave her a half-smile as he met her eyes. "I thought you might. Ready?"

Swallowing hard, she nodded.

"Try not to cry out or your husband will murder me," he joked.

"I'll be as quiet as a lamb."

Closing his eyes, he held his hands in front of him, palms exposed to her. A purple mist developed in the air surrounding them, becoming thicker by the second.

Was this part of the plan?

"Yes," he murmured. "Breathe it in, Roisin." His voice had turned seductive, and an appreciative shiver raced along her spine even as the hair on the back of her neck lifted. "Breathe in the mist and suck it deep into your lungs. As you inhale, imagine it coursing through your body and spreading outward to the tip of every finger and toe."

His hypnotic instruction was impossible to ignore, and Roisin became lost in his bewitching spell. Whatever he requested she do, she did, from inhaling the mist to visualizing her skin as smooth as it once was. Her muscles loosened, and each disc in her spine plumped back to a healthy, non-ruptured state. In the locations of all her scars, a fierce burning started, and she bit her lip to keep her scream at bay.

"Not much longer, dear girl," he said, and the compelling tone of his voice put her back into a mesmeric state.

She could feel the pounding of her pulse as blood rushed to the right side of her face. An instant later, her skin cooled and her heart rate returned to normal. When he wove his fingers into her hair, she wanted to purr in pleasure. That lasted only a moment until his thumbs settled on her temples and he started reworking the wiring of her brain.

The pain started behind her eyes, like a tension headache, growing in epic proportion until she was sure her head would explode.

"Almost done, my dear," Damian said. And again, her fear receded.

Within two minutes, he was done, and all she wanted to do was curl up to sleep for a week or more. "Why am I so knackered?" she asked on a yawn.

"Your body did in ten minutes what some might take years to do." He smiled warmly as he helped her to her feet. "I'll take you to the guest suite and have your husband join you shortly."

Tentatively, she touched her smooth cheek and gasped when she realized she was seeing him with both eyes.

"Oh, Damian!" The overwhelming relief and joy came in a tidal wave of tears. She was barely aware of his arms gathering her close or of him holding her in his lap as she cried for all she'd lost, then regained. He rubbed her back and murmured sweet little nothings that her mind could scarce comprehend as the sobs wracked her body.

When she wound down, he dabbed her wet face with a hand-kerchief as he looked over his handiwork. "Most people simply thank me and go on with their day," he said dryly.

She gave a watery laugh as she accepted the damp hanky to blow her nose.

"Sure, and I suppose you're ready to hand me off to Carrick as fast as you can to be rid of me."

"The thought did occur to me, but then he'd want to know why I made you cry." He helped her to stand and gave her a quick hug. "You may want to glamour away the evidence and avoid telling him about this, or I'm going to have an irate husband on my hands."

"Not Carrick. He owes you as much as I do."

With a firm hand on her lower back, he led her toward the door. "No, my dear. Neither of you owes me a thing. The only payment I require is that you be happy and the two of you be the best parents possible to that amazing son of yours."

As soon as Damian opened the door, they saw Carrick holding a sleepy Aeden securely against him and leaning against the far wall.

"He woke and wanted his mam," he said with a one-shoulder shrug.

CARRICK'S SHARP-EYED INSPECTION MISSED NOTHING. NOT HER tears or her closeness with Damian. He hadn't expected to feel the pang of jealousy, but it was likely he'd always be territorial when it came to her. Roisin was his as he was hers. Anything that threatened that, however remotely, would get his back up, to be sure.

She wasted no time hugging him and Aeden in a tight embrace. And when their son reached for her, Carrick wrapped his arms around them for added support.

"I was just about to show your wife to the guest suite. If you'd like to follow me, you can all have family time together." Damian smiled and gestured down the hallway.

"I think I'd like to take them home if you wouldn't be offend-ed." Carrick kissed the top of Roisin's curly head.

The Aether frowned and opened his mouth as if to speak, but his face lost expression as he turned toward the far windows. It was as if he was seeing or hearing someone else in the distance, and Carrick was chilled.

Shaking off whatever had taken hold of him, Damian returned his stare. Some of the warmth had fled, but he was just as courteous as always when he said, "Not at all, Mr. O'Malley. Of course, you'd want to return home."

"What just happened there, man? Are you all right?"

"To be perfectly honest, I'm not sure." Again, the Aether frowned. "It's as if someone walked over my grave, and yet, as hard as I try, I can't seem to find the source."

Carrick began to sweat, and his heartbeat doubled in speed. "Another threat? You think Moira has returned?"

"Possibly. But if she has, she'll find it impossible to break through my wards." Damian shook his head slightly as if to rid himself of his thoughts. "Give me time to scry and search your home for danger. Then you can return to your place, all right?"

"Maybe we should stay the night, Carrick." The worry on Roisin's face bothered him. It was as if she felt a disturbance, too.

"Let Mr. Dethridge do what he intended, and we'll discuss it after. If there's a problem, I'll leave Aeden here with you and check on Cian and Bridget myself."

"Not without me, you won't," she said firmly. "I'm comfort-able leaving Aeden here where he's the safest, but you'll not go home alone to face an unknown threat."

"We don't even know that there is one, Ro," Carrick reminded her. Yet he knew what she meant. Too many times in the past, he'd acted on their behalf without considering that she'd want to be part of the decision-making. "But yeah, moving forward, we'll face whatever might come—*together.*"

Her luminous smile was his reward. "Thank you."

$\mathcal{I}$t took the Aether roughly twenty minutes to give the all-clear for Roisin and her family to go home. When they arrived back at their place, she used her returned magic to illuminate the house without the need to go from room to room, turning on the lights.

Aeden, surprisingly, had decided to have a sleepover with Sabrina Dethridge, and Roisin was thrilled the two children had formed a fast friendship. Of course, it could be the trauma of what happened that afternoon. The two had bonded over the attack by Seamus and Moira.

Roisin said as much to Carrick.

"You could've knocked me over with a feather when he said he wanted to stay there tonight." He shook his head, a look of bemusement on his face. "I can't say I haven't played over the question if we should've stayed a million times since I declined the Aether's invitation."

"Me, too." She kicked off her shoes, sat heavily on the couch, and hugged a pillow. It would've been nice to tuck Aeden into bed and read to him as she had in the years before the accident.

To get back to a new normal. "Do you think she'll continue to bother us now her plans have been foiled?"

There was no need to elaborate on the "she" since Moira was the only woman out for everyone's blood.

Carrick settled next to Roisin on the sofa and wrapped an arm around her shoulders. "Doubtful, but there's no telling. We all know the woman is mad. With insanity comes unpredictability."

"We'll need to be on guard until the final part of the prophecy is concluded." Roisin didn't feel they could relax yet, and she couldn't understand why. Perhaps it was the residual effects from earlier or a culmination of the last few days. A PTSD of sorts.

"Yeah." He rested his cheek on the top of her head. "I doubt I'll sleep at all tonight." Lacing his fingers with hers, he lifted their hands and kissed her knuckles. "Maybe we should find another way to pass the time."

She snorted a laugh. Leave it to Carrick to turn amorous the instant things calmed down. "I'm not sure I'm in the mood," she lied as she shifted to lean back on the pillows and positioned her legs over his thighs. After a fake yawn, she said, "I'm knackered."

A wide, engaging grin played on his supremely kissable mouth. "Well, if you're knackered…"

Using one foot, she lightly shoved his chest. "Maybe if you rubbed my poor, tired feet…"

"Mmm." He inched the thick wool sock off her foot as if performing a striptease, then ran a thumb along the arch, applying just enough pressure to make her moan her pleasure. He massaged her foot in silence for a few minutes, and she rewarded his efforts with appreciative little noises.

Because she was watching his face closely, she saw the moment he turned serious, and she braced for the question she'd rather avoid. "Are you all right with what you did today, Ro?"

He hadn't looked at her, and she was left to wonder if her vicious act bothered him. Withdrawing her foot, she sat up and tucked her legs under her to remain facing him. She took time to think about her response, not wanting to come across as a cold-hearted bitch.

When he looked at her, his eyes only displayed concern, and she released a sigh. "I'm all right with it," she said. "Seamus was responsible for all of Aeden's woes, for Meg's death, and for the loss of ten months of our lives."

"Not to mention all the pain he put you through," Carrick reminded her in a hard voice.

"Sure, and that, too. But it's beside the point. The man tried to kill our son today. For that, he needed to die." She met his stare head-on. "And I'd do it again a million times over, without any regret, if it would keep him from harming another."

Carrick watched her for a moment longer, then nodded. "Sure, and I love that you're a badass." He grinned and grabbed for her other leg, whipping off her sock when her foot was secure in his grasp. "Now, I've a job to do."

"What's that? Rubbing my feet?"

"Spoilin' my woman."

She laughed and blinked away the relieved tears building behind her lids. "Spoil away, darling."

After giving her feet the royal treatment, he reached for the button on her jeans. "There are other areas that need massagin'."

Feeling like a girl of twenty again, she jumped up and raced for their bedroom with Carrick hot on her heels. He tumbled her onto the bed and kissed her with all the pent-up passion they'd denied themselves this year. Pulling back, he stared deeply into her eyes, and she absently noted his were close to their standard emerald shade.

"I love you, Carrick O'Malley. I've loved you from the moment I saw you, and I'll love you until the moment I shut my eyes in permanent rest."

A beautiful smile curled his lips. "You plucked the words straight from my own mouth, Ro." He brushed the tip of her nose with his. "This year has been the longest of my life, and it's grateful I am that you're back where you belong."

The mood shifted, and all the things she once believed needed saying faded away to nothingness. All that mattered was here and now.

They tore at each other's clothes, needing skin-on-skin contact to reaffirm their love. With his mouth and hands, he started at her temple and began to worship the healed skin of her face.

Kissing the lid of her previously blind eye, he chuckled.

She raised her brows. "What?"

"I'm simply amazed at the Aether's abilities. He's like a god, isn't he?"

"Yeah." She ran her hands over Carrick's bare shoulders. Memorizing the texture and savoring the feel of him.

"I'll admit to being jealous he could help you when I couldn't." Carrick didn't meet her eyes as he said it and instead trailed his fingers over the pale skin of her breast.

"We were never meant to have power like his," she said gently, cupping the side of his jaw and guiding his face up so he'd see her sincerity. "He's a tool designed by the Goddess to keep people like Moira and Seamus in check. You've no need to be jealous, Carrick. It's you I love."

"You weren't seduced by him at all?"

"No." She smiled. "He's too beautiful for me. It's bad enough I've to fight women off to keep you. Can you imagine being *his* wife? The poor thing must be exhausted. It's no wonder they never leave their estate." She dropped a quick kiss on his lips. "It's thrilled I am that you're jealous. It means you still want me for your own."

"Always, Ro." Carrick captured her mouth and kissed her thoroughly. *"Always."*

. . .

211

CARRICK DREW BACK AND STRADDLED ROISIN. SHE DIDN'T TRY TO hide from him, and she had no reason to. Her body was perfection. Restored to its original form prior to the accident. He ran his fingers over her lower abdomen, noting the faint stretch marks from Aeden's birth were absent.

"I'm sad to see those gone," he admitted.

She raised up on her elbows and glanced at her belly. Gasping, she touched herself then shook her head. "Should I look in the mirror? Did he make me twenty again?"

"You don't have a wrinkle on your lovely face," Carrick said with a smile.

"Are you sayin' I'm the prettier of the two of us now?"

He laughed and gave her a light shove so she was flat on her back. "You always have been, Ro. Only *you* never saw it."

"It's not something I'll ever believe. You're too pretty for words." She shifted and wrapped her shapely legs around his waist. "Enough comparison. It's time you got to spoiling your woman."

"Yeah?" He bent and nuzzled the hard tip of her breast, drawing it into his mouth and rolling his tongue along the pebbled nipple before lightly biting it. "Prepare yourself to be wowed, darlin'."

She rocked against him as he rubbed his hard length against her wet core. "You always wow me, Carrick."

"Sure, and you say that now, but your memory might be faulty."

She wrapped her hand around his dick and gave him a light squeeze. "No, I'd say I remember exactly right."

With a groan, he removed her hand, placed a light kiss on her knuckles, and guided it to the pillow next to her head. "Tonight is about you, Ro. All about you."

Leaning in, he kissed her. There was passion in the kiss, but he wanted to convey so much more. Carrick wanted her to feel what she truly meant to him. Not just for sex or as a mother to their son—although both things were intertwined, but he wanted her to experience their connection again. To see it never truly left them, that they'd forever be one, and that he'd never want another.

When he broke their kiss and lifted his head, Roisin's eyes were misty with unshed tears, as if she sensed what he was trying to relay. Her smile, when it came, was luminous, and he grinned in return. Yes, she understood.

He caressed the pale skin of her long, graceful neck and followed it with his lips, trailing gentle, worshipful kisses down the path his fingers had traveled. For the next fifteen or twenty minutes, he did this over her entire body, and not an inch of her was ignored.

Her soft moans filled the air, and with each gasp, each sharp inhale of breath, she encouraged him to love her more. When she was frantic in her movements, digging her fingers into his arse as she lifted her hips to grind against him, he allowed himself the pleasure of sinking into her welcoming wet warmth.

Roisin locked her legs around his waist, spreading her thighs wider and pressing her pelvis to his. Their eyes met, and he slowly pulled back, inch by agonizing inch, then thrust again. On and on it went, neither speaking, simply concentrating on one another as their souls reunited in this simple act of lovemaking after all this time.

Her hands became intimately familiar with the hard planes of his body, stroking, petting, loving, and he felt his balls tightening. He was a trigger hair from coming, barely holding himself in check.

With an arm around her waist, he drew her up until he was sitting on his heels and she was straddling him. He was completely embedded inside her, and it felt like heaven. She gasped at the sudden fullness brought on by his move but adjusted quickly enough. He used his free hand to touch her intimately, circling and applying the right amount of pressure to her clit to have her breath hitch and her eyes lose focus.

"Come for me, Ro. Come for me now."

And she did. The silky walls of her vagina contracted as her orgasm rocked her. The continual pulse added to his own pleasure, and he followed her over the edge after a couple more hard pumps of his hips.

Because he couldn't let her go yet, he wrapped both arms around her, holding her tightly, and buried his face in her neck. She clung to him, breathing hard. Slick skin pressed so closely together it would've been impossible to tell where he ended and she began. No words were needed.

He didn't know how much time passed as the two of them embraced, but eventually, the cramp forming in his left butt cheek informed him it was time to shift. Easing her back on the pillows, he followed her down and brushed the damp curls away from her temples. Placing his forehead against hers, he shook his head slightly back and forth, butterfly kissing her nose with his, then he nibbled her lower lip.

"Feeling spoiled?" he asked with a husky whisper.

She grinned up at him. "Feck yeah. Sure, and you can spoil me like that anytime."

CHAPTER 28

$\mathcal{L}$ight peeked between the blinds as Roisin lay curled in Carrick's arms, her body humming from making love for the third time. She smiled as she savored the feel of togetherness. They'd gotten little sleep, but neither cared since they used the remainder of the night to reaffirm their love. Aeden's gift to them, she was positive.

Her cellphone dinged with an incoming message. She stretched across Carrick, pressing her breasts into his chest as she reached for the device.

Before she could get to her destination, he cupped her ass with one hand and drew her head down for a good-morning kiss. "Mmm."

Laughing, she rained little kisses on his face. "Let go so I can check the phone."

"I don't want to." He sounded like a pouty child, and she giggled at his petulant expression.

"If you hand it to me, I'll scrub your back in the bath."

"Deal! And don't think I won't be holdin' you to that promise," he said in a mock-stern voice.

"Yeah, yeah, yeah. Give it here."

When she had it in hand, she silently read the text. "We've until half-past before Damian intends to bring Aeden home."

Carrick took her device, tossed it onto the end of the bed, and rolled atop her. "Perfect!"

She giggled as he nuzzled her neck, then gasped as his hand delved between her legs. "Carrick, we don't have time for this," she warned.

"For all *you* know! I can be done in five minutes."

"Yes, but will I?"

His dark head came up, and he narrowed his eyes.

She giggled.

"Challenge accepted," he growled, then buried his face where his hand had been. She meeped at the first flick of his tongue. Yeah, it wouldn't take nearly that long to get her off.

Twenty minutes later, they were in the tub with Roisin positioned behind Carrick to scrub his back. "Remind me to challenge you often," she said and dropped a kiss between his shoulder blades.

"Even if you don't, I'm likely to pounce on you any chance I get, all the same." Carrick shifted around and drew her up to straddle his lap. His erection became intimate with her belly.

"Again?"

"Can't help it. It's been too long, and I feel like a fecking boyo again."

"They'll be here in about ten minutes, and I know for a fact, after the first time, you take much longer to get off the second."

"You and your practical mind, woman." He groaned as she climbed to her feet. "Then you put temptation right in my face."

She covered her mound as he surged forward, and she pushed him backward with a laugh. "I'll not greet the Aether naked at the door."

Carrick stood and drew her into his arms to drop a light kiss on her mouth. "He might like that."

"Sure, and I might, too—if you and Aeden weren't home."

"Hey!"

Giggling, she dried off and padded to the bedroom to dress.

At exactly half past the hour, the doorbell rang. Hand in hand, Roisin and Carrick crossed the living room, but before they could reach their destination, a premonition struck her.

"She's here," she said grimly.

"Who?"

"Moira." She let go of his hand. "Give me one minute, then answer the door." She didn't allow him time to argue, immediately teleporting to the park across the road. She'd chosen a spot where she was hidden by the tree line and crept forward, where the threat felt the strongest.

Moira had somehow acquired a gun and was aiming from behind a copse of trees.

In front of Roisin's home, Damian squatted, seemingly listening as Aeden chatted away. Abruptly, they stopped, and Damian slowly rose to his feet and faced the direction of the threat, just as Carrick whipped open the door.

Roisin's heart was pounding so hard, she was sure Moira would hear her at any second. But the other woman was too intent on her target. Acting on instinct, Roisin eased down and selected a hefty branch from the ground, testing it for weight. She inched closer as Damian quickly pushed Aeden into Carrick's arms and used his body as a shield for her small family.

Mouthing a small prayer to the Goddess, Roisin lifted the branch and prepared to slam it into the back of Moira's head. As if sensing danger, the other woman spun around, her lips curled back in a feral snarl. She brought the gun around and pointed it at Roisin's heart.

"I'd planned to pay you back for Seamus by taking your son's life, but you'll do," Moira said.

"Oh, *please*. As if you gave one feck for him." Playing it cool looked much easier in films. Concentrating on the earth beneath her feet, Roisin sent a silent request to the tree roots closest to her to come to the surface. But as the ground rumbled beneath them, Moira held out a hand, palm down, and stopped the action cold.

"You think you're the only earth elemental, Roisin O'Malley?" Her brittle laugh skated down Roisin's spine. "Stop where you are, Damian Dethridge, or I'll plug her full of bullets."

Although Roisin caught movement in her peripheral, she didn't take her eyes from Moira to check Damian's progress. "You're outnumbered, Moira. Give it up, and I won't kill you like I did your evil cousin."

Wrong thing to say.

Moira snarled, and the report of the gun sounded.

Distantly, Roisin heard a man shout, and she had the impression it was Carrick's voice.

Damian was beside her in an instant, but Moira was already gone.

With frantic hands, Roisin patted her chest and abdomen, then her face and scalp. She hadn't felt the punch of an impact, but her adrenaline was high.

"Looking for this?" Damian asked, holding up a small metal object.

"How... why... how...?" She looked down at the bullet and then up into his amused eyes.

"I'm the Aether."

He shot a look around, and she assumed it was to see if Moira hadn't gone far. Placing a warm hand on her lower back, he guided her toward the street. "Let's get you home."

CARRICK AGED A LIFETIME IN THE MINUTES IT TOOK DAMIAN TO cross the road and bring Roisin back.

"What the fucking hell do you think you were doing?" Carrick yelled when she was secure within his embrace. "Are ya mad, Ro? You'd take on a killer with no concern for your own safety?"

"Carrick, I'm fine."

"Sure, and it's no thanks to your recklessness, now is it?" He gripped her head between his palms and stared down into her beautiful, beloved face, unable to relay how frantic he'd been when she disappeared the way she had. "You could've been killed, Ro," he whispered harshly. "Then what would I have done?" She opened her mouth to speak, but he cut her off. "I'll tell ya! I'd have lost my fecking mind for good. My heart would be a pile of dust, and every time the wind blew, the particles would surf the current, looking but never finding you."

He gave her a shake. "Don't ever go after that bleedin' bitch again, yeah?"

"Carrick—"

"You'll not be getting around it with your soft-spoken 'Carrick'. Right now, you'll promise me, Ro."

"I can't make that promise," she said, her voice full of regret.

His heart seized, and he knew she'd do it again if it meant protecting Aeden. And he couldn't fault her for it because he'd do the same. Frustrated beyond measure, he dragged her close and tucked her face in his throat as he rested his cheek on her golden riot of curls. "You'll be the death of me, pet."

"Let's not talk about death," Damian said dryly. "Not unless it's Moira's."

"She needs to be stopped," Carrick told him.

"She will be." Damian ruffled Aeden's blond hair and smiled down at him. "But I suspect she'll never get the drop on your family again. Between Anu giving early warnings to Aeden and Roisin's premonitions, I think you'll be just fine."

"Premonitions?" Carrick drew back and looked down at Roisin. "What premonition is he talking about, Ro?"

She shrugged and smiled sheepishly. "He might've given me a gift yesterday."

"Might've or did?"

"Did."

With a snort, he caressed her cheek. "Then it's glad I am of it. But I forbid you to go after her again." When her brows shot up, he cursed himself for a fool. "Here, and what I meant to say, is that I wish you would consider Aeden and not go after her again," Carrick amended.

Damian laughed. "Seems like you have everything under control here, Mr. O'Malley. I'll be in touch."

With that, the Aether was gone, and Carrick was left alone with his wife and son. He opened his arms to them, and they rushed into his embrace. He never intended to let them go again.

EPILOGUE

*M*oira flipped open another trunk lid and swore when she didn't find what she was looking for. Ronan had concealed the damned Sword of Goibhniu too bloody well. She'd searched every potential hiding spot in this hideous pile of stones, and still, it eluded her. If she could find it, she'd stop the final part of the O'Malley prophecy without having to encounter the Aether again.

It had been two days since she'd tried to take her revenge on Roisin O'Malley, and Ronan hadn't returned yet. She could only hope the black magic attached to the blade she'd used on him had done what it was supposed to. If not, there would be nowhere she could hide that he wouldn't find her and extract retribution. There was a slim chance he survived because he had Damian Dethridge on his side. The possibility lent urgency to her search.

She sat back on her heels and stared into the trunk. "Think, Moira!" she scolded herself.

"You have to ask yourself, girl, if you were Ronan, where would you hide it?"

Gasping her shock, she spun around and stared in stunned disbelief at the newcomer. "Uncle Loman!"

His cold gunmetal-grey eyes narrowed on her, and he summed up her alarm in an instant, as indicated by the satisfied smile on his handsome visage. His was a face at odds with the personality it disguised. The man looked like an angel but had the soul of a demon.

"Ronan said you were locked up."

Wrong thing to say.

His expression darkened, and he straightened away from the doorjamb to his full six-foot-four height. Moira froze in fear, like a mouse in a hawk's sights.

"I'll deal with my wayward son in due time, girl. Never you worry. And as for you, you'll tell me now, where is my family?"

She could lie, give him false locations, and teleport at her earliest opportunity to some godforsaken island where he'd never find her. Except he would—*eventually.* Loman O'Connor liked to keep his family under his thumb to use as pawns in whatever ridiculous chess game he happened to be playing at the moment. They'd all been given a reprieve when the Witches' Council had locked him away, but now, the time was at hand. She'd need to pay the piper for betraying him, just as Ronan would if he managed to survive her poisoned blade.

"Seamus is dead. Ronan was on his way to being, last I saw him."

His dark-blond brows shot up. "You're the lone survivor?"

"Aye."

He threw back his head and laughed.

She hated the sound. It was evil, pure and simple.

"No, girl. Ronan wouldn't have made it that easy for you."

"How did you—" She clamped her lips shut, damning herself for a fool. Sure, and she'd just given herself away. She'd be lucky if he didn't slit her throat.

"Where did you leave his body?"

She didn't dare prevaricate. "On the property bordering the Aether's land."

"Then Dethridge has found and helped him." Loman pinned her with a hard stare. "Lucky for you."

Tucking her trembling hands under her thighs, she asked, "What do you intend to do?"

"What you and my son should've done to begin with—kill the O'Malleys."

"I've tried. It's harder than it seems," she said sullenly.

He crossed the room and held out a hand to help her up. Easily a foot and a half taller, her uncle terrified the feck out of her. Where Ronan held an edge of ruthlessness, he maintained a code that didn't allow him to target those he believed weaker than himself. His father's moral compass was the polar opposite; he didn't care who he hurt to gain what he wanted. Loman's cruelty was legendary.

Before he released her, he tightened his hand over hers to the point of discomfort. She did her damnedest not to show it hurt.

"I'll not be losing my magic to the O'Malleys." His cold-eyed stare was that of a sociopath and set the warning bells to clanking in her brain. "I'll kill anyone who stands in the way of my goals."

Moira jerked her hand away and hid it behind her back. "Then you'll be putting your son at the top of your hit list. He's gone soft. Sure, and he betrayed the entire O'Connor line by protecting Roisin O'Malley and her little demon spawn."

Loman looked thoughtful for a moment, then his shark-like smile emerged. "I won't kill him, but he'll be reforming when I get him. It's time the boy remembers what loyalty to family means."

Moira almost felt sorry for Ronan. She might've if he hadn't locked her in the tower room for a month or foiled her plans to kill the brat at every turn. He'd probably prefer death by her poisoned blade to whatever Loman had in mind for him.

She certainly would.

Unable to help herself, she asked, "What is it you intend to do?"

His amused chuckle raised the hair on her body, and she wished she hadn't asked.

ANU, STANDING BESIDE HER CONTEMPORARY, ISIS, WATCHED THE conversation between Loman O'Connor and Moira Doyle without giving away the turmoil she was feeling inside. Or without giving it away *much*. Her stress tended to roll out by way of rain clouds and soak her beloved *Éire* until she could get her stronger emotions under control.

"For so beautiful a man, Loman is rotten to his core. Similar to an apple with a shiny red skin on the outside but spoiled flesh inside."

Anu nodded in agreement with Isis's analogy. "And he's unpredictable in nature."

Isis flipped back a wave of her thick black hair, and her amber, kohl-lined eyes narrowed as she studied him. "I don't know about that. I'd say he's extremely predictable."

"Oh?"

"He's driven by greed and power. You can always trust him to do the dastardly thing."

"True." Anu sighed and sauntered over to the stone bench on the rise above the pond. After she sat, she looked around at the paradise Isis had created. All creatures, big and small, could be seen in varying stages of rest, feeding, or in some cases, like the rabbits under the birch trees, mating. People like Loman O'Connor never appreciated the beauty in life. He was too far gone with his need to destroy anything he perceived as weaker than himself. His son, Ronan, included.

As they'd watched the events surrounding the O'Malleys unfold, Ronan's role became clearer. The Three Sisters of Fate had given Anu and Isis another cryptic clue about where all this would lead.

Isis joined her. "You seem disturbed, my dear Anu. Are you truly surprised by Loman's villainous nature?"

"No. Perhaps I'm simply tired of the conflict humans create. Maybe if we removed all magic, they'd have nothing to go to war over anymore."

The other goddess patted her hand. "Men will forever find reasons to go to war. It's in their contrary makeup. You've only to look at the gods and remember man was created in their image."

"I want to see the good guy win," Anu confessed. "To see the O'Malleys thrive and regain their magic. To see the Loman O'Connors and Moira Doyles of the world fail in their quest for murder and mayhem."

"As do I, my friend. As do I." Isis sighed. "Do you trust Ronan O'Connor to do the proper thing moving forward?"

Anu gave her a sharp look. "How do you mean? What are you planning?"

"If we return magic to him, make him stronger than the others, do you believe he will fight for the side of good, or like his father before him, turn to evil?"

She took the time to think about Isis's question. There was no ready answer. Based on what she'd seen of him, she'd bet he was true to his word in wanting the magic to destroy his father. But power did strange things to men.

"We would need to discuss restoring Ronan's magic with The Three," she said. "If it goes against what is fated, they'll not be happy." Anu kissed her cheek and stood. "But we have time yet. Unless I miss my guess, Loman is a planner. He won't be spontaneous or reckless like Moira and Seamus before him."

"Yes. And speaking of Seamus McCleary, I suppose he's been in the holding area long enough. Do we send him straight to hell, or would you rather try to reform him?"

Anu looked over her shoulder, through the veil at the waiting area. Seamus was huddled on the ground, his arms folded over his knees with his forehead resting on them. "He appears to regret hurting the boy, and yet, I'd say he'd do it again if given the chance."

"I'm of the same mind."

"Send him to hell and be done with it. Perhaps the tortures there will help him to live a better life the next go around."

Isis smiled, and her ordinarily kind eyes grew frosty as she focused on Seamus. "Consider it done."

THANK YOU FOR READING CARRICK AND ROISIN'S STORY. IF YOU want more of the O'Malley family, keep reading for an excerpt of *Beer & Broomsticks*, book 3 in *The Unlucky Charms* series!

When the Enemy at the Gate is welcomed by the Keeper of the Sword, all that is lost shall be restored.

Chapter 1

BRIDGET O'MALLEY LOVED RUAIRÍ O'CONNOR. SHE HAD SINCE the day they'd accidentally met by the garden gate dividing their properties. At the time, she was four years old and didn't understand she wasn't supposed to love him. She was *supposed* to hate him with every fiber of her being as every O'Malley had hated every O'Connor since the family feud started two-hundred and fifty years before.

Despite his betrayal when they were only twenty—the one she still couldn't bear to think about some seventeen years later— she found it difficult to call up the hate. Oh, for sure, she wasn't happy with him, and she'd spend every hour of every day making him aware of the fact if she could, but she didn't hate him. Not even a little.

"Good morning, *mo ghrá.*" Ruairí had a deep, raspy tone that never failed to reach in and tickle her girly parts.

Bridget cast an irritated glance toward the stone fence where that good-for-nothing O'Connor stood sipping his morning coffee. Her standard sneering response was done more out of habit these days. "I'm not your love, Ruairí. I'm not your anything."

"Oh, but you are. Have been since the day I first set my eyes on you thirty-three years ago."

They were of an age. Both bonded as children and spent their youth sneaking out to meet at the same time they were being taught to despise one another. They'd continually laughed at their parents' attempts to poison their hearts and minds.

Until the day Ruairí had poisoned hers against him.

He'd done what her parents and grandparents hadn't been able to.

Snorting her derision, she turned her attention back to the rosebush she was pruning.

"We aren't getting any younger, Bridg. When are you going to forgive me?"

Her heart flipped in her chest, and her mouth went dry. If she faced him, she knew what she'd see. Six feet of contrite male with shaggy blond hair and a knicker-melting smile. She didn't turn around because she couldn't afford to lose her only clean set of drawers. Which reminded her, she needed to get the laundry on before heading to work at the pub today.

Goddess, she needed a clone.

"Yer not plannin' on answering, *mo ghrá*? Can you not see your way past a wee mistake?"

That asinine comment brought her head around. "Wee mistake? Are you mad, Ruairí?" She chucked her pruning shears at his head, and lucky enough for him, he had rabbit-fast reflexes. Oh, if only she had the magic of a normal witch, she'd blast him to hell and back. And wasn't that another blame she could lay at his door? If it hadn't been for his bloody family, they would *all* be enjoying a taste of the Goddess's gift right now, instead of just her brothers.

Sometimes she dreamed about having abilities. What wouldn't she do with a spot of magic? Where wouldn't she go if she could teleport from one place to another in the blink of an eye like her brothers were beginning to do?

Fecking prophecy.

And fecking O'Connors for causing all their woes!

"You got a temper on you, ya do!" Ruairí shouted as he tried to mop up the coffee he'd spilled down his shirt when he dodged the shears.

Bridget experienced a pang for the discomfort he must've felt from the hot liquid, but she couldn't stop herself from running an appreciative eye over the sculpted chest displayed so nicely by the wet material clinging to each and every muscle. The blimey bastard even had beautiful nipples, small, hard, and perfectly pebbled at the moment.

With a heartfelt sigh, she turned her back, but not before calling over her shoulder, "Then feck off and don't come back, why don't you? It's not like I've asked you to hang about like a damned wraith."

"One day I won't come back. What'll ya do then, you bloody shrew? You'll be sorry for the way you treated me. You won't have old Ruairí O'Connor to abuse."

"Promise?" She gave him a hope-filled look.

The flash of his wicked grin nearly did her in, and she knelt at the base of the bush on the pretense of fluffing the dirt.

Damned weak knees!

Nothing was finer than Ruairí's face when he was amused by her. His blue eyes twinkled. Paired with that dimpled smile and the mussed white-blond hair that always seemed to need a barber, those peepers of his had the ability to melt even the steeliest of hearts. Cold, hard determination was no match for his roguish charm. And didn't that beat all?

"What are you doing here, Ruairí? Don't you have a job to see to?"

"It's Saturday."

She frowned and ripped out a weed. Her days all ran together now that her family had opened O'Malley's Black Cat Inn. Between the pub and their bed and breakfast, Bridget was run ragged. Soon enough, her brother Cian and his new bride, Piper, would return from their honeymoon and relieve her of the burden of running two places.

"What time do you want me at the pub tonight, *mo ghrá?*"

Ruairí had stepped in a few months back—despite Bridget's objections—and taken over bartending while she prepared the occasional meal and bused tables. He'd initially done it as a favor to Cian, but he'd never left.

She couldn't say Ruairí was a terrible worker; hell, he'd turned out to be a godsend. But she didn't have to like it, and she sure as hell wouldn't praise or thank him for his timely help.

"Four-thirty should do." If she could stand to have him around, she'd have told him an hour earlier to help prep for the evening ahead. However, it was essential to her mental wellbeing that she avoid spending as much time with him as possible. "Now go away. I've things to do."

RUAIRÍ STARED AT THE RIGID BACK BRIDGET PRESENTED TO HIM. The woman was as stubborn as the day was long. She refused to listen to any apologies or explanations of the past, convinced he was in the wrong.

And maybe he had been, *once*. But now? Now, he deserved to be heard. Having dealt with her frigid stares and scathing remarks for the better part of seventeen years, he was working up to a fine temper.

Her brothers, Cian and Carrick, were convinced she'd mellow if Ruairí remained in close proximity. Sure, and they were wrong. If anything, Bridget had reinforced the walls of her heart and effectively barricaded it against him. Convincing her that he sincerely regretted his fool mistake was getting harder by the day.

She tossed back her shiny red hair with a simple flick of her wrist and cast him a withering glare. "Still here?"

For some odd reason, he found the gesture humorous, but he dare not laugh where she could see, or she'd skin him alive. He couldn't resist saying the one thing he knew would irk her. "Aye, *mo ghrá*. It's difficult to part ways with one so lovely."

"Sure, and you didn't have a problem movin' on when you decided to stick your lying tongue down Molly Mae's scrawny throat."

Ah, finally. Bridget was ready to address the ever-present issue.

"Molly Mae kissed *me*, Bridg. Not the other way 'round."

She snorted. "From my vantage point, the kiss went on for a good day, and you weren't shoving her away, now were you?"

"She used a spell on me."

Her severe frown rivaled the dark clouds of the fiercest winter storm. "Spell? What kind of spell?"

"One designed to freeze me in place," he improvised. "I'm telling you now, Bridg, I never knew she had magic powerful enough to control me that way."

Bridget squinted as she weighed his words.

Ruairí did his best to look innocent.

Yes, he'd kissed Molly Mae down by the stream under the large oak where he and Bridget used to meet in secret. He'd employed a whole lot of stupid with a huge heaping of arrogance when he'd come up with the idea to make Bridget jealous and force her hand. The decidedly dumb plan to convince her she couldn't live without him had backfired on an epic level. Seventeen torturous years later, he was still dealing with the fallout.

"Do you know your left eyebrow twitches and you grimace slightly before you lie, Ruairí?"

His hand flew to his brow, but he dropped it just as quickly when he saw the smug satisfaction on her face. Goddess, he was still three steps behind Bridget on a good day.

Order Beer & Broomsticks today!

ALSO, IF YOU HAVEN'T ALREADY SUBSCRIBED TO MY NEWSLETTER, tmcromer.com/newsletter, or joined my Facebook reader group, tmcromer.me/vip-readers, I encourage you to do so. It's the best way for you to stay current on upcoming stories. After I'm done with the O'Malleys, I'll be introducing the Aether and friends, and you won't want to miss it.

Books in The Thorne Witches Series:
SUMMER MAGIC
AUTUMN MAGIC
WINTER MAGIC
SPRING MAGIC
REKINDLED MAGIC
LONG LOST MAGIC
FOREVER MAGIC
ESSENTIAL MAGIC
MOONLIT MAGIC
ENCHANTED MAGIC
CELESTIAL MAGIC

Books in The Unlucky Charms Series:
PINTS & POTIONS
WHISKEY & WITCHES
BEER & BROOMSTICKS (July 2022)
COCKTAILS & CAULDRONS (Nov 2022)
WINE & WARLOCKS (Mar 2023)

Books in The Holt Family Series:
FINDING YOU
THIS TIME YOU
INCLUDING YOU
AFTER YOU (Sept 2022)